D0710971

continued ...

GOODNIGHT,
Sweetheart

Suzanne Simmons

BERKLEY SENSATION, NEW YORK

THE BERKLEY PUBLISHING GROUP
Published by the Penguin Group
Penguin Group (USA) Inc.
375 Hudson Street, New York, New York 10014, USA
Penguin Group (Canada), 10 Alcorn Avenue, Toronto, Ontario M4V 3B2, Canada
(a division of Pearson Penguin Canada Inc.)
Penguin Books Ltd., 80 Strand, London WC2R 0RL, England
Penguin Group Ireland, 25 St. Stephen's Green, Dublin 2, Ireland (a division of Penguin Books Ltd.)
Penguin Group (Australia), 250 Camberwell Road, Camberwell, Victoria 3124, Australia
(a division of Pearson Australia Group Pty. Ltd.)
Penguin Books India Pvt. Ltd., 11 Community Centre, Panchsheel Park, New Delhi—110 017, India
Penguin Group (NZ), Cnr. Airborne and Rosedale Roads, Albany, Auckland 1310, New Zealand
(a division of Pearson New Zealand Ltd.)
Penguin Books (South Africa) (Pty.) Ltd., 24 Sturdee Avenue, Rosebank, Johannesburg 2196,
South Africa

Penguin Books Ltd., Registered Offices: 80 Strand, London WC2R 0RL, England

This is a work of fiction. Names, characters, places, and incidents either are the product of the author's imagination or are used fictitiously, and any resemblance to actual persons, living or dead, business establishments, events, or locales is entirely coincidental.

GOODNIGHT, SWEETHEART

A Berkley Sensation Book / published by arrangement with the author

PRINTING HISTORY
Berkley Sensation edition / April 2005

ISBN: 0-425-20193-7

BERKLEY® SENSATION
Berkley Sensation Books are published by The Berkley Publishing Group,
a division of Penguin Group (USA) Inc.,
375 Hudson Street, New York, New York 10014.
BERKLEY SENSATION and the "B" design are trademarks belonging to Penguin Group (USA) Inc.

PRINTED IN THE UNITED STATES OF AMERICA

10 9 8 7 6 5 4 3 2 1

For Cindy Hwang—
editor extraordinaire

WELCOME TO SWEETHEART, INDIANA
WHERE EVERYONE IS YOUR FRIEND
POPULATION: 11,238

Chapter
one

A friend in need was a pain in the ass, even when that friend was his best friend and older brother.

However, at the moment, the greater pain was in Eric Law's head: an intense throbbing behind his eyes that competed with the big brass drum playing timpani on the back of his skull.

" 'Anything that can go wrong, will go wrong,' " he groused as he opened the glove compartment and reached for the bottle of Bayer. *At least according to Murphy's Law.* He tapped two of the aspirin into the palm of his hand, threw the pills into the back of his throat, and washed them down with the last few drops of tepid water left in the bottle he had found underneath his car seat.

He wasn't a patient man, but Eric knew better than to fight a headache. Part of his winning strategy in life— sometimes as the result of an intelligent and well-thought-out decision on his part; sometimes by following his gut instincts; at times, to be perfectly honest, through sheer dumb luck—had been knowing when to fight and when to forego that pleasure.

He leaned back against the leather headrest and closed his eyes, trying to give the aspirin time to work its medicinal magic. A few minutes later he opened his eyes, sat up straight, and demanded of himself, "Okay, what the hell did you do with it?"

He patted down the front of his tuxedo shirt. There weren't any pockets, just formal pleats sewn into vertical rows on either side of the pearlized buttons.

He tried his black dress pants next. The right front pocket contained an eighteen-carat-gold money clip engraved with his initials: E.A.L. The *A* didn't stand for *Alan* or *Andrew* or even *Anthony*, as everyone assumed. It was for *Anscomb*, a name his mother, a dyed-in-the-wool romantic, had once read in a book.

His father, always the pragmatist of the family, had warned her that their youngest offspring would pay a price for having such a distinctive name. Devoted teacher and Anglophile that she was, Judith Law had insisted that Anscomb was an honorable name, a proud name, a noble name that meant "an unusual man who dwells in a special place."

In the end she'd gotten her way (his mother usually did), and he had been christened Eric Anscomb Law. But his father had been right, too. Growing up he had been taunted with a variety of nicknames, including everything from "ants-come" to "ass-comb."

"Sticks and stones may break my bones, but words will never hurt me."

Whoever had coined that piece of traditional folk wisdom obviously didn't have a degree in modern psychology, or a clue about kids. Kids could be cruel. Vicious. Merciless. In the first dozen or so years of his life he'd fought *and* won more than one bloody battle over his unusual middle name.

On the other hand, Eric reflected as he dug deeper into his pants' pocket, maybe a certain amount of adversity in childhood was a good thing. Maybe it had helped to prepare him for the adult world in which he lived and worked: the sometimes ruthless, always highly competitive world of corporate attorneys, ambitious politicians, and society's "movers and shakers."

He rummaged around and found a package of Listerine cool mint breath strips, a handful of loose change, and a small Swiss army knife with a miniature corkscrew.

Never know when you might need to open a miniature bottle of wine, he thought.

In his left front pocket was a ring box in Tiffany & Company's signature blue color. It was empty. He had already fulfilled one of his primary duties as best man: He had handed over the custom-designed wedding ring at the appropriate moment during the ceremony so Sam could slip it onto his bride's finger. As a matter of fact, his brother now wore a matching gold band.

Eric tossed the empty Tiffany's box onto the passenger seat and kept looking.

In his back right pocket was his billfold. Fashioned from the finest Italian leather, the trifold wallet was as soft and smooth as a baby's bottom. He usually kept his driver's license, some cash, and his credit cards inside his suit jacket to foil pickpockets, but, according to the signs posted at the outskirts of town, this was SWEETHEART, IN-DIANA, WHERE EVERYONE IS YOUR FRIEND, POPULATION: 11,238 (give or take), not Boston or New York.

Besides, he understood that pickpockets and petty criminals were pretty much nonexistent around here thanks to his cousin, Ben. Benjamin Law was a breed apart. He was also smart, tough-as-nails, and determined to do his job to the letter of the law. Most criminals, petty or otherwise, quickly learned that it was better not to have a run-in with the newly elected sheriff of Sweetheart County.

Eric continued with his search. His back left pocket contained a folded linen handkerchief. Clean. Pressed. Monogrammed. Ready in any emergency. As a matter of fact, he had everything on him but the one thing he needed.

No phone.

A thorough inspection of his car was the next order of business. He rummaged through the glove compartment. He checked the space between the bucket seats. He dug down into all the creases and crevices. Nothing. Nada. Zip.

That's when it hit him. "Brilliant. Just brilliant, Law. You left your cell phone in the jacket of your tuxedo. And where is your jacket? Back in town, of course."

Which was where he was supposed to be.

Murphy's Corollary: "Left to themselves, things tend to go from bad to worse."

It had all started less than an hour ago with a small favor, an innocuous favor: Leave the celebration just long enough to drive out to the Flying Pig, retrieve a briefcase, containing his brother's passport and the airline tickets for his honeymoon, and bring it back to the wedding reception. Not too much to ask.

Eric had climbed into his Porsche 911 and inserted the key in the ignition. He had listened with satisfaction as the powerful engine sprang to life. Then he'd shifted into gear and driven off down the street, heading west out of town.

One touch of a button on the center console, and the side windows had descended, the hood had opened, and the roof over his head had folded into the back compartment. The whole process had taken a total of twenty seconds. Tops.

The drive out to the Flying Pig had gone quickly and smoothly. With no one else in sight he had pushed the pedal to the floor. Even going ninety the Porsche hadn't broken a sweat.

The briefcase had been precisely where Sam had told him it would be: dead center on the kitchen table of the farmhouse, right next to a basket of plastic purple plums.

Eric had retrieved the forgotten leather case and headed back toward Sweetheart. He had been humming along at a good clip when the car's engine had suddenly started to make never-before-heard noises. He'd pulled over to the side of the road just as the engine sputtered twice and quit on him.

Another goddamned Murphy's Corollary: "If there is a worse time for something to go wrong, it will happen then."

"Eighty thousand dollars worth of powerful, precision-engineered sports car and you conk out on me now, Red," he said aloud to his customized tomato-red Porsche.

Eric got out of the sports car, slammed the door shut behind him—the sound rattled his teeth—and gave the front tire a jab with the toe of his dress shoe.

"Son of a bitch," he swore under his breath, reaching up to tug the formal bow tie from around his neck; he pitched it onto the passenger seat beside the empty ring box.

Without a car or a cell phone, he was pretty much up shit creek without a paddle.

The sun was a blazing yellow ball high in a bright blue sky. There was only the merest suggestion of a cloud here and there on the horizon. The afternoon temperatures had soared well into the eighties: warm for mid-June in Indiana.

He took off his dark-tinted sunglasses for a moment and mopped his forehead with the monogrammed handkerchief. His dress shirt was already damp and clinging to his back. He undid the top button or two. His shirtsleeves were next. He rolled them up to his elbows.

Well, this was a fine how-do-you-do. Here he was playing the Good Samaritan, trying to help his brother out of a jam, and now he was the one in a jam. A pickle. A hell of a fix.

Eric told himself to relax and breathe, just breathe. He inhaled deeply, filling his lungs and his nostrils with the scent of country air: a mixture of dark, dank earth, thick green vegetation, and sweet clover that grew wild alongside the road. Then he slowly exhaled.

Actually it was the first time today he'd felt like he could take a deep breath. That wasn't quite true, he realized. It was the first time since he'd driven into Sweetheart three days ago.

The problem was weddings.

He hated weddings.

They were right up there at the top of his list with root canals, traffic jams, and exorbitant taxes. Ironically, there had been a virtual epidemic of weddings in the past eighteen months since his divorce was final. He'd personally been a member of no less than four wedding parties in the last year alone.

"It must be something in the air, or the water, or maybe it's the result of global warming," he said cynically, turning and leaning against the car door. The metal was hot at his back. He pushed his sunglasses up his nose and stared off into the distance.

Let's be honest, Eric. It isn't just weddings that make you uncomfortable. It's Sweetheart, Indiana. You definitely have a love-hate relationship with your hometown.

Little wonder. Growing up he'd been wild, undisciplined, incorrigible, the black sheep of the family, the bad apple in the bunch, the kind of boy mothers warned their daughters about. Teachers, ministers, neighbors, even law-enforcement officials—including his own father, who had been the sheriff of Sweetheart County at the time—had thrown up their hands in frustration when it came to the youngest of the Laws.

Stifled. Smothered. Suffocated. Bored. Restless. Misunderstood. Rebel without a cause. That's how he would have described himself as a teenager.

He'd been the exact opposite of Sam and his sisters. In fact, the differences between himself and his three older siblings had been like night and day. They had all been excellent students, star athletes, and model citizens.

In his senior year Sam had been captain of the football team and had earned a full-athletic scholarship to Purdue. A year later Allie had been the editor of the school newspaper, on the honor roll, and headed to the University of Chicago, while Serena, her twin, had been the president of the student body and voted most likely to succeed, which she did at Stanford. Two years later he'd had the dubious distinction of being voted the *numero uno* "party animal" of his senior class.

At the time Eric knew his family had been disappointed in him. Hell, he'd been disappointed in himself.

The turning point had come the summer after graduation. He'd taken a job in a local factory. The pay had been excellent at eighteen dollars an hour, plus overtime and incentives, but he had found himself slaving away twelve hours a day, six days a week, on an assembly line building truck transmissions.

The worst part wasn't the physically demanding labor, although on a typical summer afternoon, even with huge fans blowing the air around, the temperature had soared above the one-hundred-degree mark inside the outdated manufacturing plant.

No, the worst part had been the mind-numbing monotony. It had driven him crazy.

He'd realized that he had reached that proverbial fork in the road. There had to be a better way and a brighter future for him. The very next week he'd applied to military school and been accepted on probation for the fall semester. For the first time in his life he'd worked hard at his studies, become a disciplined student, and earned straight A's. A year later he had the grades to transfer to Purdue University. Three years after that he had graduated summa cum laude in pre-law. Then, following in his brother's footsteps, it had been on to Harvard Law School.

Funny how everybody had always wanted him to be like Sam, Eric thought, and now in many ways he was. He'd succeeded beyond his wildest dreams or anyone else's. In fact, to the outside world he appeared to be more successful than his older brother.

After graduating at the top of his class at Harvard, he had been inundated with job offers on both coasts. In legal circles from San Francisco to Washington, D.C., he'd been reputed to be worth his weight not in gold, but platinum. In the end he had accepted an invitation to join one of Boston's most prestigious law firms.

His rise within the legal field had been meteoric. He had been on the winning side of one high-profile court case after another. He'd been written up in the *ABA Journal*, *The Young Lawyer*, and the *Boston Globe*. He had even been featured in a regional publication as one of New England's "fifty most beautiful people," a takeoff on the *People* magazine list.

And the crowning glory: He'd become the youngest partner in the history of Barrett, Barrett & Hartmann, with offices overlooking the city and the harbor.

Eric knew what was said about him behind his back: He wasn't just good at his profession, he was brilliant, gifted, fearless, and utterly ruthless. Within the hallowed mahogany halls of Barrett, Barrett & Hartmann, he was referred to as "Eric the Red," not for the color of his Porsche, but for his killer instincts. There weren't many in *or* out of the courtroom who had the guts to take a shot at the hotshot of BB&H.

Murphy's Military Law (learned firsthand during the year he'd attended military school): *"There is nothing more satisfying than having someone take a shot at you, and miss."*

Anyway, once his career was on track, he had set similar goals for his personal life. He'd married one of the senior partner's daughters: an educated, accomplished, and socially prominent young woman. Soon after they had moved into a million-dollar home in an exclusive Beacon Hill neighborhood. He'd bought an expensive sports car. He had been making an obscene amount of money. By anyone's standards he had finally been doing everything right.

Then two years ago it had all started to unravel . . . beginning with his marriage.

Don't go there, buddy. It's water under the bridge. Nobody can change his past.

Eric suddenly realized his headache was fighting back against the aspirin. He opened the car door on the driver's side, reached across to the glove compartment, and took out the Bayer again. The water bottle he had found underneath the seat was empty, so he tossed two more pills into his mouth and chewed them up dry. The bitter taste suited his mood perfectly.

So why was he in Sweetheart?

Because Sam had called him up on the telephone last November and asked him to come, that's why.

"I'm getting married next summer," his older brother had announced without preamble. "I want you to be the first to know."

Eric had leaned back in his sleek European-designed office chair and swiveled around to gaze at the spectacular view he had of Boston Harbor. He couldn't resist teasing Sam a little. "I hope I'm not the very first to know. You have informed the bride-to-be, haven't you?"

Sam's laughter had echoed in his ear. He sounded happier than Eric could ever remember. "Okay, you're the second to know, although I think Mom has her suspicions."

"Then I assume the lucky lady is Gillian Charles."

"How did you guess?"

He had snickered softly into the telephone. "You're kidding, right? There aren't any secrets in Sweetheart. There certainly aren't any secrets in our family."

He could almost imagine Sam smacking himself on the forehead with the flat of his hand. "What was I thinking, little brother?" They had both chuckled at that since Eric was the taller of the two by several inches; he'd sprinted past his "big" brother sometime during their college years. Then Sam had turned serious. "I've waited a long time for this."

Eric had responded in kind, his voice soft, emotion-charged. "I know you have."

"I'd like you to be my best man."

A funny lump had formed for a moment in his throat. "I'd be honored, Sam."

It was true. Only for Sam would he agree to be the best man. Only for Sam would he return to Sweetheart. Not just return for the wedding, but agree to take some long-overdue vacation time and stay for a few weeks, maybe for the rest of the summer and keep an eye on things while the bride and groom went on an extended honeymoon to Tuscany.

"Yeah, well, Sam won't be going to Tuscany, or anywhere else for that matter, if you don't get back to town pronto with his plane tickets and passport," Eric said, pushing off from his car and doing a three-hundred-and-sixty-degree turn.

Behind him there was a cornfield not quite "knee high by the Fourth of July," but then it was only June sixteenth. There was another field across the asphalt road, and row upon row of corn or soybeans as far as the eye could see.

Overhead, a flock of black birds swooped in formation and then silently lighted on a steel cable strung between two utility poles; they were lined up like some kind of macabre scene out of an Alfred Hitchcock movie. The only sound was the distant caw of a single crow.

There hadn't been a car or a truck or even a tractor drive by since his Porsche had stalled. That was going on thirty minutes now. Apparently his chances of being rescued anytime soon were somewhere between slim and none.

Murphy's Last Word on the Subject: "You never run out of things that can go wrong."

Eric stood there at the side of the deserted road, folded his arms across his chest, and muttered under his breath, "I'm beginning to think Murphy was an optimist."

Chapter

two

 Sydney St. John remembered the day her aunt Minerva had informed her that she was blessed with the Bagley Curse.

"What's the Bagley Curse?" she'd asked as her aunt had taken a clean tissue from the pocket of her apron and wiped away the tears from her ten-year-old face. (To this day, Sydney could close her eyes and still see that apron: big red poppies printed against a bright yellow background, with splotches of white flour dotting the front.)

Minerva had put an arm around her waist and walked with her toward the kitchen at the back of the house. Sunlight had flooded the big cheerful room through a wall of windows. The smell of fresh-baked cookies had filled the air.

Minerva Bagley had never been one to hurry a conversation, especially a heart-to-heart conversation with her niece. She had made a pot of tea, taken two of her best china cups and saucers from the sideboard, and poured the fragrant brew into each delicate teacup before she had continued. "There are those in our family, going as far back as your great-great-grandparents," she'd said, offering Sydney a warm chocolate chip cookie, "who claim the Bagley Curse is actually a blessing."

"Yes, but what is it?" Sydney had insisted, her curiosity an almost palpable force. She'd already forgotten about the taunts that had followed her home from school earlier that afternoon.

Minerva had sat down on the opposite side of the antique oak plank table and gazed out at the large backyard, the herb garden and the greenhouses beyond. Then she had repeated very deliberately, "What is the Bagley Curse?"

Sydney had waited with bated breath.

Her aunt had tapped one finger against her lower lip, leaving a smudge of flour behind. There was another telltale powdery streak across her right cheekbone. "Why, it's brains, big feet, and freckles, of course." An emphatic nod of her head had sent several bobby pins hurling into space. "Lots of freckles."

Sydney had repeated the words as if they were a mantra: "Brains, big feet, and lots of freckles."

She had all of those things. She was the smartest one in her class; everybody said so. She already wore a size eight shoe. She had freckles in abundance.

"And that's just from your mother's side of the family." Here Minerva had paused to take a sip of rose hips tea, said to be beneficial for anything from a cold to a sore throat, from stress to hemorrhoids.

"It's your side of the family, too."

"It's mine, too," Minerva had agreed. "From your father's side, the St. John side, you have also inherited an offbeat sense of humor, an analytical mind that rarely strays from a literal view of the world, and a strong sense of conviction."

Sydney had understood what her aunt was talking about; that alone made her unusual for a fifth grader.

Of course, she'd heard her father's favorite quote so often (it was something Winston Churchill had said), that the words were forever imprinted on her young mind: *"Never give in, never give in, never, never, never, never—in nothing, great or small, large or petty—never give in except to convictions of honor and good sense."*

Minerva had cleared her throat and gone on to expound on the curses that might be blessings in disguise. "You're tall. Tall women are taken more seriously. Tall women command more attention and respect. Tall women carry their weight better."

Sydney had piped up with "Tall women play professional basketball and tennis and golf and even professional beach volleyball. And they can become supermodels, too." She'd been watching ESPN, and sneaking an occasional peek at her older brother's copy of *Sports Illustrated*, the swimsuit issue.

"Yes, I suppose they can," her aunt had said with a wistful sigh as she'd helped herself to another cookie.

That's when it had dawned on Sydney that Aunt Minerva might be feeling a little disheartened about being plump and rather diminutive for a full-grown woman. Of course, she had been willing to bet Minerva had never been called hurtful names like "bean pole," "goose neck," "giraffe girl," or "Bigfoot," either.

"I have exceptionally large feet for my age," she'd offered as consolation to the kind soul sitting across from her.

Never one to feel sorry for herself for long, Minerva had perked right up and said, "You have the perfect size feet for the statuesque woman you will be as an adult. Small feet would look silly on you. You'll grow into your feet."

She'd fervently prayed, *I hope so*.

"You have auburn hair and freckles, which someday you'll learn to appreciate and make the most of. You will be beautiful, I promise, but yours won't be a cookie-cutter beauty. Oh, no, nothing so ordinary for you, my girl." Here a floured finger had been wagged at her. "You will be different and you will celebrate that difference."

"Do you really think I'll be beautiful some day?" she'd said, doubting her aunt's prediction.

Minerva had apparently noticed the flour spilled down the front of her apron. She'd brushed it away with an emphatic swipe of her hand. "I know so. Look at your mother."

Sydney had gobbled down the last bite of her cookie. "Mom is beautiful." Although her father always claimed it was her beautiful mind that had first attracted him.

Minerva had reached out and gently dabbed at a piece of chocolate chip that was clinging to the edge of her niece's mouth. Then she'd gone on with genuine affection in her voice, "You look very much like Abby did when she was your age."

Sydney's spirits had immediately lifted. "I do?"

"Yes, you do. I remember it as clearly as if it were yesterday. I was twelve and your mother was ten, although she was already taller by several inches. My hair was plain old brown and straight as a board. I kept it cut short, hoping nobody would notice. Your mother's hair was like an angel's; it curled around her face in soft waves, and reflected all the glorious colors of the setting sun: ruby and russet and persimmon."

Aunt Minerva's words had sounded like poetry.

"But my hair isn't auburn, or any of those lovely things you said. I hate my hair," Sydney had groaned, her shoulders slumping. "It's red and curly."

Minerva had been quick to point out, "Exactly like your mother's was when she was ten."

Maybe there was hope for her yet.

Bespectacled brown eyes had regarded her with a serious air. "You've also inherited a double dose of brains. That means you have the potential to do great things."

Sydney had always known that people expected a lot from her, and her brother, when it came to academics. After all, their parents were doctors *and* brilliant scientists.

Dr. Abigail Bagley and Dr. Matthew St. John specialized in cutting-edge pharmacology. They were experts in their field and as a team had made any number of important scientific breakthroughs. Their research required them to travel all over the globe. In fact, they were presently spending a month in the Amazon studying rare plants and their possible medical applications.

"I know one thing. I don't want to be a scientist when I grow up," Sydney had blurted out to her confidante.

Minerva had taken that statement in her stride. "What would you like to do?"

She'd shrugged her thin shoulders and reached for another cookie. "Maybe I'll stay right here in Sweetheart, and grow sage and bayberry, ginger and licorice root like you do." Turning her head, she had gazed out at the plants so carefully and lovingly tended by her aunt. Now that she was older, and could distinguish between herbs and weeds, she was allowed to help in the garden and the greenhouses. Those were often her happiest moments.

Minerva had patted her niece's hand and said encouragingly, "Well, you have plenty of time to discover what your destiny is, and where it will lead you."

"Destiny." She'd liked the sound of that word; she had said it over and over to herself. *Destiny. My destiny.*

"Thank goodness you have a sense of humor, which should keep you from taking those brains of yours, or yourself, too seriously." Then Minerva had leaned closer and looked her straight in the eye. "You are the luckiest girl I know, Sydney Marie St. John."

She remembered blushing with pleasure. "I am?"

Another nod of her aunt's head had sent hairpins flying in all directions. "The very luckiest."

She may not have believed every word Minerva had said to her on that long-ago afternoon, but in the intervening twenty-three years Sydney had learned that almost anything in life had the potential to be a blessing or a curse.

And that included brains, big feet, and freckles.

She turned to the dog strapped into the passenger seat next to her. "What do you think, Sneaker? Am I the luckiest girl in the world? Or am I cursed, after all?"

Sneaker gave a soft, inconclusive woof and cowered

down in his Port-a-Pooch. Unlike most dogs, certainly most Shelties, he did not enjoy riding in the car.

"Good answer," Sydney said, reaching across to give him an affectionate pat on the top of his beautiful black-and-tan head. "Diplomatic, too."

After all, discretion *was* the better part of valor. Silence *was* golden, at least most of the time. The truth *did* set you free. And a *dog,* not diamonds, was a girl's best friend.

Still, was it a blessing or a curse to return to her hometown of Sweetheart, Indiana?

Was it a blessing or a curse to leave her job without having a Plan B? Or, for that matter, a Plan A.

Was it a blessing or a curse that she had been the one to discover the irregularities in the company's financial records and report them to The Powers That Be?

She was a little older and a whole lot wiser than she'd been several months ago, that was for damned sure. But she had not given in. She had not compromised her integrity. And she had not run away in the face of the firestorm that had followed her discovery.

She had, however, learned a few hard truths. Nobody liked a whistleblower. People did blame the messenger. In striving to be trustworthy, people had grown to distrust her. Her personal integrity had been questioned. Her motives had become suspect. Her entire life had been scrutinized. In trying to do the right thing, it was assumed that she had done something wrong. In the end it had been a no-win situation. At least for her.

To add insult to injury, she'd been unable to avoid overhearing the rumors, innuendoes, and name-calling in the hallways and around the coffee machines at Saddler Consultants.

"Who died and put her in charge?"

"Where'd she get the frigging halo?"

"Goody Two-shoes."

"Tattletale."

"Mole."

Sometimes *"Conniving bitch."*

Sometimes just: *"Bitch."*

"If this was Survivor, *guess who'd be the first to get voted off the island?"*

Comments like that might be funny coming from teenagers or perhaps even Generation Xers, but these were supposedly honest, intelligent, and mature adults: her colleagues and coworkers and, she had thought at the time, her friends.

When Gary Saddler, founder, president, and CEO of Saddler Consultants, had arranged a meeting in his elegant thirty-ninth-floor office, with its priceless antiques and its panoramic view of Chicago and Lake Michigan, Sydney had assumed her hard work and diligence were going to be rewarded with a bonus, or possibly a promotion, or at the very least with an official commendation. Instead, she had been met by the company's senior executives and a bevy of fast-talking attorneys.

Before the meeting was over, it had been strongly suggested that she accept a buyout, for the sake of Saddler Consultants and for the sake of her own career.

That's when she'd finally understood: You can do everything right and still lose.

"Probitas laudatur et alget," Sydney said under her

breath as she drove toward town. " 'Honesty is praised and starves.' "

Sneaker's head suddenly appeared above the corner of his travel carrier. He let out with a pitiable whine.

"Don't worry, boy. I would never allow you to starve, or go without your favorite treats," she said, reaching over to give him a quick scratch behind one ear.

Sneaker did not seem reassured. He was, after all, inordinately fond of his treats.

"Maybe it's time we got a couple of things straight. First, I walked away with a very nice severance package, so neither of us has to worry about where our next meal is coming from."

Her field of expertise was finance and negotiation, and she'd made certain that her contract with Saddler Consultants was airtight. It had cost them plenty to get rid of her.

"Second, we are not running back home with our tails tucked between our legs. We're simply going to spend a little R and R in Sweetheart, Indiana, where people still know right from wrong. Where honesty is the best policy. Where it's also the rule and not the exception. Where a man or a woman's word is their bond. Where people aren't afraid of the truth." Sydney's next breath stuck in her throat. "Where life is sweeter and simpler."

Without taking her eyes off the two-lane highway ahead (although, heaven knows, traffic had been virtually nonexistent for the past half hour), she rummaged around in the oversize handbag at her elbow and located her sunglasses. She slipped them on before pressing the button for the sunroof.

It was the middle of June, and the gently rolling fields to

either side of the highway were planted with corn or soybeans. There was the familiar sense of earth and sky and
brilliant sunlight that she remembered from her previous,
if infrequent visits. Around the next bend in the road was
the Flying Pig, with its distinctive weathervane *and* with its
distinctive odors.

Sneaker's nose began to twitch wildly. There was a look
of distaste on his canine features.

"I'd forgotten about the barnyard smells," Sydney said,
quickly closing the sunroof over their heads and nudging
the air-conditioning up a notch. "You don't know what to
make of it, do you, boy? You're a city dog born and bred."
Her voice softened. "I wonder how you'll like living in the
country."

That was the lovely thing about having a dog for your
companion. You could talk out loud to yourself and pretend
you were holding a conversation with your Yorkshire ter-
rier, or your shih tzu, or your Shetland sheepdog.

Dogs were excellent listeners. They were nonjudgmen-
tal. They were generous of spirit. They were forgiving. They
didn't care if you were short or tall, thin or not-so-thin. And
your dog was always happy to see you at the end of the day.

Of course, those were only a few of the reasons she was
grateful for Sneaker's company. He was also a loyal and
faithful companion, and he gave her unconditional love. She
hadn't experienced that in her life apart from Aunt Minerva.

It's your own fault, Sydney.

She had taken a different path from the one originally envisioned for her by her mother and father. She'd chosen a
profession that was generally misunderstood and largely un-

appreciated by the scientific minds in her family, especially since her older brother had followed in their parents' footsteps and was now a brilliant medical researcher himself.

In fact, she was the first Bagley or St. John to graduate with an MBA, and then proceed to dive into the murky waters of commerce. For the past decade she had invested all of her time, energy, and passion into her business career.

"You put your job first, and now that it's kaput, you're feeling a little lost, a little afraid—okay, maybe more than a little—and you're wondering what in the world you're going to do with yourself." She took in a deep breath, and then slowly released the air in her lungs. "Let's face it, Sydney Marie St. John, you're thirty-three years old, unemployed, and the 'man' in your life is a dog."

Sneaker's head suddenly popped up again. There was a neon green shoelace dangling from one corner of his mouth. He spit out the shoelace just long enough to utter several sharp yelps.

"What?" she said, baffled. "I shut the sunroof. I aired out the car. I did my best to get rid of the smell."

Sneaker was not appeased.

"Is it the music? I thought you enjoyed Yo-Yo Ma. Okay, maybe you're tired of listening to the cello. I guess I've had enough, too." She hit the Eject button on the CD player. The sound of music was immediately replaced by the voice of a local deejay.

"*Good afternoon, Sweetheart!*" came the announcer's mellifluous baritone. "*It's a beautiful day out there in Heart country. Unseasonably warm at eighty-eight degrees. The humidity a slightly uncomfortable seventy-six percent. The barometric pressure is twenty-nine point eleven and rising. Later this evening it will cool off to a good-sleepin' sixty-two. So open your windows tonight, folks, and enjoy the fresh air, since there is no precipitation expected through the remainder of the weekend.*

"Your afternoon forecast here at WHRT, The Heart, ninety-eight point nine on your FM dial has been brought to you by the Sweetheart Bed and Breakfast and Art Gallery. You're cordially invited to come in and browse the latest display of watercolors and award-winning drawings by Davison 'Doodles' Weaver, Sweetheart's very own Norman Rockwell.

"In addition, there will be a special herbal tea tasting presented by Miss Minerva Bagley, owner of Water from the Moon, this Wednesday at three-thirty on the verandah, and each Wednesday afternoon during the summer. Reservations for this perennially popular event can be made by calling the B and B.

"At ten minutes past the hour it's time for a 'blast from the past.' What year is it? Richard Milhous Nixon is president of the United States. Detroit automakers redesign cars to run on unleaded fuel. Congress lowers the voting age from twenty-one to eighteen. The Beatles split up; the Fab Four are no more. And the Kansas City Chiefs beat the Minnesota Vikings in the Super Bowl. If you guessed 1970, Heartlanders, you're right on the money.

"This request is from Paula and is going out with her love to Paul. It's time for a little 'Sweet Baby' James Taylor, singing his 1970 hit, 'Fire and Rain.' " ←

Sydney heaved a long sigh. For some reason this song reminded her of a boy she had known back in high school . . . about a million years ago. She couldn't remember who it was.

Liar. You remember. It was Eric Law.

Okay, but she didn't know why this particular song reminded her of Eric.

Oh, yes, you do. Because it was playing on the radio that night.

She'd like to forget that night since it had been one of the most embarrassing moments of her adolescence. She supposed everybody had some*thing* or some*one* in their past they never wanted to come face-to-face with again.

Well, hers was Eric Law.

She blew out her breath and reminded herself to loosen her stranglehold on the steering wheel.

Good grief, Sydney, you haven't even caught a glimpse of him in years.

In fact, the last time she had seen Eric had been the summer after their graduation from high school. She'd heard he was working on the assembly line at the transmission plant. She had been getting ready to leave for her freshman year at Bryn Mawr.

He hadn't noticed her as she'd cruised through town. He had been standing on a street corner with his arm casually draped around the shoulders of a pretty girl in a pink dress. Their heads had been close together—Sydney had almost been able to taste the kiss they were sharing—as he'd urged his willing partner into the seductive shadows of a nearby alleyway.

At eighteen Eric Law had been everything she could never imagine herself being: wild, uninhibited, spontaneous, dark, and dangerous. He'd reeked of pure male sex appeal. She may have been the definitive high-school nerd, but in one respect she'd been no different from any other girl in Sweetheart and the surrounding three-county area: She had made a perfect fool of herself over him.

That was a long, long time ago . . . *in a galaxy far, far away.*

Years later she had heard through the grapevine that Eric was married and living in Boston. (Okay, it had been a newspaper clipping enclosed in a letter from Minerva.)

"And that, as they say, is pretty much that," she said, pressing her foot down on the accelerator with the toe of her black alligator Manolo Blahniks.

Some people might find it a little odd that she was dressed to kill for the long drive from Chicago to Sweetheart: She was wearing a designer suit, designer shoes, and her lucky diamond earrings that she'd bought as a present for herself when she had signed her first major contract nearly a decade ago. But frankly, arriving home in style was doing wonders for her morale.

As she swung around the next corner, Sydney noticed there was a red sports car stopped by the side of the road. She eased her foot off the gas pedal. There was usually only one explanation for somebody to be standing out here in the middle of nowhere: car trouble.

She turned her head as she slowly approached the scene. The man was tall and broad-shouldered, with dark curly hair that was blue-black in the bright sunlight. He was dressed in formal clothes—white shirt open at the neck, black tie missing, shirtsleeves rolled up to the elbows— and leaning against a low-slung *and* expensive Porsche.

His face was partially obscured by the sunglasses he

was wearing. Yet there was something familiar about the shape of his head, the chiseled features, the jut of his chin, the way he stood there, arms casually crossed, feet firmly planted. Sydney could almost see the piercing blue eyes behind the dark lenses.

Her heart began to do something odd in her chest. Her breathing suddenly became shallow. She would have known Eric Law anywhere, she realized.

He straightened and raised his hand to get her attention. Just for a moment Sydney was tempted to turn tail and run. Instead, she hit the brakes, pulled over onto the shoulder of the road, and said to Sneaker, "I think my luck just ran out."

Chapter
three

The cavalry had arrived.

Although Eric hadn't expected it to be in the form of a sleek silver BMW sedan with a young woman behind the wheel. As she slowed down, he caught a glimpse of long auburn hair and a pair of tortoiseshell sunglasses. She turned her head for a moment and took a good look at him.

He made a mental note: *Fair skin. High cheekbones. Nice mouth. Bright red lipstick.*

Another few yards down the road she finally pulled over onto the berm. He didn't blame her for being cautious—you could never be too careful these days—but he really needed a ride.

The door on the driver's side opened. The first thing to emerge was a pair of stylish high heels—very stylish and very high—then a pair of slender ankles, followed by long, shapely legs. The woman gracefully exited the front seat and stood beside the Beemer.

She was tall and willowy, beautifully dressed and beautifully groomed. Eric wondered if she was a model, although she didn't seem to have the self-awareness common to those in the modeling profession. Maybe she was simply one of those attractive women who was all the more attractive because she was something of a mystery.

Her shoes were no mystery. He was willing to wager they were Manolo Blahniks at five or six hundred dollars a pop, maybe more. Her silk suit was a brilliant shade of red that seemed to enhance the color of her auburn hair and her pale skin. The suit was undoubtedly high-end designer as well. Maybe Armani. Maybe Dior. Maybe classic Chanel. She looked expensive.

Eric knew more than his fair share about expensive women. His ex-wife had been born with a silver spoon in her mouth *and* grasped in each perfectly manicured hand.

Water under the bridge, buddy.

So what was a woman like that doing in a place like this?

Not that he would dream of using a cliché like that with a woman like this. Despite rumors to the contrary, he'd stopped using clichés and pickup lines on the female of the species a long time ago. His reputation with the opposite sex had always been more fiction than fact, anyway. These days he was more apt to employ his persuasive skills in the courtroom than in the bedroom.

Truth was, he hadn't had any interest in women since his divorce. *Once bitten; twice shy.* It had been his experience that women were more trouble than they were worth.

Still, this particular woman was attractive—okay, stunning—in a very different kind of way. And she had legs that seemed to go on forever. Eric let out a soft whistle under his breath. He'd always been a sucker for long legs.

His musings were interrupted by the sound of a dog barking somewhere nearby. Then a small furry head appeared briefly over the back of the passenger seat. It seemed his Good Samaritan already had someone with her.

The woman stood by the silver sedan, not coming any closer, but not showing any signs of apprehension, either.

Maybe her dog's bite was worse than his bark.

"Car trouble?" she said, her voice low and husky.

"You can say that again." Eric knew he sounded irritable and out-of-sorts. Probably because he was. It was also hotter than Hades out here in the afternoon sun, although he noticed the new arrival was as cool as a cucumber.

"What happened?" she inquired.

"Red just up and conked out on me."

Her perfectly arched eyebrows rose a fraction of an inch above her dark glasses. "Red?"

He thumbed in the direction of his Porsche. "That's the nickname of my sports car."

Her response was a noncommittal, "I see."

His mouth curved humorlessly. "I was going to call for help, but it seems I've left my cell phone back in town."

"Pity."

"Yes, it is."

"Inconvenient, too," she pointed out.

He gritted his teeth. "Very."

She tossed back her hair and it fell into a perfect framework around her face. "Is that where you're headed? Sweetheart?"

"Yes," he said with an exasperated sigh. "And if I don't get back there pretty damned quick, the bride and groom won't have their airplane tickets or his passport so they can leave on their honeymoon."

She pressed her lips together. "Well, we wouldn't want to hold up the honeymoon, would we?"

"No, we wouldn't."

She paused and gave him a sideways look. "You didn't mention who's getting married."

"My brother. Actually he's already married." He glanced down at the Rolex on his wrist. "The ceremony ended a little over an hour ago. Right about now hundreds of guests are gathered under a huge air-conditioned tent for a late luncheon of finger sandwiches, assorted salads, cold shrimp, and lobster on ice flown in from God-knows-where, imported Beluga caviar on toast points, Ben and Jerry's ice cream for the kids, and any adults who wish to indulge, sodas and kegs of cold beer, wedding cake, and, of course, Cristal champagne."

"Sounds delicious."

He agreed. "Unfortunately I had to leave before the food was served." As if to prove that last point, his stomach made a low rumbling sound. It was either hunger, or the aspirins he'd taken without the benefit of food or water.

"In that case, I'm sure you're in a bit of a hurry. Would you care to borrow my cell phone to call for a tow, or do you want a lift back to town first?"

"If you don't mind, I'll take the lift. I really need to get Sam's briefcase to him."

She took a step in his direction; her stilettos made a distinctive sound on the gravel. Then she stopped and asked, "Where are they going on their honeymoon?"

"Tuscany."

"Tuscany," she said, and gave a wistful sigh. "The light in Tuscany is different from any other place on earth."

"Now you sound like my sister-in-law. That's exactly how she talks about Tuscany. In fact, it's the reason they chose Italy for their honeymoon: Gillian wants to show Sam the light."

"And the fabulous art."

"And drink the Chianti."

"And eat the wonderful food," she said.

Eric realized he was having difficulty judging the woman's mood. Admittedly he couldn't see her eyes since they were concealed behind dark glasses. Her posture had remained the same—uncompromising—since she had stepped out of the automobile. Her left hand was resting comfortably—no sign of fidgeting—on the open car door. Yet he was getting mixed signals from her, as if she were both relaxed *and* ill-at-ease with him.

It was the darnedest thing.

But he'd learned to trust his gut instincts when it came to reading people's emotions. He was legendary for those instincts when it came to jury selection or grilling witnesses on the stand.

"I'm ready to go whenever you are," the woman said, indicating the passenger side of her sedan.

"I'll get Sam's briefcase and lock up my car." He made fast work of what needed to be done and then walked around to the far side of the Beemer. He stopped and placed his hands in plain view. "Are you sure you're okay with this?"

"With what?"

"Giving a stranger a ride into town."

"I think I can trust your story," she said, giving him one of those Mona Lisa smiles that really wasn't a smile at all.

Eric discovered he was curious. "How do you know I'm telling you the truth?"

She paused a beat. "You could always volunteer to show me the passport and the airline tickets in the briefcase."

"I could if I had the combination to the lock," he said.

"But you don't have it."

He confirmed, "But I don't have it." Then he added, "Frankly I didn't think I'd need it."

She tapped a bright red fingernail against her bottom lip. "Well, you're dressed in a tuxedo. Part of a tuxedo, anyway. That gives some credence to your story about a wedding."

"I suppose it does."

She continued to make her case. "For another thing there are rose petals in your hair."

Eric reached up and raked his fingers through his hair. A few petals fell to the ground.

"I've always preferred throwing flower petals to rice at weddings," she said.

"So have I," he agreed.

She said, "It's more environmentally responsible."

"Less lethal, too."

Something tugged at the corners of her mouth. "I assume you're speaking from experience."

He put the question to her. "Have you ever been hit in the face with a handful of rice?"

"I can't say that I have."

"Well, I have. Trust me, rose petals are a much better choice." Eric rocked back on his heels. "In fact, I'm something of an expert on the whole subject of what should and should not be thrown at weddings. Besides traditional rice, I've also experienced heart-shaped designer rice that claimed to be bird and animal friendly, confetti made from old-fashioned ticker tape—the bridegroom was a Wall Street stockbroker—butterflies, balloons, bubbles—we were all blowing like mad—and on one particular occasion, the release of several hundred white doves."

"Several hundred doves would make for a lot of . . ."

"Dove droppings?"

"Yes."

"In that instance, trust me, you only hope and pray they have a poor aim," he said.

"How many weddings have you been to?" she asked.

"I've lost count over the years. But this is the fourth wedding in the past year that I've been suckered into playing some kind of role, whether as an usher or a groomsman or . . ."

"A flower girl?"

She had a sense of humor. He chuckled. "However, this is my first time serving as the best man."

"For your brother."

"I'd only do this for Sam."

They stood there for a moment.

Then she said unexpectedly, "You also have an honest

face. That's another reason I'm offering you a ride into town."

"Are you always such a good judge of character when it comes to men?"

She laughed and it wasn't entirely from amusement. "I think I'll take the Fifth on that one."

It was her right; as a lawyer he should know.

"By the way, you'll have to share the front seat with Sneaker. The trunk and backseat of my car are jam-packed with suitcases and boxes," she said.

"I take it Sneaker is the dog I heard barking."

"Yes. He's a Shetland sheepdog. But don't worry he only weighs fifteen pounds."

Eric had known cats that were bigger. "I think I can handle a fifteen-pound dog."

"I'll come around and hold him while you fold up his travel case and stow it behind the passenger seat, along with your brother's briefcase. There's just enough room back there for two small items. You don't mind if Sneaker rides on your lap, do you?"

Did he have a choice?

He waited while his Good Samaritan came around the sedan, reached in and lifted up the black-and-tan fluff ball, and then stepped to one side. Two half-concealed eyes regarded Eric suspiciously. He could have sworn the dog was giving him the once-over.

"Now, Sneaker, behave yourself. The man needs a ride into town and we happen to be going in that direction anyway." The woman nuzzled the Sheltie for a moment, burying her face in his soft fur. Then she turned to Eric and said, "If you'll just grab the sneaker—"

He frowned. "I beg your pardon."

The redhead indicated an object in the travel carrier. He bent over and retrieved a large white sneaker with a bright green shoelace dangling from one eyelet.

"It's his security blanket," she said. "While I'm away at the office, the dog sitter found that Sneaker was much happier if he had something of mine to keep near him."

"Dog sitter?"

Her nose went up in the air a fraction of an inch. "He also attends doggie day care and has a dog walker mornings and afternoons." She went on to answer the question he hadn't asked. "Well, I could hardly rescue him and then leave him alone all day."

"I see your dilemma," he said as he stowed the dog's travel seat and Sam's briefcase in the back.

"If you'll please get in and buckle your seat belt, I'll hand you Sneaker and his—"

"Sneaker."

"Precisely."

Eric settled himself in the passenger seat and was handed the dog and the Nike version of a security blanket. As he'd suspected, the Sheltie was more fluff than substance.

Sneaker peered up at him and growled.

"I don't think your dog likes me."

"It's not you."

He wasn't so sure. "You aren't just saying that to spare my feelings, are you?"

"It's nothing personal. Sneaker doesn't like men in general. I can only assume that it was a man who mistreated him before Sheltie Rescue rescued him."

It made sense, he supposed.

"It might help if you took off your sunglasses so Sneaker can see your eyes."

Eric reached up and removed his dark glasses.

This was quickly followed by another suggestion. "You might try smiling at him."

He flashed the ball of fur on his lap his best courtroom smile.

Sneaker bared his teeth.

"I don't think it's working," he said as the elegant woman climbed behind the wheel, strapped herself in, and eased her car back onto the blacktop.

"Don't worry. Sneaker never bites."

That was reassuring.

"By the way, I should have introduced myself," he said belatedly. "I'm Eric Law."

"Yes, I know," she said, and took off down the road in the direction of Sweetheart.

The good news was: Eric Law hadn't recognized her.

The bad news was: She was going to have to tell him who she was in a minute or two, anyway, or risk appearing even more foolish than she had back in high school.

He'd changed, of course. He was older: It showed in the lines on his face and in the self-assurance with which he carried himself. His shoulders were broader. He had grown a few inches. He was taller than she was, although she was wearing her highest heels. His hair was darker and Sydney thought she'd glimpsed a smattering of gray at the temples.

Eric had always had that lethal combination of dark curly hair, bedroom eyes, perfect teeth, a killer smile, and a killer body. He exuded pure male sex appeal. That hadn't changed. It was a little more subtle now. Either that, or she'd changed.

Well, of course she had changed. She wasn't a silly, impressionable seventeen-year-old girl anymore.

Her passenger sat very still for a moment before he said, "You know who I am?"

"Yes."

His eyes narrowed. "Have you known all along?"

Sydney decided to fudge a little on her answer. There was no earthly reason Eric had to know that she had recognized him instantly. "I thought there was something familiar about you as I drove by. That's the reason I pulled over. I knew for sure when I heard your voice."

"Then you have the advantage," he said, obviously not entirely pleased to find himself at a disadvantage. "Because I don't have a clue who you are."

For some reason that made Sydney laugh. Turnaround was fair play. Well, perhaps not always fair, but she wanted to enjoy Eric's discomfort just for a few seconds.

"We went to high school together," she said, providing him with his first clue.

"Sweetheart High School?"

She nodded. "I'm originally from this area, but I haven't been back very often, and for the past few years I've been living and working in Chicago."

"I've been in Boston myself."

"So I'd heard."

"Through the grapevine?"

"Actually I read it in a newspaper clipping my aunt sent to me when you were married."

Sydney glanced down at his left hand. *No wedding ring.*

Eric must have guessed what she was thinking. "Apparently your aunt didn't send you the newspaper clipping when I got divorced."

She bit her lower lip. "I'm sorry. I had no idea."

He was suddenly tense. Visibly so. Sneaker immediately became agitated.

"What's wrong with your dog?" he asked.

"Dogs are very sensitive to human beings and their emotions. Sneaker senses you're upset. He can tell by your breathing, and your tone of voice, and by the way you're holding him."

"Sorry, boy," Eric said, giving the dog a friendly pat or two. He turned his head. "Better?"

"Much better." Sydney could almost feel his midnight blue eyes fixed on her.

Then the man beside her snapped his fingers. "Wait a doggone minute. I know who you are."

Sydney discovered she was holding her breath. "Was it my hair that gave me away?"

"No," Eric said. "It was your laugh. You always did have a distinctive laugh, Sydney St. John."

Chapter
four

She looked like a million bucks.

Her hair was darker: It was long and wavy and a rich auburn color, not the mop of red curls he remembered from fifteen years ago. With the afternoon sun streaming in through the car window, Sydney's hair was like silk on fire. Eric was tempted to reach out and touch it, to see if it would burn his fingers.

He seemed to recall that she'd had a lot of freckles as a kid. It was impossible to tell if she still had any of those freckles; her skin was flawless and her makeup was impeccable.

She was tall. She had always been tall. Tall and skinny, although slender was a better description now that she had filled out in all the right places.

It was obvious that she'd done well for herself. He wondered whether it was the consequence of marriage, or divorce, or the result of her own talent and hard work. No doubt the latter. He was also fairly confident that the family fortune, *and* the family inclination, didn't extend to the designer clothes she was wearing or to the fancy car she was driving.

The Bagleys—Bert, while he was still alive and the leading attorney in town, and Minerva, his niece—weren't fancy folks. The Bagleys never had been. And Sydney's parents had always been more interested in raising funds for medical research than spending money on luxuries. At least that's what he'd heard from Mrs. Goldman.

Gossip was a favorite pastime in Sweetheart. In Mrs. Goldman's case it was more than a pastime or even a hobby; it was an art form. Yet Goldie's tools were simple and few: the telephone, the ability to eavesdrop almost anywhere (including under the hair dryers at Blanche's Beauty Barn), and a pair of binoculars.

Eric had heard several juicy tidbits from his parents' nosy neighbor in the three days he'd been back in town. However, not a single word regarding Sydney St. John had passed Goldie's lips. Maybe Sydney hadn't told anyone she was returning to Sweetheart.

What did he remember about the girl he'd once known? *She was smart.*

While he was flunking first-year Latin—he never once bothered opening the textbook—Sydney was acing chemistry, calculus, and advanced placement English.

He dozed off during the SAT exams; Sydney scored a perfect sixteen hundred.

He went to their high school commencement only because he made a promise to his mother that he would attend. Sydney graduated at the top of their class and gave the traditional valedictorian speech.

At a time when he couldn't have qualified for the local beauty college, Sydney was being aggressively recruited by a dozen universities across the nation.

She was a geek.

In high school he was into video games, grunge rock, fast cars, and faster girls. His nickname was "the Heart-breaker." She studied classical music and took violin and piano lessons. He couldn't recall that she'd ever had a date.

She was intimidating.

Not only because she was smarter than anyone else in their class, but because she knew what she wanted and how she was going to get it. He remembered thinking at the time that was pretty damned gutsy for a seventeen-year-old girl.

Enough about the past. Don't just sit there like a lump on a log. Say something. Anything.

For whatever reason Eric found himself utterly out of practice when it came to making small talk: a ridiculous situation for a man who lived, breathed, *and* died (metaphorically speaking, of course) by the spoken word in the courtroom.

Yeah, but when was the last time you really tried talking one-on-one with a woman?

Eric cleared his throat and brushed away the soft fur clinging to his chin. "Tell me, what do you do in Chicago?"

Sydney kept her eyes fixed on the road in front of them. "I'm a financial consultant."

Apparently she hadn't followed in the footsteps of her parents or her older brother.

"You didn't choose science or medicine?"

There was a definite edge to her voice when she said, "No. I didn't." Without any further prompting from him she went on to say, "During college I discovered what fascinated me was money. Not having money per se, but understanding how it works. So after undergraduate school I went on to get my MBA at Wharton in corporate economics: financial forecasting, stocks and bonds, investments, leverage buyouts, IPOs . . . that kind of thing."

"Sounds interesting."

"It is." She immediately corrected herself. "It was."

"Was?"

Frown lines formed around her mouth. "As of one week ago I'm no longer with the company I was working for."

His curiosity was aroused. "What happened a week ago?"

Her lips thinned. "Let's just say that Saddler Consultants made me an offer I couldn't refuse."

Eric sensed he was treading on very thin ice. "I see."

She was frank. In fact, downright blunt. "I doubt it. You see, I discovered that several of our company's divisions were involved in highly questionable dealings. I believe the politically correct term these days is 'unusual accounting practices.' Anyway, what they were doing was definitely unethical and very possibly illegal, so I reported my findings to top management."

"You did the right thing."

"Yes, I did." Sydney reached out and flipped on her turn signal. "But it wasn't universally appreciated."

Eric put two and two together and came up with four. "That's when you were forced out."

"Not in so many words," she said.

Maybe he had misunderstood. Maybe she had resigned voluntarily. Either way, he wondered if Sydney had any idea how tightly she was clutching the steering wheel. Her knuckles were turning white.

She picked up the thread of their conversation. "*Forced out* wasn't the precise phrase that the CEO or other high-level managers used during the meeting we had. They left the dirty work to a cadre of fast-talking attorneys."

He winced. "Ouch."

Sydney glanced at him out of the corner of one eye, then down at Sneaker, who was sitting quietly on his lap. She bit her bottom lip and inquired delicately, "What do you do in Boston?"

She was quick.

"I'm what you would call a 'fast-talking attorney,'" Eric said without sarcasm.

"Oops." She reached up and adjusted the rearview mirror. "Sorry about that."

"There's no need to apologize." He heaved a long, drawn-out, and rather theatrical sigh. "Ninety-nine percent of the lawyers ruin it for the rest of us."

It was a second or two before Sydney reacted. Then she began to laugh. It was unrestrained and unself-conscious laughter. It was the laughter Eric remembered from high school. It was also contagious. He found himself laughing along with her.

"Now what?" he asked a few minutes later.

"Now I'm coming back to Sweetheart for a little R and R. I've been wanting to spend some time with my aunt Minerva, and this seems like the perfect opportunity."

Keep her talking.

"Mrs. Goldman mentioned that your parents are currently somewhere in Africa."

"They're working with Doctors Without Borders in the Nuba Mountains. That's in the central region of Sudan." Sydney switched back to the subject of Mrs. Goldman. "I take it Goldie hasn't lost her touch in the gossip department."

"Nope. She's still the undefeated cham-pi-on," Eric said, straightening his shoulders and leaning back against the leather seat. It was a welcome relief to find that his shirt was no longer damp and plastered to his back. The air-conditioning inside the Beemer had not only cooled him off, but dried out his clothes.

They were another mile or two down the road before his Good Samaritan said, "So, you ended up becoming a lawyer."

"I thought about a number of different career paths, but law seems to be in the blood."

"Hasn't a Law always been the sheriff of Sweetheart County?" she said.

"For the past fifty years, anyway. First, my grandfather for almost three decades. Then my dad for another twenty-plus years. And recently my cousin, Ben, was elected to the job." Eric watched as Sneaker's eyes drifted shut. Maybe this was his big chance to slip his sunglasses back on without the Sheltie noticing. "I knew from the start that I wasn't cut out for law enforcement. I just never imagined I'd follow in the footsteps of my three siblings and become an attorney."

"Yet in the end you did," Sydney commented.

He nodded. "I can't conceive of doing anything else now."

"Then the law is your true calling."

He nodded a second time.

"Are you successful at it?" she asked.

"Yes."

Sydney continued with her cross-examination. "Are you a good lawyer?"

He didn't even hesitate when he told her, "The best."

Her distinctive laugh filled the luxury automobile again. Sneaker opened his eyes, double-checked to make sure nothing was amiss, and then slowly closed them once more.

"You never were one to hide your light under a bush, Eric Law," she said.

He'd made her laugh.

She hadn't expected that.

She hadn't expected a lot of things, Sydney realized. She hadn't expected to feel comfortable with Eric. She hadn't expected to find him so easy to talk to. She hadn't expected him to be a professional anything, let alone a very successful attorney. And she certainly hadn't expected him to be single. That meant Eric Law had just regained his title as Sweetheart's most eligible bachelor.

The irony was that she had been carrying an image of Eric around in her head for the past fifteen years, and it had just been smashed to smithereens in a matter of minutes. He was definitely *not* the boy she remembered from high school.

Then maybe he's forgotten all about that night.

Maybe he'd forgotten it a long time ago. Maybe he'd put the incident out of his head before the night had even been over. Maybe it had meant nothing to him. Less than nothing. Her most embarrassing moment—so vivid in her own mind that she could still smell him, taste him, feel him—and he didn't even remember it.

The joke, it seemed, was on her.

They were approaching the city limits and there was the familiar sign: WELCOME TO SWEETHEART, INDIANA, WHERE EVERYONE IS YOUR FRIEND, POPULATION: 11,238.

Someone had recently x-ed out the last number and printed a five where the eight ought to be. Graffiti had been spray-painted in bold black letters across the bottom of the sign: PORKY DID DRUGS. NOW PORKY'S NO MORE. POPULA-TION: 11,234.

It was traditional for graduating seniors to spray-paint jingles on the Sweetheart signs at the end of the school year. The temporary "vandalism" had been going on for as long as anyone could remember and was largely over-looked by the authorities. Most of the local citizens (many of whom had done the same thing in their day) considered it a rite of passage from the "glory days" of high school to whatever lay ahead.

Sydney turned to the man beside her. Sneaker had been surprisingly content in his arms.

Who wouldn't be?

Now, that's one thought you shouldn't be entertaining even for an instant, Sydney.

It was time—past time—to deliver Eric Law to his des-tination. "Where is the wedding reception?" she inquired as she slowed down to the posted speed limit.

"You can't miss it: It will be the only large white tent set up in the middle of the city park."

"Where they hold the annual May Dance?"

"That's the place." Eric surprised her by suggesting, "Why don't you come with me?"

"Where?"

"To the wedding reception," he said. "You're dressed for the occasion. Most of the guests are people you know. In fact, Minerva and Goldie were about to sit down at a table with the Weavers as I was leaving." His final argument was "And I'll bet you haven't had any more to eat today than I have."

"I haven't been invited."

"I'm inviting you." Eric assumed that would take care of any misgivings on her part.

Sydney licked her lips and tried to marshal her thoughts. "I've got Sneaker with me."

"Sneaker can come, too. He's well behaved. Besides, he won't be the only dog there."

"He won't?"

"Nope. Max is the guest of honor."

"And who is Max?" she asked.

"Sam's dog." That statement was almost immediately rescinded. "Gillian's dog." Her passenger rubbed the back of his neck and tried a third time. "Sam *and* Gillian's dog. It was Max who brought the two of them together."

She chuckled. "Ah, dog as matchmaker."

"Something like that." Eric's voice took on a humorous undertone. "As a matter of fact, according to my brother, Gillian married him for his dog."

A look of healthy skepticism flickered across her face.

"That's the story I heard," Eric said, holding up three fingers. "Scout's honor."

Sydney made a half-disbelieving, half-amused sound. "You were never a Boy Scout."

"Maybe not," Eric said, his mouth curving into a wry smile, "but I was once made an honorary Girl Scout."

I'll just bet you were, Sydney thought as she pulled into the nearest parking space she could find in the downtown area.

Apparently a number of the wedding guests had wisely made their way on foot from the church on the corner—there were wedding flowers still draped over the arched doorway—to the luncheon reception in the park.

"We aren't going to take no for an answer," Eric informed her as he opened his car door.

"We?"

"Sneaker and me. I'll bet he's never been to a wedding reception before. It's time he got out and about more." Eric shot her a questioning glance. "Leash?"

"Under the front seat," Sydney heard herself reply before she could think better of this crazy idea. "Although Sneaker will be happier in his Port-a-Pooch."

"Then you hold Sneaker while I grab his travel carrier, his sneaker, and Sam's briefcase. Let's go join the party: It's time to eat some delicious food, drink a few glasses of expensive champagne, and maybe even dance a little."

Damn, if she hadn't been talked into going along with him, Sydney realized as she locked her car doors.

How had Eric Law managed it?

Because he's a fast-talking attorney-at-law. That's how.

"How like my brother," Samuel Law said to his bride in an amused tone. "Eric leaves the wedding reception to do me a favor and returns an hour later with a beautiful woman."

He swung Gillian around in a circle so she could get a discreet look at the newcomer. "Who is she?"

A crease formed between Sam's eyes. "I have no idea." He paused for a moment in mid-waltz. "Although there is something vaguely familiar about the red hair."

"I'd say it's more auburn than red." Gillian nibbled on her bottom lip. "She's quite stunning."

"Tall, too."

"Not too tall for Eric," she pointed out.

"No, not too tall for Eric," Sam echoed absentmindedly. "I feel as if her name is on the tip of my tongue."

"An old girlfriend, perhaps," Gillian said saucily.

"I don't remember ever dating a redhead. In fact," Sam said, gazing down into her upturned face, "I can't seem to recall any other women before I met you."

His bride smiled up at him, her face glowing with happiness. "That, Mr. Law, is the perfect answer. And the perfect way to begin your honeymoon."

"*Our* honeymoon, Mrs. Law. Although I'll admit I was getting a little worried we might not be able to leave for the airport on time. Thank God, Eric also returned with my briefcase." Sam shook his head from side to side in bewilderment. "I still can't understand how I forgot something as important as my passport and our plane tickets back at the farm. It's not like me to be so disorganized."

Gillian patted his arm reassuringly. "I think you can be forgiven under the circumstances."

Sam frowned. "What circumstances?"

She smiled beatifically. "It's your wedding day."

He broke into a broad grin. "Yes, it is. And it's the best day of my life."

"So far."

"So far." There was the promise of even better days to come in his wife's blue-green eyes.

"I do think it's generous of James to drive his limousine all the way to Sweetheart just so he can turn around and chauffeur us to the Indianapolis airport," Gillian said.

Sam dropped his voice to a caress. "I'll never forget that first night when your big black stretch limo pulled onto Main Street, and I watched as you got out of the backseat." There was a meaningful pause. "Right then and there I knew my life was going to change."

"You were standing at the window of your office."

"You saw me?" He laughed good-naturedly. "You never told me that before."

His bride informed him, "A woman is entitled to have her little secrets."

Sam could deny her nothing. "I suppose she is."

"By the way," Gillian related, "the woman who came in with Eric seems to be making a beeline for Minerva Bagley."

Sam snapped his fingers together. "Of course, that's who she is: Minerva's niece, Sydney St. John." A moment later he added as an afterthought, "My mother once suspected Sydney had a crush on Eric back in high school."

"You don't agree?"

"If memory serves me right, Sydney was smart. In fact, brilliant. She graduated at the top of their class. I can't see a girl like that being infatuated with a boy like my brother."

"The heart isn't always logical," she said. "Besides, that was then. And this is now."

"True," he said thoughtfully.

"From what you've told me, Eric has changed a great

deal since he was a teenager. I'm sure Sydney has as well," Gillian said, putting in her two cents' worth.

"No doubt you're right," Sam readily acknowledged. "You usually are."

One blond eyebrow arched with amusement. "Usually?"

"Okay, always."

Then his bride of less than two hours said in a suspicious tone, "Sam, what are you thinking?"

He tried to appear innocent. "Who says I'm thinking?"

"I do. I recognize the look on your face."

He attempted to be disarming. "Will you do me a small favor later, my dear wife?"

"What is it?" Gillian asked.

"When the time comes, try to toss your bridal bouquet in Eric's direction."

"Eric's?"

Sam's expression was unapologetic. "Ten to one, he turns right around and gives the flowers to Sydney."

"You, my dear husband, have a devious mind."

"Hey, it can't hurt to give Fate a little helping hand now and then, can it?"

"I suppose not," she said. "However, I got the distinct impression during the past several days that Eric has sworn off women."

Sam was in total agreement. "See, doesn't that strike you as odd for a man who was once known as 'the Heartbreaker' of Sweetheart *and* the surrounding three-county area?"

"I also believe your brother doesn't like to fail, and he now has a failed marriage on his résumé."

"He's not alone. Lots of people don't make the right choice the first time out." Sam gazed down into his wife's luminous eyes. "Some of us are lucky, very lucky, the first and only time we marry."

"Yes, some of us are." Gillian went up on her tiptoes and placed a kiss on the edge of his mouth.

"So, how's your aim?"

She put her head back and looked up at him with amusement. "Excellent. I threw out my line and caught you, didn't I?"

Sam laughed with contentment, with happiness, with joy. "I believe it was the other way around."

"Whatever you say," she sweetly conceded. Then she put forth another idea. "For all you know, Eric may already have designs on Ms. St. John."

Sam rubbed his chin. "Hmm, that possibility hadn't occurred to me. But he'd be a fool not to."

Gillian bit the edges of her mouth against a smile. "You know what they say, darling."

Sam brought her closer. "What, sweetheart?"

His bride was a little breathless when she answered him. "There is no difference between a wise man and a fool when they fall in love."

Chapter
five

 "I must confess, Minerva, I don't understand young men today," Elvira Goldman said to her longtime friend as they sat sipping champagne from fine crystal goblets. Every now and then one of them would pause and take a bite of a canapé, or a forkful of shrimp salad, or a morsel of succulent cold lobster.

"I've never understood men, young or old. Today, or back in our day," Minerva Bagley admitted in a rare expansive mood as she helped herself to another crab puff.

Goldie adjusted the hat pinned precariously to the top of her head: It was pink and feathered and the latest fashion for summer weddings, at least according to Bernice down at Bernice's House of Hats. "I think that therapist is right."

"What therapist?"

"The one who writes those books."

"Which books?"

"The books about how men are really from Mars," said Goldie.

Minerva hid a smile behind her glass of champagne. "Oh, those books."

Elvira Goldman took another bite of lobster. Then she raised her napkin and dabbed at a dollop of dill sauce that had somehow missed her mouth and landed squarely on her chin. Lowering her voice, she said in a confidential tone, "Sometimes my Herbert behaved as if he were from another planet."

Minerva wisely held her tongue.

Goldie was in fine form, helped along by several glasses of vintage Cristal. "He would go out to that workshop of his in the garage and tinker for hours and never have a thing to show for it." A long-suffering sigh raised and then lowered an ample bosom. "Whenever I asked him what he was doing, he just shrugged his shoulders and answered 'nothing.' He never did have much to say." She reached over and patted Minerva's hand: *pat-a-pat-pat*. "I know I shouldn't complain, especially now that dear Herbert has gone to his final reward."

Minerva Bagley bit down hard on her tongue. Maybe getting away from Elvira and her endless chatter, by whatever means were necessary, had been Herbert Goldman's final reward.

Not that she would ever say anything so unkind to her friend. After all, the two of them had known each other for nearly fifty years. Longevity accounted for something in this life.

Goldie took another sip of bubbly. Her plump cheeks

were flushed a bright shade of pink that perfectly matched the bright pink plumage perched atop her head. "At least I've been married," she said. "While you, poor dear . . ."

Minerva was determined to head her companion off at the pass. "You were lucky enough to find the right man."

The woman sighed and said, "Yes, I was."

Minerva realized she had more to say on the subject of marriage in general and men in particular. "I've always believed that marriage to the right man means freedom, while marriage to the wrong man is like a prison sentence. The trick, of course, is recognizing who is Mr. Right and who is Mr. Wrong."

"How true," Goldie said, nodding her head a little too vigorously and sending a plume of feathers flying to one side. Her hat was quickly taking on the appearance of a rather exotic and bedraggled bird. "You know," she confided to her fellow luncheon guest, "marriage is always something of a prison for a woman."

"In that case," Minerva said, "perhaps I was lucky to escape."

"Perhaps you were at that." Her lifelong friend appeared curious, in spite of herself. "Didn't you ever consider marrying?" It was the three glasses of champagne talking. Not even Elvira Goldman would have had the nerve to ask her that question under normal circumstances.

Minerva took in and let out a deep breath before she replied. "Yes, I considered marrying."

A speculative glance came her way. "I'll bet one, or both, of the Pearson cousins proposed to you."

She let a moment pass. "Walter P. and Walter E. have been trying to outdo each other all of their lives. No woman with an ounce of common sense would put herself between those two."

There was no stopping Goldie; she was on a roll. "At one time, a long, long time ago, I even thought there might be something between you and Bimford Willow."

"Bimford Willow has always preferred his trees to people," Minerva said with finality. "Hardly good husband material."

"You're such a practical soul, my dear," came Goldie's response, along with another *pat-a-pat-pat* on her hand.

Perhaps too practical, Minerva thought.

She deftly steered the conversation away from herself. "I believe Sam has found the right woman." The two of them watched, smiles on their faces, as the bridal couple waltzed around the dance floor. "He seems very happy."

"Sam and Gillian both seem very happy," Goldie said, accepting another glass of champagne from the handsome young man in a tuxedo who had been looking after them during the sumptuous meal. "Gillian makes a beautiful bride."

"Yes, she does." Minerva realized she was feeling utterly content. She liked to think that she had played some small part in bringing Samuel Law and Gillian Charles together.

"Who would have thought our Gillian would turn out so well?" Goldie mused over the rim of her crystal flute. "I don't mind telling you that I had my doubts when she first arrived in Sweetheart. That young woman," she said, wagging her finger, "is living proof that we mustn't judge a book by its cover."

"She is, indeed," Minerva said.

"I do believe Gillian will settle down nicely and become one of us now. Well, as soon as she and Sam get back from their honeymoon. Isn't it exciting that her grandmother, accompanied by Esther Warren, will be joining the newlyweds in Italy at the end of the summer?"

"Yes, very exciting," she agreed.

"Think of all the fascinating stories Anna and Esther will have to tell us when they return."

Minerva nodded her head and made an occasional "hmm" sound while the woman beside her rattled on non-stop. Every now and then a word registered.

Florence.

Da Vinci.

Vineyards.

Cricket festival.

Then Elvira Goldman came to a halt in mid-sentence, craned her neck, and declared with an audible gasp, "My word, Minerva, I can't believe my eyes."

"What is it?"

Goldie was rarely astonished and never speechless. But it was a full ten seconds before she managed to continue. "I think that's Sydney who just walked into the reception."

Minerva spun around. "*My* Sydney?"

"Yes, *your* Sydney." The woman's mouth dropped open.

Minerva sat forward eagerly in her chair and surveyed the large party tent. "Where is she?"

"There." Limp feathers flopped forward over her friend's eyes, making it impossible for her to tell in which direction Elvira was staring. "And she's not alone."

"What do you mean she's not alone?"

Goldie blew out her breath and swept the errant

plumage back from her face with both hands. "She's with Eric Law."

Sydney could feel a dozen pairs of eyes fixed on them. All right, maybe it was more like two or three dozen. Obviously she and Eric had created a stir by entering the reception together.

That had not been her intention. This was someone else's wedding celebration and all eyes should be focused on the bride and groom dancing together in the middle of the floor, especially when Eric's brother and his wife made such a striking couple.

For a moment her gaze swept the large and exquisitely decorated tent. There were bright summer flower arrangements, pristine white linens, elegant china and silver place settings, and sparkling crystal chandeliers. The setting was breathtaking: formal, yet relaxed.

At one end of the room there was an orchestra playing. A number of couples had joined the bride and groom for the next dance. Several hundred other guests were seated at intimate tables around the perimeter, while a staff of waiters discreetly served food and refilled glasses.

A group of children were happily playing in one corner. There was a dog in their midst, soaking up all the attention. It could only be the honored guest and matchmaker *extraordinaire:* Max.

Aunt Minerva, where are you?

Her prayer was immediately answered. There were her aunt and Mrs. Goldman sitting at a table directly across from where she was standing. They were sipping champagne and nibbling on what appeared to be gourmet seafood.

Her stomach growled, reminding her that she hadn't eaten since breakfast. It had been a very light breakfast at that: a small container of yogurt and half of a banana. The cupboard had been bare back at her apartment since she had made the decision to sublet the space for the foreseeable future.

"I've spotted my aunt," she said to Eric. "She isn't expecting me, so I'd better let her know I'm here. Besides, you have Sam's all-important briefcase to deliver."

Eric nodded. "There are a few 'best man' duties I need to see to, but I'll be back to claim that dance."

Sydney opened her mouth to say, "*What dance?*" but Eric had already turned and was making for the head table on the other side of the reception tent.

"Come on, Sneaker, I have several ladies I want to introduce you to. I think you may come as an even bigger surprise to them than I will," she said to her companion as he cowered in his traveling case.

Sneaker had never been to a formal party before. It was apparent that he didn't know what to make of the music and the dancing and the general commotion. However, the Sheltie was no fool. He was suddenly alert, his nose in the air, sniffing. He recognized lobster and crab and steak when he smelled them.

"Aunt Minerva," Sydney said, approaching their table. Her throat was suddenly thick with tears and her eyes were misty. She realized that she'd never been so happy to see someone in her entire life. She also realized belatedly that she should have called her aunt and told her she was coming to town.

"My dear girl, I wondered if you would arrive in time for the wedding reception." Minerva's kind, brown eyes were asking questions, but she was too perceptive to voice them aloud with Goldie sitting there, listening to every word.

"I wasn't sure exactly what time I would get into Sweetheart," she said, bending over to give her aunt a hug, followed by a kiss on the cheek. Then she straightened and greeted the other woman. "Hello, Mrs. Goldman."

"Mrs. Goldman?" There was a slight slurring to the words. "Why, so formal after all these years, Sydney St. John? You call me Goldie like you always have."

"Hello, Goldie."

"That's better" was accompanied by an emphatic nod that sent pink fuzz flying.

Minerva patted the empty chair next to hers. "Sit here, Sydney. The Weavers were making the rounds, but I see they're on the dance floor now. I don't expect they'll be back any time soon."

Goldie peered down at the dog staring up at her from his Port-a-Pooch. "What, pray tell, do we have here?"

"This is Sneaker," Sydney said, making the introductions. "He's a Shetland sheepdog."

Elvira Goldman's forehead wrinkled, giving her the appearance of a Chinese shar-pei. "A dog at a wedding reception?"

"Eric Law assured me it was all right to bring Sneaker, and that he wouldn't be the only dog here."

"That's correct," Minerva spoke up in her defense. "Max is here somewhere. Probably playing with the children."

"Or being fed that fancy prime beef at thirty dollars a pound," Goldie said with a disapproving *harumph*. She leaned closer. "What in the world is that green thing dangling from your dog's mouth?"

"It's a shoelace." An explanation seemed called for. "It's attached to his sneaker, which goes with him everywhere. Like Linus and his security blanket."

Goldie screwed up her face. "Linus?"

"The character in the *Peanuts* cartoon."

"Oh . . . *that* Linus."

"I'll bet that's how Sneaker got his name," Minerva said, taking Sydney's hand in hers and squeezing it affectionately.

An attentive waiter suddenly appeared tableside. He hovered behind Sydney's chair and inquired, "May I bring you a plate of selections from the buffet, Ms. St. John?"

"Yes, thank you."

"And a glass of champagne?"

"Please."

He nodded, neatly turned, and disappeared as discreetly as he had appeared.

"I wonder how our waiter knew your name," Goldie said as if she were pondering one of life's great mysteries.

Sydney knew how. In two words: Eric Law. That's how.

It was some time later, over a plate of shrimp salad garnished with slivers of avocado, artichoke hearts, white truffles, and hearts of palm that the inquisition began.

"Minerva failed to mention to me you were coming to town," Goldie scolded.

"My vacation plans were up in the air until very recently," Sydney responded. It was more or less true. She was on a vacation of sorts and her plans had been uncertain until the past twenty-four hours.

"I also hear that you work too hard at that fancy-smancy job of yours."

"I suppose I do." *Did.* "That's why I've decided to take some time off from the corporate world."

Goldie stared at Sydney's left hand and, without batting an eyelash, inquired, "Why aren't you married?"

She was tempted to give the Busybody of Sweetheart one of those stop-them-dead-in-their-tracks responses she had recently read about in a newspaper advice column.

"Beats me. Why aren't you skinny?"

Or: *"Why would I want to ruin a perfectly good sex life by getting married?"*

And her personal favorite: *"Dang, I knew there was something I forgot to do."*

Instead, Sydney chose diplomacy. "I suppose I've been too busy to give marriage much thought."

Everyone knew that Goldie fancied herself an expert on the subject of wedded bliss. After all, she had been married for more than four decades to Herbert Goldman.

Sydney felt herself being scrutinized from head to toe. "You're too tall, of course" came the expert's pronouncement. "No man likes to be towered over by a woman. You're also too independent and too smart. I always said you had more brains than were necessary or wise for a girl. I must say you've turned out to be surprisingly attractive . . . in a different sort of way. You used to be such a carrot top. Now your hair is a lovely reddish-brown color." Goldie had one last piece of advice to give. "Just don't get too fussy or particular about men, or you'll end up an old maid like Minerva."

Sydney felt rather than heard the intake of air from the

gentle creature sitting beside her. She would gladly have strangled Elvira Goldman on the spot. The woman's only excuse for such thoughtlessness was the one too many glasses of fine champagne she had indulged in.

Sydney abruptly changed the subject. "I wonder if our waiter would bring me a small piece of chateaubriand without the bernaise sauce."

"Still hungry, dear?" Minerva said, obviously relieved to have the topic of marriage dropped.

"It's not for me. But Sneaker would certainly enjoy a small bite or two."

That was an understatement: The Sheltie was still licking his chops when Sydney happened to glance up and see that both Minerva and Goldie had their eyes fixed on something *or* someone over her left shoulder.

Before she could turn around, a familiar voice said, "I believe this is the dance you promised me, Sydney."

Chapter

six

Sydney turned around.

Eric could read her mind. Or maybe it was her body language telling him loud and clear: *I don't remember promising to dance with you. I don't want to dance. Besides, I'm not going to desert Sneaker, and I'm certainly not going to leave my aunt when I just got here.*

Minerva Bagley must have sensed that Sydney was about to refuse him. "Go on and dance with Eric, my dear. Enjoy yourself. Have some fun with the other young adults at the party," she urged her niece.

With a quick glance down at Sneaker, Sydney opened her mouth to speak.

Minerva beat her to the punch. "Goldie and I are perfectly happy to sit and watch. We'll keep an eye on your dog for you." The Sheltie was curled up in his Port-a-Pooch carrier, nose buried in his sneaker, shoelace dangling from one side of his mouth, eyes heavy with sleep. "Sneaker seems content since he's taken a walk in the park and had something to eat and drink."

Apparently Sydney still wasn't convinced. "Are you sure?"

Minerva smiled at her niece. "I'm sure."

"But . . ."

There was the *but* that Eric's gut instincts had warned him was coming.

Elvira Goldman sat up straight, righted the feathered concoction on her head, cleared her throat, and went on to broadcast the latest goings-on: "I see that Mary Kay and Davison Weaver are heading in this direction, each with a plate of food and a drink in their hands. They'll need someplace to sit while they eat."

"There's plenty of room for all of us," Minerva said with a pointed look at Goldie. "I'll simply ask the waiter to set up several more chairs at our table."

"Meanwhile, it's the perfect time for us to dance." Eric reached down and offered Sydney his hand. She finally accepted and stood up. As he guided her through the crowd, he leaned closer and said, "Besides, they're playing our song."

Her mouth twitched in what might have been a smile. "We don't have a song."

"We don't?" he said, feigning surprise.

Sydney gave a ladylike snort of amusement. "You know darn well we don't."

Eric cocked his head to one side and listened to the music for a bar or two. "As luck would have it, the orchestra is playing a classic that's tailor-made for us."

"What classic is that?" she asked.

He took her in his arms and began to move to the slow, sensual rhythm. " 'You Don't Know Me.' "

She pursed her lips. "Ray Charles."

Eric felt his face dissolve into an acknowledging smile. "The one and only."

After the briefest of pauses, Sydney said, looking rather baffled, "But we do know each other."

His mouth curved up at the edges. "Maybe. Then again, maybe not," he said.

They danced for a minute or two without speaking. It wasn't a comfortable silence, Eric realized, but it wasn't exactly uncomfortable, either. The good news was, his headache had disappeared sometime in the past hour.

A moment later Sydney's foot bumped into his. "Sorry. I haven't danced in a long time," she said by way of an explanation.

"Neither have I," he admitted.

She knitted her brows. "Not even at all those weddings you've attended?"

He was going to have to enlighten Sydney St. John on the finer points of member-of-the-wedding-party etiquette. "Those dances were what I call 'duty dances.' "

She gave him a look of polite inquiry. "Isn't dancing . . . well, dancing?"

"Not by a long shot. Not when they're duty dances." There was a short pause. "First, there is the danger involved."

Sydney gave a light laugh. "I've heard of dirty dancing, but never dangerous dancing."

"Believe me, it exists," Eric said in a deadpan tone. "I have personally tripped the light fantastic with bridesmaids who trampled on my toes until they were black and blue *and* bloodied. I have waltzed with aged grandmothers who barely came up to here on me"—he indicated a spot midway up his chest—"leading to a permanent crick in my lower back. I have danced the Twist and the Watusi and something called the Fish with anyone and everyone, from childhood friends to former college roommates of the bride who felt compelled to divulge indiscretions pertaining to *a*: the bride, *b*: the bridegroom, or *c*: both the bride and the groom, after imbibing too much champagne."

"I see what you mean by dangerous," Sydney said facetiously. "I had no idea."

"And that's not the half of it," he told her.

Hazel eyes, tigress eyes flecked with brown and green and gold, stared up into his with interest. "What else?" Sydney inquired.

He had her now. She was curious.

Curiosity was a funny thing. It could be cunning. Sly. Seductive. Even addictive. He had used that aspect of human nature to his advantage on numerous occasions both in *and* out of the courtroom. But In his opinion, the whole subject had been best expressed by the humorist Dorothy Parker: *"Four be the things I'd been better without: Love, curiosity, freckles, and doubt."*

"Let me see." Eric searched for the right words. "I wonder if there is a delicate way of putting this."

Sydney caught the tip of her tongue between her teeth. "Would it have anything to do with females between the ages of nineteen and ninety hitting on you?"

He felt the heat rise in his face. Strange. He couldn't remember the last time he'd been embarrassed. He wasn't sure why he was feeling embarrassed now.

"I won't deny it hasn't happened," Eric said, without mentioning any specific incidents, "but I was thinking more along the lines of the volatile and often unfortunate combination of too much food, too much alcohol, and too much energetic dancing."

Small creases momentarily formed on a porcelain forehead. "I don't understand."

Apparently he was going to have to be a little less delicate and a lot more blunt. "Let's just say that I've held more than one young woman's head while she threw up *a*: in the ladies rest room, *b*: in the bushes, *c*: all over my shoes, or *d*: all of the above."

Sydney's mouth formed a perfectly round O.

It was time to change the subject. Eric gazed down at her. "You're not as tall as I remember."

Nice out.

"I'm exactly the same height I was at seventeen," Sydney informed him. "You're the one who's taller."

"As a matter of fact, I grew three inches after we graduated from high school." He paused a beat, then decided to proceed. "This may sound conceited"—*nice opening argument, Law*—"but I always thought you liked me back then."

Sydney raised and lowered her elegant silk-clad shoulders. "I liked a lot of people."

Eric didn't think she was being intentionally obtuse. It was just the way Sydney was. "I meant *liked* as in 'had a crush on.' "

"High school seems like a lifetime ago," she said, without refuting or confirming his claim.

"Water under the bridge, huh?"

She moved her head: It was a definite yes. "Under the bridge and out to sea." As an apparent afterthought a zinger was added. "Besides, my taste in men has matured."

"Damned shame," he muttered under his breath as the orchestra concluded one song and segued right into the next.

A bright red mouth toyed with a wry smile. "We all have to grow up sometime."

"It took me a long time," Eric admitted as he maneuvered between the couples crowding the dance floor.

His partner let out a sigh. "I'm positive it took me longer than anyone else in our class. I was the definitive 'late bloomer.' "

"Not from where I stood."

Sydney gave him a questioning glance. "Where in the world were you standing, then?"

Eric was determined to be forthright with her. "Even as a kid, and certainly as a teenager, you seemed to understand what was important and what was trivial. You were smarter than the rest of us put together, and yet you studied harder than anyone else in our class. You didn't follow the crowd. You marched to your own drummer. You had the guts to be different."

Sydney fixed him with a steady gaze. "It's not as if I had a choice. I *was* different."

"Different can be good."

"Not when you're sixteen or seventeen," she said, her dark auburn brows drawn in a thoughtful frown. "It was as if everybody else was in on the joke and I was clueless."

"I said it was good to be different. I didn't say it was easy," he gently corrected her.

Sydney stared over his right shoulder for a moment. "I was smart about some things and dumb about others."

"Weren't we all?"

She confessed, "I was socially immature."

"For my money, that's better than being socially precocious. Or even worse, promiscuous." The words came straight from his gut. God knows, he'd started down that path himself and had thankfully put the brakes on in time. "There were girls and guys in our class who would sleep with anyone, anytime, anywhere. Aside from any moral considerations, or the risk factors associated with that kind of behavior, sex becomes commonplace, mundane, even prosaic, when it should be something very special between two people."

"I couldn't agree more." She cast him a sidelong glance and said, "Okay, now it's your turn to 'fess up."

No problem.

"I was a late bloomer"—that was the understatement of the decade—"when it came to academics. I rarely cracked a book. I never took getting an education seriously. I basically pissed away my entire four years of high school and then had to run like hell to catch up."

Sydney appeared genuinely interested. "What turned it around for you?"

"Working in a factory one summer, followed by a year spent at a military academy. I was just darned lucky I woke up and smelled the coffee before it was too late. Some of our classmates never did. They're still working down at the corner gas station making minimum wage, or worse, laid off from the transmission plant." Eric shook his head and said with conviction, "Better to be a late bloomer than to look back on high school as your 'glory days.'"

Sydney's expression changed and her voice grew fiercely adamant. "High school was never my glory days. In fact, I used to think I hated high school. Later on I realized what I hated was feeling like a square peg in a round hole."

"Me, too. I never felt like I fit in anywhere." Eric brought her closer as they circled the dance floor. "I never imagined we had so much in common. I always assumed we were poles apart."

"I guess in some ways we were and in some ways we weren't," she said.

The Ray Charles song had hit the nail on the head: He hadn't really known her. She sure as hell hadn't known him. That pretty much summed up their past.

"By the way," he went on, "thanks again for the lift into town."

"You're welcome."

"Sam and Gillian asked me to thank you on their behalf as well. They're relieved *and* thrilled that they get to leave for their honeymoon on schedule."

"I was happy to help. Tuscany should not be kept waiting." Sydney threw her loose auburn hair back from her shoulders. "What about your sports car?"

"Even as we speak, Ernie should be towing Red back to the garage." Ernie had better be handling his Porsche with kid gloves, too, considering the tip he'd been given.

Sydney's tone was one of bemusement. "After all these years Ernie is still in business?"

"Yup. He's still owner, proprietor and sole employee of

Ernie's Towing and Tattooing. Although I understand he's recently had a new motto painted on the side of his tow truck."

"Which is?"

Eric paused for effect. " 'Wreck a-mended.' "

They both groaned and then laughed.

It was a minute or two later that he reiterated, "You did me a big favor today. I'll find a way to pay you back."

"There's no need," Sydney assured him. "You would have done the same for me."

Something niggled at him. "Come to think of it, I did do the same for you once, didn't I?"

The woman in his arms stiffened ever so slightly. "Did you?" she echoed.

Memories stirred of a night long ago. Eric started to think out loud. "I was driving home from a party and suddenly there you were standing in the middle of the road like a startled deer caught in my headlights. You were soaking wet and covered with mud. As I recall your car had skidded off the highway into a drainage ditch."

Sydney gave him a veiled look. "I'd almost forgotten about that night."

It was coming back to him in bits and pieces. "It was raining cats and dogs, wasn't it?"

She nodded. "I must have hit a slick spot on the road—probably an oil patch—and I lost control of the steering wheel. Once my car landed in the ditch, it was stuck. I couldn't get any traction under the tires."

Eric cocked a brow. "When I arrived on the scene, you were pretty upset."

"I remember being cold and wet and discouraged and frustrated," she said with a sigh.

Eric knew there was a wry smile on his face. He realized he was actually enjoying himself. "I had a chain in the trunk of my old Mustang. I hooked it up underneath the frame of your family's sedan and managed to pull it back onto the highway."

"Yes," was all Sydney said.

He chuckled. "Before the night was over we were both soaked through and covered with muck. But, as I recall, no harm done beyond a small dent to the back fender."

"No harm done," she echoed in a slightly strained voice.

Eric rubbed the back of his neck with one hand. "Lucky I came along that night. In those days we didn't have cell phones to carry around with us." Of course, owning a cell phone hadn't done him much good this afternoon.

"Aunt Minerva always claimed I was lucky." Sydney seemed to breathe easier. "You rescued me what . . . sixteen years ago? I finally repaid you today."

"Well, you know what they always say." He gave his partner a spin as the music changed to a tune with an upbeat tempo.

"What?" Sydney asked as he caught her hand and twirled her in another circle around him.

Eric laughed, brought her in closer to his side, and said, "One good turn deserves another."

Chapter
seven

 Sydney was standing at the rear of the crowd when the bride threw her "tossing bouquet." Gillian had chosen to perform this part of the traditional wedding celebration midway through the reception, rather than wait until the last minute when she and Sam were ready to leave on their honeymoon.

Anyway, no one seemed more surprised than the bride's brother-in-law when the bunch of pale pink roses, decorated with pale pink silk streamers, came flying through the air straight toward him. Eric's reaction was instinctive: He raised both of his hands and made a perfect catch.

The assembled wedding guests broke into loud cheers and delighted laughter. The bride and groom were both grinning from ear to ear as if they had managed to pull off some clever stratagem of their own. The best man stood there for a moment staring down at the bouquet in his hands before he realized he was being surrounded by a dozen young women vying for both the flowers and his attention.

Eric politely waved them aside, made his way through the throng of well-wishers, walked up to Minerva and presented her with the bouquet of roses. Then he leaned over and whispered something in her aunt's ear. Whatever he said brought a smile to her face.

In fact, Aunt Minerva was positively beaming.

The two of them—the tall, dark, and drop-dead gorgeous man in the prime of life and the unpretentious middle-aged woman—spoke privately for several minutes before Elvira Goldman tottered back to the table and interrupted them.

Naturally, Sydney had no intentions of sticking her nose in where it didn't belong. Whatever had passed between Eric and Minerva was their business and nobody else's. Although she had to admit that her curiosity was aroused.

For the remainder of the afternoon she caught only an occasional glimpse of Eric. At one point he was conferring with a distinguished-looking gentleman she assumed was the catering manager. Another time he was standing on the far side of the party tent deep in conversation with his brother.

He never once looked her way.

Why should he, Sydney? You aren't really his guest. You weren't even officially invited to the wedding reception. It was all happenstance. You did the man a favor. He returned the favor by including you in the party.

And wasn't it only earlier this afternoon that you were hoping you wouldn't run into him again . . . ever?

Maybe people change. Maybe they don't. But let's face it, the last thing you need is to go looking for trouble. And Eric Law has always been trouble. Big trouble.

"Far better and certainly far safer for you if you go your way and he goes his," she said under her breath.

Besides, his duties and responsibilities as Sam's best man would undoubtedly keep Eric busy until the last party-goer had called it a day. Or more accurately, had called it an evening.

The newlyweds had slipped away at some point during the afternoon and changed into their travel clothes: Sam and Gillian were casually dressed when they made their farewells. Then they were whisked away in a black stretch limousine that had been waiting to take them to the Indianapolis airport. Soon after, the first of the wedding guests began to take their leave.

"This has been a perfect day," Minerva said with a contented sigh, the tossing bouquet still clasped in her hand. She raised the roses to her face and inhaled deeply, then said, "Hmm." Adding, "Wasn't it thoughtful of Eric to present me with the bridal flowers?"

"Yes, it was." Sydney realized it had been thoughtful. In fact, surprisingly thoughtful for someone who had once been completely self-centered in her book.

And who isn't self-centered and self-absorbed at the age of sixteen or seventeen or even eighteen?

"Eric used to be such a wild one." Her aunt shook her head and hairpins went flying as they invariably did. "I always felt a little sorry for him when he was growing up."

Sydney wondered aloud, "Why?"

Bespectacled brown eyes were filled with sympathy and

understanding. "He seemed so lost to me. Yes, that's what he was: a lost boy."

"Well, he's not a boy any longer," Sydney said with more feeling than she had intended.

"I don't believe Eric is lost anymore, either," the older woman said. "I hear he's done very nicely for himself."

Her response was succinct. "Apparently."

Her aunt leaned closer, placed a hand on her arm, and lowered her voice to a confidential level. "Do you know what he said when he gave me the roses?"

Sydney shook her head, although she assumed it was the kind of question that didn't really require a response from her.

"He quoted a line of poetry. French. Sixteenth century. Imagine a handsome man of Eric's age spouting French poetry to me at my age." Minerva's cheeks were flushed with pleasure. "Let's see if I can remember how it went." There was a pause and then she recited, " *'Une rose d'automne est plus qu'une autre exquise.'* "

Sydney got the gist of it, but still inquired, "Which translated means . . . ?"

Her aunt was more than happy to oblige. " 'More exquisite than any other is the autumn rose.' "

"Why, that's lovely."

"Yes, it is. I'm not certain I understand what it means, but it is lovely, isn't it? Then Eric thanked me for being kind to him at some point in the past when he claimed he didn't deserve it. I reminded him that's when we all need kindness the most."

Sydney reached over, took her aunt's hand in hers, and gave it an affectionate squeeze. She felt her throat tighten and she tried to swallow before she said, "No one has a better heart or a more generous nature than you do."

Minerva seemed taken aback, even a bit embarrassed, by the compliment. She dabbed at something in the corner of her eye with a luncheon napkin. "My goodness, look at the time. I should be getting Goldie home."

Sydney made a point of *not* looking at the woman sitting across the table from them. Admittedly Elvira Goldman's eyelids were shut and she appeared to have dozed off. But Goldie's reputation for eavesdropping—when people least expected her to be listening—made both of them cautious.

"She seems a little the worse for wear" came out as a barely perceptible whisper on Sydney's part.

It was the hat.

What remained of the woman's hat, anyway. It had been shedding feathers and bits and pieces and whatnots since Sydney had arrived earlier that afternoon. The remaining plumage resembled some sort of fantastical hybrid creature: half pink flamingo, half bald eagle.

Minerva mouthed, "No doubt she's feeling under the weather. One too many . . ." She pantomimed holding a glass to her lips. "Thank goodness, I'm driving."

Sydney stifled a yawn. "Sneaker and I should be on our way, too. It's been a long day. We left Chicago early this morning, but between road construction and traffic jams it turned out to be a seven-hour trip." She rose from her chair and began to gather up her handbag, the Sheltie, his sneaker, and his Port-a-Pooch.

"We'll walk out with you." Minerva Bagley raised her voice a notch or two. "Goldie, the party's over."

Elvira Goldman's eyes flew open. Her mouth immediately followed suit. "Beautiful bride. Magnificent wedding." She scarcely caught her breath before she rambled on. "Lovely party. Delicious food. Wonderful champagne." She stood up on wobbly legs, steadied herself against the chair back, adjusted her hat (to no avail), picked up the matching pink handbag, and muttered to no one in particular, "Must have cost a pretty penny."

Minerva ignored that last comment and said to Sydney, "Where are you parked?"

"Just down the street." Once they were outside she pointed in the direction of her car. "It's the silver sedan."

"Why, I'm only three parking spaces from you."

They deposited Goldie in the passenger seat of Minerva's car, helped her buckle up, and closed the door.

"Are you sure you'll be able to manage Mrs. Goldman by yourself?" she asked her aunt.

"I'm sure. It isn't the first time I've had to take Goldie home; it won't be the last." An explanation quickly followed. "Not that she makes a habit of overindulging, because she doesn't. It's just that weddings seem to make Elvira sentimental." There was a pause and a sigh. "I think they remind her of how lonely she is without Herbert."

Sydney almost blurted out: *Don't you ever get lonely?*

Her aunt stepped up onto the grassy curb, wrapped an arm around her waist, and changed the subject. "Something tells me we have a great deal to talk about."

"We do," Sydney said, speaking softly. "I hope I didn't make it awkward for you in front of Mrs. Goldman by showing up without any warning."

Minerva waved that consideration aside with one hand.

"Your business and my business are none of Goldie's business."

"Still, I'm sorry I didn't let you know I was coming back to town. I only decided yesterday."

"It wasn't necessary, you know that." The woman beside her was solicitous. "You look tired."

Sydney stifled another yawn. "I was up half the night packing. And I didn't expect to spend most of the afternoon and evening at a wedding celebration."

"I admit I was surprised to see you walk into that tent, especially with Eric Law in tow," said Minerva.

Sydney decided to clear up the reason for their sudden appearance. "I was on my way home. Just west of town I ran into Eric and offered him a lift."

"So that's why you were together this afternoon." Minerva smiled. "You two created quite a stir."

Sydney gave a tired laugh. "Believe me, it wasn't intentional."

Eyebrows flecked with gray were arched in curiosity. "Why did Eric need a lift?"

Sydney kept the explanation short and sweet. "Apparently he was running a last-minute errand for his brother and developed car trouble. I found him stranded out on State Road Three."

"Then he was very lucky you came along."

There was that word again.

Lucky.

Luckier.

Luckiest.

You are the luckiest girl I know, Sydney Marie St. John.

An expression of concern settled on Minerva's usually pleasant features. "Are you sure you're all right?"

Sydney gave her head a shake. "I'm fine."

"Truly?"

"Truly," she said without hesitation. *Or I will be once I've slept for a week or two.*

Minerva glanced at her passenger: Goldie's head had fallen back and her lips were parted; she appeared to be snoring. "Let's have a long chat when we can talk in private. And once you've had a chance to settle in and get your bearings."

Sydney was relieved. "Thank you for understanding," she said. "You always do."

Minerva took the car keys from her handbag. "Well, you know you're welcome to stay here in town with me."

"I know, but . . ."

But she wanted nothing more than to get back into her car, drive the short distance remaining to the Woodlands, unload the one suitcase from the trunk that she would need tonight, gather up Sneaker and the few things he would require, let herself into her parents' house, and fall straight into bed.

Minerva extended her customary hospitality. "If you change your mind, your old room is ready and waiting."

Sydney acknowledged the offer, but said, "I think I need the peace and quiet of the country for a while." She stared off into space. "And the solitude. I have a lot of decisions to make about my future."

Minerva appeared concerned. "Surely you don't need to start making them right off the bat."

She gave a shrug. "Perhaps not."

Her aunt made a suggestion. "Why not give yourself some time to just do nothing? Perhaps sleep in for a few mornings. Maybe even spend a whole day in bed. Curl up in the hammock with a good book. Sit on the front porch and sip homemade iced tea. Enjoy the summer flowers in the garden. Stroll through the woods. The change of pace would do you a world of good."

"Yes, it would." Sydney's voice vibrated slightly. "How did you get to be so wise?"

"Wisdom comes from making mistakes." After a brief pause Minerva tempered that statement with "Well, at least it does if we learn from our mistakes. I'm nearly twice your age, so you can imagine the huge number I've managed to rack up."

Sydney scoffed good-naturedly. "I don't believe I've ever seen you make a mistake, whether it was baking cookies, or whipping up a fancy soufflé, or helping me with a problem when I was growing up, or even in your own life."

"Oh, my dear, you always did see me through rose-colored glasses." Her aunt reached up and touched her face with soothing fingertips. "I have missed you."

"I've missed you, too." Sydney suddenly felt guilty. "I should have come home to see you more often. I'm sorry I didn't this past year. I meant to. My intentions were good." She heaved a sigh of regret. "But I kept getting caught up in my work to the exclusion of anything *or* anyone else." *For all the good it did you in the end, Sydney.*

"Shhh. There's no need for apologies. We each do our best. No one can ask more of us than that." Minerva gently patted her cheek. "Now go home and get some rest. Call me when you feel like talking."

"I will. I promise."

The woman beside her paused, turned her head, and said in a hushed tone, "Listen."

The soft strains of a familiar song were coming from the large white party tent. The orchestra was playing the same piece of music that had signaled the last dance of the evening in Sweetheart for the past sixty years and more: "Goodnight, Sweetheart."

"The party is officially over," said Sydney.

"Yes, it is." The music came to an end. There was a smattering of applause for the orchestra. Then Minerva turned and said to her, "Drive carefully."

Sydney hastened to reassure her. "My one glass of champagne wore off hours ago."

Minerva went up on her tiptoes and kissed her cheek. "Good night, my girl."

Tears welled. Only her aunt called her *"my girl."*

It was a moment or two before Sydney managed to say in return: "Good night, Aunt Minerva." Then she watched until the tan sedan disappeared around the next corner.

"We'll be home soon," she said to Sneaker as she settled him in the passenger seat of her car and buckled in his Port-a-Pooch. "I just need to make a short pit stop for coffee and a few essentials."

Before it was said and done, a "few essentials" ended up filling two large grocery bags. After all, she did prefer her coffee generously laced with cream and sugar. And the blueberry muffins in the bakery case by the checkout counter had proven to be irresistible, not to mention the homegrown sweet corn and muskmelons, tomatoes and cucumbers. There was barely room on the floor in front of Sneaker's travel carrier for the bulging brown paper sacks.

Sydney slowly made her way through the businesses that bordered downtown. She caught a glimpse of Jayne's Epicurean Delights (the only vegetarian restaurant within a fifty-mile radius), Stella's Nails (a large outline of a hand in the front window advertised a special on painted acrylics: THIS WEEK ONLY: TROPICAL PALM TREES $19.95, RHINESTONE COWBOYS $20.95), and Ann's Art Gallery and Scrapbook Supplies ("Memories are made of this 'n' that").

She went past what used to be Weaver's Emporium (it had been converted a few years ago to an antique mall), then the Sweetheart County Courthouse with its spotlights all aglimmer and its flowers in full bloom: A colorful mixture of geraniums, pansies, and impatiens were planted on each of the four corners of the town square.

She drove on by McGinty's Pub—she must remember to stop in and say hello to her old friends and one-time employers Mike and Hilda—and then the Sweetheart Bed & Breakfast & Art Gallery, according to a discreet sign posted on the front lawn of what had once been Sweetheart's one and only mansion.

On the outskirts of the city limits was the No-Tell Motel, looking as rundown and as dilapidated as it had back when she was in high school. There was a beat-up tin sign to one side of the potholed gravel drive: PATRON PARKING IN REAR. It was common knowledge that rooms at the No-

Tell were for rent by the night . . . or by the hour. *What happens here, stays here.*

Across the road was a hamburger joint the locals called the "Greasy Spoon." Sydney didn't think the eatery had a real name. An orange neon light dangled precariously in the front window of the restaurant and flashed between two messages: EATS and OPEN. Several of the neon letters were burned out and the center of the *E* was broken off. The *O* had been repaired with what appeared to be duct tape, so the message repeated as CATS . . . UP . . . CATS . . . UP . . . CATS . . . UP.

The more things change, the more they remain the same.

The St. John family homestead, established in 1842, according to the date carved into one of the older structures on the farm, was five miles due east of Sweetheart. The setting sun was well behind her by the time Sydney reached the familiar fork in the road and the discreet sign that read: THE WOODLANDS.

She turned onto the country lane. Deciduous trees—ash and elm, sugar maples and Golden Raintrees—formed a natural canopy overhead. The air was still; there was barely a whisper of a breeze. The evening sky was gradually fading from cerulean, streaked with scarlet and orange and cerise, to deep indigo blue. There was a solitary light blinking in the distance.

She had forgotten how quiet and how isolated it was out here in the country.

"Isn't that what you claimed you wanted: peace and quiet? To have some time alone?" she said to her reflection in the rearview mirror. "Well, that's what you're going to get."

Sydney tried to console herself with the thought that she wouldn't *really* be alone. There were several other occupied dwellings on the property, including the log cabin Bimford Willow had built deep in the woods where he could be near his beloved trees; trees he considered more his than her family's. It was Bim's job to look after the Scotch pine, the Fraser fir and the Douglas fir, the white pine and the spruce. The Woodlands had always been a working property.

She was nearly to the end of the lane—the house would soon be in sight—when she became aware of another vehicle ten or fifteen car lengths behind her. By the height of the headlights in her mirror, it was either an SUV or a pickup truck. Maybe it was Bim. Or his sister, Mrs. Manderley. Maybe it was the farm manager or one of the handful of people who lived at various locations around the acreage.

With the sun below the horizon, a blue mist seemed to seep from the woods and roll across the fields, hovering several feet and more above the ground. In front and to either side of her sedan the landscape was awash with shadows: dark, drifting, ghostly. The headlights of the vehicle behind her scarcely pierced the gathering fog.

Pinpricks stung the back of her neck. She shivered, and goose bumps covered her skin.

"Don't be silly, Syd," she said out loud, trying to quell a rising sense of apprehension. "This is a country lane on the outskirts of Sweetheart, Indiana, not some dark and foreboding back alley, and certainly not something out of one of those god-awful fright movies."

Sneaker was suddenly on the alert. He stood up in his

Port-a-Pooch and put his front paws on the edge of the carrier. His eyes were wide open. His nose was in the air. His fur was ruffled. He growled long and low in the back of his throat.

"You're not helping matters, you know," she said to him with a slightly nervous laugh.

This was crazy. She was allowing her imagination to run away with her. After all, for the past decade she had taken care of herself while living in Chicago and during business trips to any number of big cities where the dangers were real, not imagined. And she'd done a damned fine job of it, too.

Nevertheless, she kept one eye on her rearview mirror and the vehicle behind her.

Sydney steered around the last bend in the road, and there was the house she'd grown up in, the house she had always thought of as home, the house she was coming back to now by herself.

Home was a sprawling three-story white farmhouse built on the rise of a hill and surrounded by trees; it had a bright red front door and newly painted black shutters on the windows. The wraparound porch, with its ornate Victorian balustrades, had been added during an era when porches were meant to be a place of welcome, a place to sit and socialize, a place to cool off on a hot summer's eve; a fan in one hand and a glass of cold lemonade in the other.

The side yard was large and fenced in on three sides. Flowers were everywhere: filling numerous terra-cotta pots and neatly edged mulched beds, spilling over a wooden garden gate and rambling over the decorative wheelbarrow placed in the center of the lawn.

Sydney pulled up by the side door and shifted into park.

A white pickup truck stopped a short distance away. A man got out and walked toward her.

It was Eric Law.

She hit the button for the driver's side window and said, "Are you following me?"

He kept coming. "Yes and no."

Chapter
eight

 Murphy's Law of Ornithology: " 'Winging it' is for the birds."

Even with the last remnant of daylight fading away and the rising moon no more than a pale presence in the night sky, Eric could make out the expression on Sydney's face. He was pretty sure her emotions mirrored his: She was as surprised and as startled as he was.

In addition, her body language made it clear that she wasn't in the mood for guessing games.

"What do you mean yes *and* no?" she said, her hands gripping the steering wheel as if it were a lifeline.

Damn, so much for "winging it." She didn't know. Apparently, nobody had told her.

And why would they? As far as he could tell she hadn't informed anyone—not even Minerva Bagley—of her plans.

Eric stopped a foot or two from the BMW and planted his feet. It was a little like putting stakes in the ground. *This* was his territory. *That* was hers. No-man's-land was the narrow strip of gravel driveway between them. "I thought you'd be staying in town."

Sydney sat there like a stone statue, immovable and unmoving. "You thought wrong."

Exhausted as he was, Eric was determined not to lose his patience with her. "It was reasonable to assume that you'd be staying with your aunt."

Sydney didn't give an inch. "Well, I'm not."

He could read her mind: *Not that it's any of your damned business what I consider reasonable, or where I stay.*

"What are you doing here?" she finally asked.

Eric shifted the tuxedo jacket from his right hand to his left and casually tossed it over his shoulder. He kicked at the loose pebbles in the driveway with the toe of his dress shoe. Something told him Sydney wasn't going to like the answer to that question. He took in a sustaining breath and plunged headfirst into the deep end. "I live here."

A crease formed between her eyes. "You live where?"

"Here."

It still wasn't sinking in. "Where here?"

"Here, here. I've rented the apartment above the garage." He motioned in the direction of the building situated halfway between the farmhouse and a nearby barn.

Sydney stared out the front windshield. Her mouth formed a silent *ah* as she exhaled.

The headlights of her sedan cut a swath through the swirling blue mist and beyond to a stand of maple trees;

they illuminated silvery undersides to leaves that danced on the night wind and dark, elongated, shaggy bark on aged trunks.

Beyond the grove of silver maples was the barn. Closer and off to one side was the oversize three-car garage and the flight of steps leading up to the second-floor rental in question.

The efficiency apartment was one bedroom, one bath, with a small kitchen, a dining ell, and a living room Eric intended to use as a study: eight hundred square feet in all. According to the terms of his lease, the place came furnished (if a bit sparsely, in his opinion) and included a weekly change of bed linens and towels, and a bi-weekly cleaning by the housekeeper, Mrs. Manderley, who also looked after the main house at the Woodlands.

A slight breeze came up and blew a strand of hair across Sydney's mouth. She brushed it away, turned back to him, and said, "When did you rent the apartment?"

"A few weeks ago."

"Who did you lease it from?"

"I believe he said he was the farm manager. He claimed to handle the day-to-day business details for your parents when it comes to the Woodlands. His name was Popplewell."

Her brow wrinkled. "Charles Popplewell?"

"Yep, that's the guy."

Fingertips were drummed on the leather steering wheel; there was motion but no sound beyond a barely perceptible *thumpety-thump-thump-thumpety-thump-thump*. "Why?"

"Why am I renting an apartment?" He went ahead and answered the question. "Because I need a place to live."

She stared at her hands for a moment and said, "I meant why specifically here?"

That was easy. "It was the best apartment I could find in the area that didn't require a one-year lease."

Sydney glanced at him and then looked away. "Why aren't you staying with your parents?"

Was she kidding? The place was packed to the rafters with family members. It was wall-to-wall people. And right now wall-to-wall people was the last thing he needed.

What he needed, Eric realized, was to be left alone. What he wanted was peace and quiet and solitude. And lazy laid-back days without a single client appointment. And how about a week or two where the most pressing decision he had to make was whether to eat a hamburger or a hot dog for dinner.

He tried to imagine himself sitting in the shade of an old oak tree drinking an ice-cold beer on a sweltering hot summer afternoon. Or the luxury of getting six or seven or even eight hours of sleep at night for a change.

Besides, he'd lived by himself for the past two years and he liked it that way.

He tried to balance the tension in his voice with a healthy dose of humor. "It's all filled up at the Law household, I'm afraid." He forced an affable expression onto his face. "Relatives: Can't live with them; can't live without them."

Sydney turned and studied him for a long moment. "Surely your relatives will be leaving now that the wedding is over."

"My aunt and uncle and assorted cousins will gradually clear out over the next day or two. My sisters and their families will be on their way by Tuesday or Wednesday."

Hope, it seemed, sprang eternal. "Then you can move back home next week."

Eric shook his head. "No can do. It won't be long before my parents take off again."

"Take off again?"

He swung his right arm wide in an all-encompassing gesture. "They're heading somewhere out—there."

That brought a raised feminine eyebrow.

Maybe it was time for him to be more specific. "My parents are doing a coast-to-coast tour of the best of the best when it comes to roller coasters: the Beast, the Monster, the Gargantua, Godzilla, even the Wild Toad."

Sydney blinked and repeated, "The Wild Toad."

"Named for Mr. Toad."

Her forehead creased perplexedly. "Who?"

"Mr. Toad of Toad Hall. *The* Toad Hall in *The Wind in the Willows.*" She still had that blank expression on her face. "Didn't you ever read about Toad's adventures with Ratty and Mole and Badger when you were a kid?" he asked.

A silk-clad shoulder was raised in a dismissive gesture. "I suppose I must have."

Eric couldn't believe that he'd read a book that Sydney St. John apparently hadn't read. Well, the classic children's book had been read *to* him when he was no more than four or five years old, probably by his mother or one of his older sisters.

He went on to explain. "Mr. Toad has his own roller-coaster ride now based on the labyrinth that winds its way underneath the Wild Wood to the cellars of Toad Hall."

"I've never heard of the Wild Toad." Sydney seemed to stop herself from saying anymore.

"It's one of the lesser known roller coasters unless you're an afficionado like my mother," he said. "After she and my father retired, they decided to travel from one end of the good old US of A to the other. Last year they hit the choice fishing spots for my dad. This year it's roller coasters for my mom."

"I see." Sydney raised her eyes to his. "But surely once your parents have gone off to ride roller coasters . . ."

He starting shaking his head before she could even finish her thought. "As soon as they leave, Sylvia French is moving into their house for the summer and fall."

Eric could almost feel the waves of frustration flooding the no-man's-land between them.

Sydney threw up her hands. "Why?"

"For three reasons, as I understand it."

Her mouth all but disappeared. "Would you mind spelling them out for me?"

Sure. Why not?

Eric took a deep breath and began. "First, Sylvia is going to paint the entire inside and outside of my parents' house, plus the detached garage and the lawn shed."

"Second?"

"Second, while Sam and Gillian are on their honeymoon, she's going to supervise the major renovations being done to their house next door, including a new kitchen and the addition of a solarium."

"That's putting a lot of responsibility on Sylvia."

He'd thought so, too. "Apparently she's a very responsible young woman. My sister-in-law trusts her implicitly.

Gillian and Sylvia have become good friends in the past year."

"You said there were three reasons. What's the third?" she prompted him.

"Sylvia has no place else to live."

In spite of herself Sydney was curious. "Why not?"

"I don't know the whole story," he admitted, shifting his weight from one foot to the other.

Something seemed to suddenly occur to her. "Where has Sam been staying?"

"Out at the Flying Pig."

"Why can't you live out there?"

Eric snorted. "Have you ever caught a whiff of that place on a windy day?"

She sniffed and uttered a reluctant, "Yes."

"It's not exactly 'everything's coming up roses,' is it?" He was tired and he wasn't in the mood to belabor the point. "Look, no offense, but nobody knew you were coming back to the Woodlands."

"Mrs. Manderley knew."

"Since when?"

Sydney stared straight ahead and said in a soft voice, "Since I called her yesterday."

Johnny-come-lately.

Not to put too fine a point on it, but he had been here first. As a matter of fact, the legal papers had been signed, sealed, and delivered—along with his first month's rent—before he'd even left Boston. The law was clearly on his side.

Eric felt it was appropriate to inform her at this juncture, "I'm all moved in."

Well, more or less. He hadn't unpacked everything yet. As a matter of fact, most of his stuff was still in the suitcases and a couple of moving boxes that he'd shipped ahead of time.

There was a short, brittle pause.

"I suppose possession is nine-tenths of the law," Sydney finally said through stiff lips.

Well, now that she'd mentioned it: Yes, it was.

A lightbulb seemed to come on over her head. "Why aren't you on your way back to Boston?"

"Trying to get rid of me?" Within a second or two Eric realized his attempt at humor had failed rather miserably.

She frowned. "I don't understand."

He decided to play it straight. "I'm not leaving town right away."

Why not? Eric knew those were the two words on the tip of her tongue.

Sydney cocked her head and waited.

He didn't owe her an answer, but he went ahead and gave her one. "I promised Sam that I'd stay and keep an eye on his law firm while he and Gillian are on their honeymoon."

Sydney didn't mince words. "How long are you planning on staying in Sweetheart?"

Eric shrugged and shoved his right hand into his pants pocket. His fingers curled around his cell phone. "How long are *you* planning on staying in Sweetheart?"

"I don't know."

"Neither do I."

"I'm out of a job and I need time to reassess my options." Sydney gave him a speculative glance. "I assumed you still had a job."

He drew a deep breath and straightened his shoulders. "I do, but I haven't had any time off in a while." In a while? The only vacation he'd taken during the past decade was for his honeymoon, and that had been four years ago. *Water under the bridge, buddy. Water under the bridge.*

"All work and no play," she hazarded a guess.

"Something like that. It's been twenty-four/seven for months." That was only a slight exaggeration. The heavy workload had started to catch up with him, too. He had begun to hate the one thing he loved most: practicing law.

"I see."

Maybe she did; maybe she didn't. But he wasn't going to stand out here all night and explain it to her. He was tired right down to his bones. He wanted nothing more than to take a shower, crawl into bed, and sleep for the next twenty-four hours.

Sydney seemed determined to give it one last shot. "There will be gossip about us."

Eric showed the edges of his teeth. "There's always gossip in Sweetheart. There always will be. You know that, Syd."

She opened her mouth and shut it again.

It was time for him to take control of the situation. "Look, it's not as if we'll be living in the same house."

It took a few seconds for that to sink in. "But you'll be a mere twenty yards from my door," she pointed out unnecessarily.

He assessed the distance from the house to the garage. "I'd say more like thirty."

She wasn't amused.

Eric hastened to reassure her. "We don't have to run into

each other any more than we would if we were living on opposite ends of the county. You go your way and I'll go mine." He flashed her a sardonic smile. "Hey, feel free to ignore me."

Chapter
nine

 Easier said than done.

But that's exactly what she intended to do: ignore him. She would show Mr. Eric Law that she didn't give two hoots about the fact he was going to be living right outside her front door.

Okay, right outside her parents' back *door.*

The irony of the situation didn't escape Sydney. Only a few minutes before she'd been spooked by the idea of staying at the Woodlands by herself. Now, to use a favorite phrase of her great-uncle Bert's generation, somebody else would be within "spitting distance."

"Look, it's too late to discuss this any more tonight," Eric said, rubbing his hand back and forth along his jawline. Sydney could hear the soft, abrasive scrape of skin across five o'clock shadow. "Tomorrow's another day."

"Yes, it is," she said, pushing the button for the power

window and watching as it silently glided shut, creating a barrier—if only a tempered-glass one—between them. She could still see him standing there in the night, tall and dark . . . and irresistible.

Don't be stupid, Sydney.

She turned and glanced at Sneaker, who was patiently waiting in the passenger seat next to her, and resisted the urge to lean over and drop a kiss on the top of his head.

She was pretty sure Eric didn't have a dog. Therefore, anyone caught kissing theirs would undoubtedly come under the heading of "Looney Toons" in his book. Not that she was alone in showing her affection for her faithful four-legged friend. In fact, far from it. She'd read somewhere that ninety percent of pet owners kissed their cat or dog when they came home from work.

"I'll be around to get you in a minute, sweetie pie," Sydney said, giving Sneaker a reassuring *coochie coochie coo* under his chin. She turned off the ignition, grabbed the handbag beside her, and reached for the door handle.

Eric immediately stepped forward and opened the door on the driver's side of the sedan.

"Thank you," she said as she slid out from behind the wheel. Just because she was surprised to find him here— okay, discombobulated was more like it—was no reason for incivility.

"You're welcome," Eric responded with the same degree of politeness. Then he turned and tossed the jacket to his tuxedo in the direction of the white pickup truck behind him.

Her eyes followed the coat's flight through the air; it landed on the hood of the vehicle with a soft thud. "I see the auto repair shop supplied you with a loaner."

Eric contemplated that briefly and then shook his head. "It's my sister-in-law's. But since Gillian obviously won't be needing her pickup this summer, she suggested I drive it until they can figure out what's wrong with my car."

Sensible suggestion.

A quick assessing look was cast in her direction. "Speaking of driving, you must be tired after the trip from Chicago."

"I am a bit," Sydney admitted, sighing softly and sweeping the hair back from her face.

She slipped the strap of her Italian leather handbag over her shoulder and smoothed the skirt of her Armani suit. That's when she happened to glance down and notice that her high heels were sinking into the loose gravel on the driveway. Hmm. It might be a good idea to put away her Manolo Blahniks for a while. They were impractical as long as she was living on a farm.

Actually, wearing very expensive and very high designer heels hadn't been all that practical on the streets of Chicago, either, she acknowledged to herself.

Eric's face was in shadow, but Sydney noticed that his voice had deepened from its usual baritone to a basso profundo. It sounded gravelly, ragged around the edges, and noticeably hoarse, like he'd spent the past few hours trying to make himself heard over the din of an orchestra and chatty wedding guests.

Which he had.

"How about I help unload your car?" he volunteered. "It'll go a lot faster if I carry the heavier boxes and some of the suitcases into the house for you."

His offer caught her off-guard. Still, she had no intentions of biting off her nose to spite her face. Truth was, she was more than plain, old tired, she was exhausted. She could use his help.

You can always ignore the man starting tomorrow.

"Thank you. I believe I'll take you up on that," Sydney said as he closed the car door behind her. She headed for the porch and dug around for the house key Mrs. Manderley had told her would be hidden under the third flowerpot on the left.

She retrieved the key and unlocked the entrance that led directly into the mudroom: It was really no more than a hallway with a rack of outdoor boots on one side and a row of brass hooks for jackets and sweaters on the other. A wooden shelf overhead held an assortment of wide-brimmed straw hats and several pairs of gardening gloves. A brightly colored majolica pot served as an umbrella stand.

Sydney felt around the corner into the next room for the switch plate, and a moment later the big country kitchen was flooded with light. The first thing she noticed was a plate of cookies in the center of the table. The second was a vase filled with white bell-shaped flowers and a few sprigs of decorative greenery.

Propped up against the cut-glass container was a note written in a distinctive, spidery hand. She picked up the piece of paper and read the note aloud. " 'Welcome home, Miss St. John. I thought you might enjoy some fresh flowers from the garden and a few of my homemade cookies. Ella Manderley.' "

"That was thoughtful of Mrs. Manderley," Eric said, juggling a grocery sack in each arm. He set them down on the kitchen counter closest to the refrigerator.

"Yes, I suppose it was," she said without enthusiasm as she skirted the area around the vase.

Eric leaned over the table and took a whiff of the flowers. "Nice scent."

Sydney felt it was only fair to warn him, "Those are lilies of the valley."

A masculine eyebrow arched quizzically. "Is that supposed to mean something?"

She swayed on her feet, not altogether certain she had the energy—or the inclination—to explain. "My parents never allowed lilies of the valley in the house, especially not in the kitchen."

"Why not?"

"As a precaution." Sydney dropped her handbag onto the nearest chair and said to him, "As a little girl I found out the hard way they're poisonous."

Eric straightened. He didn't take his eyes off her. "What happened?" he asked.

"I overheard my parents talking about a salad they'd enjoyed at a fancy restaurant somewhere: It was made from edible flowers. Apparently I decided to create my own version from the plants in our garden, including a few lilies of the valley. Unfortunately, the salad I concocted made me sicker than a dog. I wound up in the hospital having my stomach pumped." Sydney knew the expression on her face matched the unpleasant memory dredged up from her childhood. "I've never cared for lilies of the valley since."

Frowning, Eric crossed his arms and studied her from the other side of the kitchen table. "Understandably."

"In fact," she went on to tell him, "just the sight of them makes me feel kind of queasy."

He unfolded his arms, reached up, and rubbed one hand back and forth along his jawline. "I guess Mrs. Manderley didn't know you'd been poisoned by them."

"She did at the time, but she must have forgotten," said Sydney. "It was almost thirty years ago."

He made a gesture in the direction of the vase. "Want me to get rid of them for you?"

She shook her head, feeling foolish for even mentioning it to him. "I'll take care of them tomorrow."

"You sure?"

"I'm sure," she said.

"Well, the cookies Mrs. Manderley baked sure smell delicious. Snickerdoodles, aren't they? I haven't had a snickerdoodle in a decade. Maybe longer." Eric went and stood in the archway between the kitchen and what was designated as the "front room" of the farmhouse—he seemed to fill the entire space: kitchen, doorway, front room, *house*—and took a cursory look around before asking her, "So, where would you like me to put your stuff?"

Sydney took a minute to consider. "I guess in the study." She indicated a smaller adjoining room. "It'll be out of the way in there until I have a chance to unpack."

"Consider it done," he stated.

Sneaker sat in his Port-a-Pooch on the porch and watched as the two of them unloaded her belongings and hauled them into the house. The job took less than half the time, and considerably less than half the effort, than if Sydney had done it on her own.

"A small token of my appreciation," she said, presenting Eric with the plate of cookies.

"Thanks, but you'd better keep a few for yourself in case Mrs. Manderley asks how you liked them."

She transferred two snickerdoodles to a small Tupperware container she found in a kitchen cupboard and handed him the rest. Then she walked him back out to the porch.

The evening had turned cooler just as the announcer on the local radio station had predicted. The wind had shifted and was blowing in from the northwest, clearing away the mist and the humidity. The shadows were slowly receding into the woods. Overhead, a midnight-blue canopy was filled with stars.

Eric was almost to the driveway when he stopped and gazed up at the sky. "It's a beautiful night."

Sydney stepped down off the wraparound porch for a better view. "Yes, it is."

"We never see this many stars in Boston."

"We don't in Chicago, either," she said, sighing inwardly.

After clearing his throat he said, "It wasn't like this the night I pulled your car out of the ditch."

What had made him think of that now?

Her response was reasonably calm. "No, it wasn't."

For a minute or two Eric stood with the plate of cookies in one hand and the other thrust into the pocket of his tuxedo trousers. His white dress shirt was in sharp contrast to tanned arms and dark hair. In fact, his shirt seemed to glow in the dark. The extra-fine material—Egyptian cotton, if hers was any guess—was pulled taut across his shoulders before tapering down to a waistline that had to be the envy of most men in their mid-thirties.

He turned and remarked to her, "I've remembered something else about that night."

Her pulse leaped. "Have you?"

Eric's expression gave nothing away. "I followed you back here to the Woodlands to make sure there weren't any mechanical problems with your car." He paused and then went on talking. "We stood on this very same walkway."

She remembered.

"The downpour had stopped, but the air still smelled of rain and damp earth and drenched trees and wet clothes." Blue eyes pinned her to the spot. "There was another thing, too."

Sydney repressed a shiver.

"When I didn't say anything this afternoon while we were dancing, you must have thought I'd forgotten about the most important part of that night."

Sydney felt her insides tighten. "The most important part?"

Eric took a step toward her and she had to remind herself to stand her ground. "You kissed me," he said.

Oh, you did a hell of a lot more than just kiss him, Sydney. You offered yourself to him—heart and soul . . . and body—on a silver platter.

Chapter
ten

Sydney realized she didn't want to be having this conversation. Not now. Not ever. But the silence was deafening. *Say something. Say anything.* "I was very young and foolish," she said.

"You were—" Eric paused, clearly searching for the right word. "Sweet."

She cringed inwardly. "Now you're being kind."

He squared his shoulders; the action smoothed out even the most stubborn wrinkle in his elegant dress shirt. "Kindness has nothing to do with it. *Had* nothing to do with it."

Sydney was too tired to argue the point. "If I remember correctly"—*and* she did—"I made a pass at you." That was considerably more tactful than saying she'd tried to jump his bones. "At least you let me down gently."

Of course, that realization had come later. At the time

she'd been embarrassed; more embarrassed than she had ever been in her entire life. She still had a vivid recollection of squeezing her eyes tightly shut and desperately wishing that she could vanish into thin air—*poof!*—right on the spot.

Eric started to gesture with the same hand he was holding the snickerdoodles with. He stopped in mid-motion, took his other hand out of his pants' pocket, and switched the plate of cookies before he continued. "I figured if I took you up on what you were offering, you'd never forgive yourself."

"Probably," Sydney said. She looked away for a moment and thought, *Possibly.*

She turned back just as the moon slipped out from behind a bank of white stratus clouds and illuminated Eric's face. He was frowning. His mouth, usually full-lipped and sensual, had thinned to a single, emphatic line. Between his earlobe and his chin, a muscle had started to jerk as if he were clenching and unclenching his teeth.

With a hint of weariness in his voice, he went on to say, "And I was afraid you'd end up hating me."

I ended up hating you, anyway, Sydney thought to herself, but she said aloud, in what she hoped was a casual tone, "I wouldn't have blamed you."

Eric shoved his free hand back into his pants' pocket and the metallic jingle of loose change could be heard. "Maybe not, but I would have blamed myself."

So would everybody else in Sweetheart wasn't verbalized, but it was clearly understood.

After all, back in high school she'd had an unblemished reputation as a moral, upright, and outstanding student who had been voted "the most likely to succeed" in her senior class. Eric, on the other hand, had been the out-Law of his own family.

It had been common knowledge that parents warned their daughters about how dangerous he was. They'd lived in fear that he'd snap his fingers and it would be their precious offspring who would be seduced into running off with him. Heaven knew where or when. Even the *P* word had been knocked around on a regular basis.

To make matters worse, by the time he was sixteen or seventeen, Eric had started to drink too much, smoke too much, and drive his souped-up Mustang much too fast. Everybody in town had the youngest Law marked for trouble.

Big trouble.

Of course, it turned out that everybody was wrong, Sydney reflected. Eric hadn't gotten a single girl pregnant (unlike some of the so-called pillars of Sweetheart society), and he'd made a big success—a huge success—of himself.

She watched him now standing there in the dark, outlined against the moon and a swath of light cast by a motion-detector on the far corner of the garage. Something must have set off the mechanism: the spotlight blinked on and the sound of rustling in the underbrush immediately followed. Maybe it was a raccoon. Or an opossum. Or some other nocturnal creature who preferred the cover of darkness.

Eric turned to her; his features were haggard. "You were so smart and so innocent, Syd. Frankly, you scared the"— she sensed he was about to use another word and changed his mind at the last minute—"crap out of me," he explained tightly.

She'd scared the crap out of him? That was nothing compared to how she'd felt at the time.

Funny thing about time. Time was money. Time was wasted. Time was saved. Time flew. Time was honored. Time lagged. Time waited for no man.

And time really *was* relative.

Sydney could recall every detail of that encounter sixteen years before as if it had happened only yesterday.

She'd thrown her arms around Eric's neck and had thrust her body up against his with what she later realized, much to her chagrin, was clumsy, virginal passion. One or both of them had uttered a sharp yelp of pain as she had proceeded to bump into his nose *and* simultaneously trample on his foot as she'd pressed her mouth to his.

Despite those initial mishaps, their lips had parted and she had tasted him on her tongue: He was wind and rain and the wild night, intermingled with a trace of beer and the scent of cigarette smoke.

His body had been as rock-solid, as hard, as uncompromising as any hormone-driven teenager's could be. It had taken her a minute or two to realize he had an erection. But all of a sudden there it had been: unexpectedly, unmistakably, outlined against her thigh. Hot. Heavy. Unapologetic.

She hadn't been able to breathe. Or think. She hadn't wanted to. She'd acted on impulse, slipping her hand between them, and then reaching down to grope the front of his jeans, scrapping her fingernail along the line of his zipper.

His body had twitched and he'd mumbled something. It had sounded like "yes," but her heart had been drumming so loudly in her ears, she couldn't be certain.

Eric's heart had been pounding as well. She'd watched

his pulse race in his throat and just below his temple. She'd felt it on the underside of his wrist and in his groin.

Electricity had crackled in the air like heat lightning. A breeze had swept through the dewy leaves overhead, sending a soft, cascading shower down to cool overheated flesh.

Neverending blue eyes had blinked open, and for an instant she'd felt as if she were peering into his very soul, and as if he was looking right through to the heart of her.

Then he had kissed her breathless, one palm cupping her breast, one urging her closer to his pelvis. Her hands had been everywhere, touching everything within their reach.

"Please want me," she'd implored in a whisper, "as much as I want you."

The next instant she had prayed, *Oh, God, I hope you didn't hear me say that.*

It had been another heartbeat or two before Eric's head had jerked up. He'd stood there staring at her, and then he had stepped back, dropping his arms to his side, breathing hard, eyes hot and dark.

"I can't do this," he'd said, swearing softly under his breath. "*We* can't do this."

Why not? she'd wanted to ask as the blood rushed from her brain, leaving her light-headed and wobbly on her feet.

"This isn't a good idea. In fact, it's a really bad idea," he'd stated, driving his fingers through his hair, leaving black curls rumpled and irrepressibly tousled. "Trust me, we'd both be sorry in the morning."

I'm already sorry, she'd wanted to tell him defiantly. But it hadn't been true.

The truth had been simple and hurtful: She hadn't been

attractive enough or sexy enough to interest Eric Law. Not with her brains and her myriad freckles and her size ten-and-a-half feet.

The bloody Bagley curse.

If only she'd been blond and petite. If only she'd known all the things the other girls in her class seemed to know about boys and how to make them want you. But she didn't know. She was different. She'd always been different.

Some part of Sydney had wanted to be swallowed up right there and then. Another part had allowed her pride to rise to the surface. Without a word, and without looking back at him, she had turned and walked straight toward the door of the farmhouse.

He'd called after her, softly, apologetically, "I'm sorry, Sydney. At least let's be friends."

"To hell with you, Eric Law," she'd said, more for her benefit than his. She had shut the kitchen door behind her and then leaned back against it for support, chest heaving, lungs gasping for air, tears of anger and frustration and humiliation running down her cheeks.

"Sydney?"

The sound of her name jolted Sydney back to the present.

"You, ah . . . scared the crap out of me, too," she said, echoing his words, while reining in her emotions.

They said there was a first time for everything. Well, this man embodied a number of firsts for her: Her first French kiss. Her first attempt at seduction. The first time she had touched a sexually aroused male and had been fondled by one in return. The first time she'd felt a hard body, in every sense of the word, pressed against hers. The first time she had been sexually aroused, herself.

Not that you're going to admit any of this to him now.

Sydney's face grew hot and her skin felt flushed and prickly just thinking about what had happened between them. It was time—oh, it was way past time—to put that long-ago night and her silly schoolgirl infatuation with Eric Law to bed.

Okay, bad choice of words: to *rest*.

She was an adult now. It was time to think and act like an adult. It was time to regain her sense of humor about what had been a ridiculous and juvenile incident.

After all, in the grand scheme of things, what was one erection, more or less?

Sydney realized she was nearly drunk with exhaustion. She felt a little giddy and she was unsteady on her feet. Her mouth started to twitch in an effort not to smile.

Too bad they didn't have cell phones back when she and Eric were in high school. Finally, all these years after the fact, she had thought of the perfect comeback.

Then she had another revelation: *Whatever you do, don't look at his crotch, or he'll know what you're thinking.*

"I know what you're thinking," Eric said.

Sydney went utterly still. Like a statue. A tall, elegant statue, its perfection marred by a disobedient—and rather endearing—strand of dark ruby hair that insisted on falling across her right eye no matter how many times she tried to brush it away with the back of her hand, or stick it behind her ear.

She looked pale without the bright red lipstick she had been wearing when she had run into him on the road this afternoon. Either that or the rosy spot in the center of each cheek made the rest of her skin look bone-china white.

Her silk suit was wrinkled—silk was apt to do that in the heat—and the hand she raised to her lips was trembling. She looked less than perfect. In fact, she looked tired and rumpled and very human.

Christ, surely you had your fill of perfection a long time ago, Eric reminded himself.

His ex-wife had given every indication of being perfection personified. Marla had always been perfectly dressed, perfectly groomed, and perfectly spoken. She never had a hair or a word or a foot out of place. In the beginning, that's what Eric had thought he needed: the perfect wife. In the end, that's the last thing he'd wanted.

Water under the bridge, buddy.

Sydney stood there looking years younger than she had earlier today. She appeared uncomfortable and uncertain of herself. Maybe even a little embarrassed.

Eric was about to reach out and give her a reassuring pat on the shoulder—maybe even tuck that errant strand of fiery hair behind her ear—when he stopped himself and said instead, "Is anything wrong?"

She shook her head too quickly.

He decided to try again. "Are you all right?"

"I'm fine," she said, sinking her teeth into her bottom lip.

She wasn't telling the truth. He could see it in her eyes and hear it in her voice, and he sensed it in his gut. Why would Sydney think it necessary to lie to him?

Maybe it was something he'd done.

Naw.

He'd carried her groceries into the house. He'd sniffed her ridiculous *and* poisonous flowers. He'd lugged her suitcases and boxes into the study. He'd even petted her dog, although Sneaker made no bones about it: The Sheltie didn't like him and didn't trust him.

Of course, you did bring up the subject of that episode back in high school again.

Maybe that was it. Maybe there something about that night he'd forgotten.

Sydney had been young and naive and surprisingly strong as she'd wrapped her arms around him like a vise and pulled his body up against hers. Her enthusiasm had almost made up for her obvious lack of experience.

Still, as he recalled, he'd started to get hard. Cripes, he'd barely been eighteen at the time. It had taken very little—next to nothing—to excite him back in those days, indiscriminate young punk that he'd been.

Eric scowled, deep in thought. Come to think of it, he was pretty sure Sydney had never dated in high school. He couldn't recall ever hearing one word in the boy's locker room about her doing anything with anybody at anytime or anywhere.

What if that night in the dark with him, clothes cold and wet and muddy, hands groping, buttons undone, zippers half unzipped, had been the sole extent of her sexual experience as a teenager?

Shit, she'd been a seventeen-year-old virgin and he'd been her worst nightmare.

Eric took a stab at an apology. "I'm sorry, Sydney. I've made you uncomfortable, haven't I?"

"Uncomfortable?" she said, sounding like she was choking on her own saliva.

That was it.

He was filled with latent remorse. "By mentioning the night we made out right here on this sidewalk?"

Sydney dropped her eyes and stared down at her feet. Her shoulders and upper body seemed to be shaking.

"Look, there's nothing to be embarrassed about," he said in an attempt to console her. "We were both awfully young at the time. And a boy's body has a mind of its own."

For that matter, sometimes a man's body did, too. Not that he'd been paying attention to his lately. He worked. He slept. He ate. And he took a lot of showers, both hot *and* cold. When was the last time he'd felt passionate about anything?

Or anyone?

The woman standing only a foot or two from him finally looked up. The last thing he'd expected to see on her face was a broad grin, yet there it was with lips slightly parted, skin flushed, and white teeth patently visible. Sydney opened her mouth wider and began to laugh. It was a big, hearty, irrepressible laugh that filled the night air.

"What's so damned funny?" Eric said, not bothering to mask his annoyance.

"If . . . if only we'd had modern electronics back when we were in high school." Sydney barely managed to get the words out. She had to pause, collect herself, and try again. "I've thought of the perfect pun for that night."

The perfect pun?

She was clearly pleased with herself. "Is that your cell phone, or are you just glad to see me?"

Oh, great, Eric thought, *Red up and quits on me, Sydney's laughing at me, and her dog hates me.*

This day just kept getting better and better.

She'd had the last laugh.

To her immense satisfaction, having the last laugh *was* all it was cracked up to be, Sydney realized as she closed the door of the farmhouse behind her, turned the key in the lock, and switched off the overhead light in the kitchen.

She leaned over and swept Sneaker up into her arms. "Time for bed, my sweet," she murmured as she trudged upstairs and headed for her old room at the end of the hallway.

Time was not only relative. It apparently stood still. Her bedroom was decorated with the same dark cherry furniture, the same cotton candy-colored drapes, and the same god-awful furry purple area rug that she'd picked out in tenth grade.

Posters of Duran Duran and a very youthful leather jacket-clad Tom Cruise (sitting astride his motorcycle in a scene from *Top Gun*) were plastered on one wall, while another was covered with copies of her favorite poems, mostly maudlin verses about love: lost, found, tragic, and, of course, unrequited.

Sydney leaned closer, squinted at one of the scraps of paper tacked to the corkboard, and read aloud: " 'Take him and cut him out in stars, and he will make the face of heaven so fine that all the world will fall in love with the night.' "

"Thank God your taste in poetry has matured as well," she said to herself as she opened her overnight bag, took out her toothbrush and toiletries, and rummaged around until she found her favorite pair of summer pajamas.

She was squeaky clean and wrapped in an oversize Turkish bath towel when she came strolling out of the adjoining bathroom half an hour later, wet hair dripping . . . *drip, drip, drip* . . . onto her bare shoulders like cool, crystalline raindrops and toothbrush sticking out of one side of her mouth. That's when she discovered Sneaker curled up in the middle of her bed, nose buried in his Nike, eyes droopy with sleep.

Sydney planted one hand on her hip. "I was going to confide my most intimate secrets to you, Sneaker, but something tells me you couldn't care less." She went right on brushing her teeth and mumbling, "Anyway, I've made an executive decision. I will never again take anything regarding Mr. Eric Law seriously: not what he says, not what he does, not what he thinks. I'm sure you will agree this is a wise course of action, my friend. In fact, I believe I detected a certain antagonism on your part toward the man right from the start."

The Sheltie turned onto his side and began to snore softly into the white tennis shoe.

"Don't let my chatter keep you awake," Sydney said as she padded back into the bathroom to spit out the last mouthful of toothpaste and rinse off her face.

Sneaker was sawing wood when she returned. She envied him. Here she'd been so tired on the drive home, and now she found she wasn't the least bit sleepy. She slipped into her pj's, opened the drapes, and stood at the window, gazing out at the night.

Moonlight gave an eerie, iridescent glow to a nearby grove of red maples. Just past the maples were a few stately elms that had managed to escape the dreaded Dutch Elm disease. In her mind's eye Sydney could see beyond the trees to rolling fields of corn and soybeans. On the far side of the cultivated fields and farther up the hill was the evergreen farm: the Scotch pine, the Fraser fir and the Douglas fir, the white pine and the spruce, all tended and cared for by Bim.

She unlatched the window, leaned over, and rested her elbows on the sill. Then she inhaled deeply: the air was brisk and refreshing and had a slight floral scent to it.

She'd forgotten how quiet the nights were in the country. There was the faint rustle of wind through the treetops. The drone of insects somewhere off deep in the woods. The hoot of a distant owl. A cacophony of frog song coming from the pond, along with the occasional flutter of wings or a loud squawk from a resident Mallard duck or one of the Canadian geese.

Life seemed—*was*—simpler, more basic, back to earth *and* down to earth at the Woodlands, which was good because she was here to simplify and clarify her life.

She'd never understood why her parents kept the farm until now. Sydney realized it was comforting to have a place to call home. She had forgotten that for a while. Then she remembered a few words of wisdom passed on by her very wise great-uncle Bert: *Sometimes we have to go home and deal with who we really are.*

"Who are you really, Sydney Marie St. John?" she whispered to her reflection in the window glass. "What do you want?"

She knew what she *didn't* want.

She *didn't* want to look back at the past anymore. A past that included her awkward childhood and adolescence, an exceedingly brief romantic encounter with Eric Law, two former fiancés—one official, one not—and her erstwhile job with Saddler Consultants. It was all ancient history now.

She *didn't* want to go on any more blind dates set up by well-meaning and usually happily married friends.

She *didn't* want to sign up for an online matchmaking service in search of "a few good men." Or put an ad in the "personals" column of the local newspaper: *SWF looking for Mr. Right.*

She *didn't* want to go on a "mini-marathon date," where a man and a woman connected for three or four minutes before moving on to the next prospect.

And she absolutely refused to attend any "My Sweet Embraceable Who?" parties, where singles—complete strangers—cuddled together for a moment of affection and the touch of another human being.

"You know what you *don't* want, Sydney. That's the easy part." She heaved a great sigh. "But what is it you *do* want?"

Sneaker rolled over, raised his head half an inch off the bed, and opened one eye.

"I know what you want, boy. Sleep." Sydney shut the window, drew the drapes, and crawled between cool cotton sheets that were splashed with a pattern of dark green leaves and deep purple lilacs. She reached over and turned off the bedside lamp, then pulled the summer-weight blanket up to her chin.

She gave her pillow a gentle punch and murmured, "You don't have to decide your future tonight, Sydney."

Suddenly she couldn't seem to keep her eyes open. She turned over onto her side. The last thought she remembered flitting through her mind was something Eric had said to her earlier this evening: *Tomorrow's another day.*

For once he was right.

Chapter
eleven

"Yes, Mrs. Freeman, each Wednesday afternoon during the summer from Memorial Day to Labor Day," Minerva said into the cordless phone propped between her ear and shoulder.

She hadn't bothered removing her gardening gloves or even putting down her hand spade when the extension rang in the greenhouse. "This Wednesday? I don't know off the top of my head. I'll have to check. It's no trouble, but it will take me a few minutes to reach my desk. Do you mind if I put you on hold?"

After an appropriate response from Elizabeth Freeman, that doyenne of Sweetheart society, in particular the Ladies Club, which met the second Tuesday of each month to play bridge, nibble salmon and cucumber sandwiches, *and* gossip, Minerva hit Hold, stripped off her work gloves, exited the greenhouse, and made her way along the flagstone path to her office.

She didn't hurry, but she didn't dawdle, either. She walked at her usual pace. Minerva had always taken life at her own speed, making certain to stay within her comfort zone. Any time she had deviated from that, she'd regretted it.

The small brick building adjacent to the main house had started its existence well over a century ago as a summer kitchen. That was back before the Civil War, back in the days when the Bagleys had a staff of hired help (including a cook and several scullery maids), back in the days when each household baked their own bread and cured their own meats, and, consequently, a separate kitchen was considered a necessity during the warm summer months.

Next, the building had served as a storage area and catchall for the "finds" shipped home from all over the world by various members of the Bagley clan, in particular the Victorians on their "Grand Tours" of the Continent during the Gilded Age.

The Bagleys—pack rats to the last man, woman, and child—had always preferred to think of their acquisitions as treasures or collectibles or keepsakes, occasionally as "curiosities," but not as souvenirs and certainly never as junk.

During her uncle Bert's heyday, in the decades following the Second World War, the storage area had been cleared out. The best of the "finds" had been moved into the house proper, the others were sold or given away or simply hauled off.

Shortly thereafter, the structure had been converted into

a sunroom, replete with green striped canvas awnings on the windows, overhead paddle fans, large earthenware pots filled with tropical plants, and white wicker furniture.

A permanent breezeway connecting the smaller outbuilding and the house had also been added at some point, and for the past twenty-odd years the former summer kitchen had served as the office for Minerva's herbal tea business, Water from the Moon.

Minerva glanced down at the engagement calendar on her desk, picked up the phone, and said, "I have that information for you, Mrs. Freeman. This week we'll be tasting white tea, green tea, and several varieties of herbal blends, including one with spearmint, elderberry, and lemon balm, and another of chamomile and apple mint. There will also be a short lecture on the health benefits of each type of tea, and a discussion about which herbs should never be brewed." She paused and listened. "Yes, that's right. Some can actually make you ill."

Certainly there were health benefits to herbal tea, but there could also be dangers. What had once been common knowledge, passed down from one generation to the next, was now relegated to specialized gardeners and practitioners like herself, Minerva thought.

Most of the population didn't know the difference between blue cohosh, *Caulophyllum thalictroides*, that widely touted healer of female ailments, and elderberry, whose shrubs contained a substance known to release cyanide.

Her maternal grandmother had always had a common sense approach to life and health in general, and herbs in particular, especially when it came to "healing" or medicinal herbal teas. "*If it tastes bad and smells bad, for heaven's sake, girl, don't drink it*," had been her advice, always voiced in a no-nonsense tone.

Minerva realized Mrs. Freeman had asked her another question while she was woolgathering. "What time? We start at three-thirty. Please call Mary Kay Weaver at the Sweetheart Bed and Breakfast and Art Gallery to make your reservation." She paused again. "There's no cover charge, but we do have limited seating. The teas are very popular."

And getting more popular by the day. No doubt in part, Minerva concluded, to the little drama that had played out at last Wednesday's gathering.

"May I help you with anything else?" she inquired politely. Elizabeth Freeman simply cleared her throat and thanked her, so she said, "You're welcome," and hung up.

Minerva left the office and walked along the breezeway to the back of the house, letting the screen door swing shut behind her. She opened the refrigerator and reached for the pitcher of lemonade she'd made fresh that morning.

She poured herself a large glass. There was no need for ice cubes since the lemonade was chilled to the perfect temperature, and ice would only dilute the recipe that had been handed down through the female line from her great-grandmother to her grandmother to her mother and eventually to her.

Minerva sat at the kitchen table, took a sip of lemonade, held it on her tongue for a moment, and then pronounced judgment. "Slightly tart, refreshing, not too sweet, yet not too sour. In short," she said with satisfaction, "just right."

*   *   *

Elvira Goldman came bearing gifts.

She'd expected to find Minerva in the garden or the greenhouse, since that's where she usually was at this time of day, checking her plants, feeding her plants, watering her plants, pruning her plants, and, her friend suspected, talking to her plants.

But no Minerva.

Goldie made her way along the stone path, skirted around the office, and headed directly for the back door of the house, peace offering in hand. She spotted her long-time friend sitting at the kitchen table drinking a glass of what appeared to be lemonade.

She knocked on the screen door and called out, "Yoo-hoo, Minerva. It's me. Goldie."

Minerva turned and said, "Come in."

"I've brought you a jar of my homemade relish. Your favorite," she said solicitously, entering the kitchen and setting the small gift basket down on the table.

"Why, thank you, Goldie. You do make the best sweet pickle relish of anyone I know. Small wonder you've taken the prize seven years in a row at the Golden Raintree Festival."

For a moment she basked in the praise. How like Minerva to mention a friend's victories and not her defeats.

Minerva seemed to belatedly remember her manners. "Would you like to have a glass of lemonade with me?"

"Oh, yes, please." Goldie heaved a sigh of relief as she pulled out a kitchen chair and made herself comfortable. Minerva was talking to her and seemed as hospitable as always, so maybe she wasn't so very angry with her after all. Goldie fanned herself with her hand and said, in an attempt to make conversation, "It's gotten rather warm this afternoon, hasn't it?"

"It is almost July," her hostess pointed out, and then the kitchen went quiet again.

Goldie took a sip of lemonade. It was cold, without being too cold, and tart without making her mouth pucker up or giving her heartburn. She set her glass down on the table in front of her and explained, "I didn't intend to drop by unannounced, but every time I dialed your number the line was busy."

Minerva brought a plate of cookies to the table. There were several varieties and they were all soft and plain and only slightly sweet—the perfect accompaniment to lemonade. Goldie was offered her choice as her friend said, "My telephone has been ringing constantly."

Goldie nibbled on a butter cookie and waited. It was an effort not to blurt out the question on the tip of her tongue. But it was important that she maintain some semblance of self-control. *For once in your life, Elvira, keep your mouth shut.*

Minerva began to fill in the blanks. "I've already had at least a dozen phone calls inquiring about this week's tea at the B and B, and here it's only Monday."

Goldie frowned. "That's unusual, isn't it?"

"Yes, it is."

Goldie waited, reminding herself that patience was supposed to be a virtue.

More information was volunteered. "Without naming names, several of the women who phoned came right out and asked if Eric Law was going to be there again this Wednesday."

"Having a young man in attendance was . . . different," Goldie said carefully, taking another bite of cookie so her mouth was full and she wouldn't be tempted to say any more.

Minerva grew more expansive on the subject. "I don't believe Eric meant to attend the tea at all. I learned later that Mrs. Ledbetter had bumped into him outside on the street and asked for his help navigating the front steps of the old mansion." A hairpin slipped its moorings and dropped onto the hardwood floor with a soft *ping*. "Mrs. Ledbetter is frail and getting a bit on in years."

"She's half-crippled and ninety if she's a day," Goldie piped up, and then wished she'd kept her mouth shut. She must be careful. Very careful. She was teetering on the edge of a precipice.

Minerva didn't seem to notice the slip-up. "Apparently Mrs. Ledbetter insisted that Eric sit beside her and keep her company for the entire program."

Goldie lost control for a moment. "Elsa Ledbetter should have known better. Eric was the only man among all those women. He must have felt terribly uncomfortable."

She certainly would have been if the circumstances had been reversed. She couldn't imagine being the only woman in a room filled with men. Despite her claims of being an expert on the subject of marriage in general and men in particular, Elvira had never quite figured out how to relate to one. Men were a mystery to her.

Minerva's head bobbed up and down. "Still, all things considered, Eric handled himself well. In fact, he was the perfect gentleman."

"Yes, he was." To the amazement of many. *Oh, bother!* This was getting her nowhere. She was going to have to chance it. "I couldn't help but notice that Eric and Sydney didn't speak to each other, or even look at each other, all afternoon."

"Really?" Minerva said as if it were news to her. "Of course, Sydney was busy helping me pour, and Eric was dancing attendance on Mrs. Ledbetter."

That still didn't explain why they had avoided each other like the plague. She hadn't been the only one who had noticed, either, Goldie wanted to tell her friend. It had been patently obvious to every woman in the room.

Which no doubt explained the gossip that had started later the same day. Not because anything had happened between Sydney and Eric, but because absolutely *nothing* had.

Goldie traced a random pattern in the condensation on the surface of her glass. "I suppose people assumed they would be friendlier since Eric is staying out at the Woodlands."

Minerva shook her head and immediately squelched that idea when she said, "Sydney mentioned to me that they haven't run into each other since the wedding."

That caught her interest. "You don't say . . ."

"Well, not until last Wednesday's tea."

Goldie took another sip of lemonade and wanted desperately to ask, *And since then?* but she didn't.

Without any prompting, Minerva said, "It turns out Sydney wasn't even aware that Eric had rented the apartment above the garage. He dealt solely with Charlie Popplewell."

That was news.

Elvira planted what she hoped was an innocent expression on her face. "So, they weren't in touch before Sam and Gillian's wedding."

"Heavens, no. They hadn't bumped into each other in years. Not since high school." Minerva turned in her chair and looked at Goldie with those bespectacled brown eyes of hers: kind eyes, gentle eyes, true, but shrewd eyes that seemed to see everything *and* eyes that expected her to tell the truth and nothing but the truth. "You haven't been gossiping about Eric and my niece, have you, Elvira?"

"No," she said, swallowing hard. But she was guilty of *listening* to gossip.

Minerva Bagley didn't mince words. "They're adults. What they do or what they don't do is none of our business . . . or anyone else's, for that matter."

She was right. Goldie told her so.

Minerva went on. "Eric and Sydney have both worked hard to make something of themselves. I'd hate to think that anything, past or present, would come back to haunt them."

Sometimes the past came back to haunt you until you made peace with it, Goldie reasoned. Which was why she'd dropped by today with an olive branch in her hand.

Just do it, Elvira.

She wasn't very good at apologies. The words always seemed to get stuck in her throat. Or they got twisted on her tongue and came out all wrong. But she had to at least try. "We've known each other a long time, haven't we, Minerva?"

"Yes, we have."

Goldie leaned forward a little in her chair. "By my estimate, for more than fifty years."

Minerva nodded. "Since the seventh grade."

They said confession was good for the soul. Elvira Goldman certainly hoped so. "Sometimes I speak before I think," she admitted. "And I say things I shouldn't."

"We all do on occasion," Minerva replied.

"You don't. You always seem to say the right thing at the right time." Goldie's throat tightened. She ran out of air and had to pause and take a great bosom-heaving breath. Then she went on in a rush. "I'm afraid the day of Sam's wedding I drank too much bubbly."

"Perhaps a little too much."

"Let's face it, I talk more than I should with or without champagne." She didn't give Minerva a chance to respond but forged ahead. "I don't know why I prattle on so."

You're here to make amends, Elvira. You're going to have to be honest with yourself and with Minerva.

"Actually, I do know why," she corrected herself.

Minerva's hand went to the bird's nest of brown and gray hair atop her head; she pushed a hairpin in here and there at random. "You don't have to do this, you know."

"Yes, I do." Goldie wondered if Minerva realized it was National Sorry Week. She'd only recently read about the event in a glossy magazine while she was sitting under the hair dryer at Blanche's Beauty Barn. The article had hit home when it said a lot of people didn't know how to apologize.

She was one of them, Goldie realized.

She drew in a lung full of air and straightened her shoulders. It was time to finish what she'd begun while she still had the nerve. "You've got your garden and your herbs and a thriving business that you created through your own talent and hard work. You're clever and interesting. You're thoughtful and you're a good listener, too. It's no wonder people are drawn to you." She paused, nervously twirling the simple gold band on her ring finger. Herbert had passed away two years ago last March, but she still couldn't bring herself to take off her wedding ring. Moistening her lips, she went on. "All I have to offer is gossip. That's why people pretend to be my friend."

Minerva looked straight at her and said, "That isn't all you have to offer, Elvira Goldman. And I don't *pretend* to be your friend. I *am* your friend."

Goldie blurted out, "That's why it's so difficult for me to admit that I'm jealous of you. I always have been."

There, she'd finally come clean.

"You're too hard on yourself," Minerva said. "We all have times in our lives when we envy what someone else has."

Goldie looked at her longtime friend with skepticism. "I can't believe that you've ever felt jealous or envious of anyone."

"Well, I have. I'm human. We're all just human," Minerva said, with a sigh.

Goldie reached over and briefly touched the other woman's hand. "Still, if I said anything, anything at all, the day of the wedding that may have hurt your feelings, I hope you'll forgive me."

"There's nothing to forgive," Minerva assured her.

Goldie was relieved and somewhat surprised. "You're not one to hold a grudge, are you?"

"Life's too short to hold a grudge," Minerva said as she

pushed her chair back, stood up, crossed to the refrigerator, and opened the door. She took out the pitcher of lemonade, refilled their glasses, and graciously offered her guest another cookie. "It's better for everyone to let bygones be bygones."

Sometimes that was easier said than done, Minerva granted after Goldie had gone. Especially in Sweetheart, where gossip was woven into the very fabric of the town's history and social life.

Not that she was concerned for herself. She wasn't. She'd been the subject of idle gossip and wagging tongues more than once in her sixty-plus years and she had survived.

Indeed, she had thrived.

Sydney, however, was another matter altogether. Minerva had watched over her niece since her childhood, and she would not stand by and let anyone sully her good name or her reputation.

Of course, Sydney wasn't a child anymore. She was an intelligent and mature young woman. She was well educated, well traveled, professionally successful, and more than capable of taking care of herself.

Still, Sydney had lost her way—at least temporarily—and she'd come home to find it again.

She was going to make damn sure her niece had that chance, too, Minerva vowed as she carried the empty glasses to the sink, rinsed them off, and put them in the dishwasher.

She glanced at the clock on the kitchen wall and then headed outside to the garden. There was ample time for her to gather a few sprigs of peppermint for the jar of mint water she liked to keep chilled in the refrigerator, and collect a leaf or two of Corsican mint to add to her herb vinegar—along with a few requisite orange peels—before the conference call scheduled for three o'clock with her business manager and Web site designer.

The afternoon sun was out in full force. Minerva plopped a straw hat on her head and slipped her feet into gardening clogs before heading into the mint patch. The fragrances seemed to steam up from the plants. She bent over and plucked a fresh sprig of pennyroyal (she grew both the European and American varieties, *Mentha Pulegium and Hedeoma pulegioides*) and held it up to her nose. She inhaled and savored the distinctively minty aroma.

The last time she'd held a flower to her face and breathed in its scent, it had been the "tossing bouquet" presented to her by Eric Law at the wedding reception. Minerva was amazed to think he'd remembered that long-ago act of kindness.

After all, it had been at least twenty years since the youngest and the wildest of the Law teenagers had been dared and double-dared by his friends to sneak into the Bagley residence and steal the antique ivory head from the library.

Eric had no way of knowing that Minerva was having one of those sleepless nights (there were far too many of them back then) and was sitting by herself in the dark. She'd caught him red-handed. In the act. *Flagrante delicto*. Carved ivory head tucked under one arm. She'd never forgotten the expression on his already handsome masculine face when she'd flicked on the library lamp: shame.

Minerva had followed her heart instead of her head that night, and she'd never regretted it. She had sat the troubled teenager down at the kitchen table and brought out a tin of her homemade cookies. She hadn't lectured him or scolded him, and she certainly hadn't threatened him. She had simply fed him and then sent him home.

Not another word had been spoken about that night or the break-in until the day of Sam and Gillian's wedding, when Eric had whispered his regrets *and* his thanks, along with the words from the French poem: *Une rose d'automne est plus qu'une autre exquise.*

" 'More exquisite than any other is the autumn rose,' " Minerva said under her breath as she straightened and rubbed a muscle cramping in her lower back.

The autumn rose. Where had the spring rose and the summer rose gone, along with her youth? For that matter, where had middle-age gone? (Although she'd recently read an article in the AARP magazine that sixty was the new forty.)

Well, she was sixty-two years old and she would soon be the "winter rose." Curious how the years seemed to have slipped through her fingers one day at a time.

Regrets.

She had her share of regrets, Minerva acknowledged to herself as she tucked the cluster of fresh mint into the front pocket of her gardening apron.

Unlike the words of "My Way," the signature song crooned by Frank Sinatra—old Blue Eyes himself—her regrets *weren't* too few to mention. But she had learned how to live with them. How to live and prosper. How to attain a degree of contentment and happiness. Well, acceptance, anyway.

Water from the moon.

The truth was harsh and irrefutable, and it was carved in stone: No one could go back and change their past *or* correct the mistakes they'd made along the way. She should know. She'd made plenty of them in her lifetime. Some real whoppers.

Minerva picked another sprig of fresh mint, raised it to her nose, took a sniff, and then popped it into her mouth for a moment.

If you weren't careful, she reflected, the past—with all of its mistakes and regrets—could eat you alive, consume you from the inside out, cannibalize you, leave you an empty shell, a shadow of yourself, a bitter old maid.

"They don't use the term *old maid* anymore," she said out loud as she spit out the mint and raised the hem of her apron to her face, wiping away the perspiration. "You're a SWFOS."

Single white female over sixty.

Water from the moon.

Everybody assumed she'd chosen the name for her company from a favorite saying of her uncle Bert's and his World War II buddy, Jacob Charles. Those two special men had certainly given her the original idea, but it was her regrets, her mistakes, her past that reminded her daily of the meaning behind the traditional Japanese saying.

"There's no use in crying over spilled milk, Minerva. What's done is done," she said, suddenly feeling impatient with herself.

She yanked off her straw hat and headed toward her office for the three o'clock conference call.

Water from the moon.

Minerva knew better than anyone that there were some things she could never have. . . .

She'd liked Sydney St. John better as an ugly duckling.

Nope. That was pure bull. She'd hated her then. She hated her now. She'd always hated Sydney St. John. Ever since the fifth grade. Maybe longer.

Back in elementary school, Sydney had been the teacher's pet, even though she'd been tall and skinny and covered with freckles and had worn Coke-bottle glasses. In fact, more than once she'd gotten their classmates to laugh behind Sydney's back, and sometimes right to her face, by claiming if they looked up the word *ugly* in the dictionary, there would be a picture of Sydney the Freak.

But more important than Sydney St. John being Mrs. Higginbottom's favorite—and far worse, in her opinion—had been the Freak's habit of raining on *her* parade.

She remembered one particularly fine spring day. It had

been during afternoon recess and she'd been entertaining their classmates with stories she had heard from her two older brothers. Some of the kids had giggled, but it'd been that scared and nervous kind of giggle. A few had groaned and said that her stories were disgusting or gross or that she must have made them up. She had always sworn that every word was true. *Cross my heart and hope to die.*

It never failed that a couple of Goody Two-shoes would pipe up and say that they still didn't believe her, but nobody had walked away. In fact, her classmates had been all ears, hanging on to every word as she'd spun her tales.

Except for Sydney St. John.

The Freak had stood outside the circle gathered around her, not saying one damn word, but staring at her with disapproval.

Anyway, on that otherwise perfect day in April she'd had the kids eating out her hand as she had told them the one about the secret ingredient in bubblegum that kept it chewy: spider eggs. They had all pressed closer, not wanting to miss a word.

She'd been on a roll after that. She had gone on to tell the story about the boy in the commercials—some kid named Mikey—who had gulped down a can of cola and then eaten a whole bag of that fizzy candy: The two had combined in his stomach and exploded, killing him. His guts had been splattered all over the walls.

She had described it in vivid Technicolor, too, hooting with delight when one of the kids had turned green around the gills and looked like he might puke. A couple of the other boys had laughed like hyenas, jostling and elbowing each other, and had even dared each other to try the same trick.

Then Mrs. Higginbottom had blown her whistle and recess had been over. As they'd marched in formation two-by-two toward the school door, several of the kids had stopped and asked Sydney if it were true about the spider eggs.

Sydney had looked down her nose at them—not that she had any choice since she was a head taller than anybody else in their class—and said, "No, it isn't true." Then she had gone on to explain what it was that kept chewing gum chewy, using big words that nobody had understood, and showing off.

The Bigelow boy had turned around, snickering, pointing at *her*, and had whispered something to the girl next to him. Then they'd both laughed behind their hands and had looked at her like she was a maggot on a dead crow.

She'd never forgiven Sydney the Freak for that.

Then there was the time Sydney had tried to help her with a math lesson, but trying to understand long division had made her head hurt and her palms sweat, so she'd finally told the Freak to shove off, butt out, hit the road, Jack. She didn't like the feeling of being dumb as a rock, and she'd always felt real dumb next to Sydney.

Besides, the Bagleys and St. Johns thought they were somehow above other folks, common folks like her family, just because their ancestors had founded the town and laid claim to most of the prime farmland in the area. Not to mention the big houses and the money and the fancy smancy East Coast university educations.

The Bagleys had always lived in one of the largest Victorian houses in Sweetheart, currently occupied by Minerva Bagley, and they owned the whole Bagley Building on the town square.

The St. John side of the Freak's family—except for the Freak, herself—were a bunch of brilliant doctors. They also had a tree farm just outside of town. Supposedly Johnny Appleseed had come through the region in frontier days, planting seeds along the way.

No doubt about it, the Bagleys and St. Johns considered themselves a notch or two above everybody else.

Of course, when they were kids, Sydney had been so self-conscious about being the tallest one in their class and having big feet—huge feet—and all that splotchy skin that burned if she stayed out in the sun for more than ten seconds, that *she* could feel how uncomfortable the other girl was just by walking by her.

At one point she'd even found herself feeling sorry for Sydney the Freak.

Except Sydney St. John wasn't a freak anymore. And she sure as hell wasn't the ugly duckling she'd been way back when they were in high school together.

High school had been *her* glory days before she'd gotten married and had the kids and divorced Billy Bob and had taken up with Ed Snelling, only to discover a few months later that Ed wasn't divorced and never intended to get divorced from that sniveling wife of his.

She'd been working two jobs, too, just to keep body and soul together, while he was gallivanting around the countryside in his souped-up pickup truck with the bumper sticker that read: MECHANICS KNOW HOW TO USE THEIR TOOLS.

She'd kicked Ed out of her trailer and out of her life on the same night. *Good riddance to bad rubbish.* Next day she'd taken on a third job working the wedding reception.

Anyway, she'd watched Sydney St. John and Eric Law at his brother's party. Dancing together. Talking. Laughing. Drinking champagne. Both tall and handsome and dressed up like they were some kind of goddamned movie stars. She was pretty sure those were real diamonds in Sydney's ears, too. Not rhinestones or paste.

She'd seen the two of them, but her former classmates hadn't seen her. Nobody had paid her any attention that day; she'd been just another waitress hired to work under the big white tent. Her duties had included keeping the buffet table stocked with fresh food, and carrying in clean silverware and dishes (with strict instructions to be careful because the fancy china plates cost a hundred bucks a piece), and wiping up any spills or messes.

It had been as plain as the nose on her face who was going to catch the wedding bouquet tossed by the bride (now, there was another one born with a silver spoon in her mouth), so she'd been as surprised as the next person when it had been Eric Law.

Eric was cut from a different piece of cloth altogether. He'd never made her feel like trailer trash. Back in their heyday he hadn't been much more than a good-looking kid with a great body and a knack for trouble. The brains must have come later. After he'd left town. She'd even heard he was a hotshot attorney now. Some claimed he was a millionaire. But that was just gossip, and you could never trust the gossip in Sweetheart.

Unless it came from Mrs. Goldman. She was the real

thing; she got her information the old-fashioned way: at
the beauty parlor, the grocery store on the corner,
McGinty's Pub, even at church. Goldie was a natural-born
busybody and snoop.

Well, *she* had learned a thing or two on her own. She'd
been sneaking around the edge of the barn one night, week
before last, same night as the wedding, and had watched
Eric and Sydney. The two of them were standing on the
walkway gazing up at the stars in the sky or some such
nonsense. She'd even managed to pick up a word or two
here and there before the damned security light had
blinked on and she'd had to hightail it into the darkness.

"*. . . scared the crap . . .*"

"*. . . you'd never forgive yourself.*"

"*I was afraid you'd end up hating me.*"

She would dearly love to know what they'd been talking about. Sounded like secrets. Must be secrets. Had to be
secrets.

Momma knew a lot of secrets. Momma wasn't real
bright in some ways, but she was a survivor and she'd been
a good teacher, at least when it came to keeping your
mouth shut and your eyes and ears open. Of course, she
knew some secrets about Momma as well.

Secrets were a funny thing. Most people were dying to
tell you their own and other people's. That was just plain
stupid. The real power was in the secrets you kept.

That was a lesson she'd learned a long time ago. There
were some secrets she'd never tell anyone . . . for Momma's
sake and certainly for her own.

She turned the light on in the bathroom: the bare bulb
overhead swung back and forth on a long piece of exposed

electrical cord, throwing the cramped room into harsh focus. The sink was stained and chipped along the rim. The mirror on the medicine cabinet had little black specks all over it, like the finish was coming off. There was a plunger sticking out of the toilet. The room smelled of mildew and worse.

She raised her eyes and stared at herself in the mirror. She felt old and used up. She looked old and used up, too. It was hard to believe that she and Sydney St. John were the same age. She looked ten years older than the other woman.

More like twenty, she thought.

"Who's the freak now?" she muttered, coughing and taking another drag on her cigarette. She squinted and watched the smoke momentarily blur the image in the mirror.

Hell, she'd never gotten a lucky break in her life. Not one. Bad luck seemed to follow her around like she was a bitch in heat. But now it was being thrown in her face: Sydney the Freak had everything and she had nothing.

Still, she had her plans and nobody was going to rain on her parade. Not this time.

Chapter
thirteen

There was a knock on his door.

It couldn't be Sydney. They had taken extra pains to avoid each other since the tea "incident" at the B & B last week.

After all, Eric reflected, he was a man of his word, and he'd promised her that they wouldn't run into each other. Sydney was free to go her way and he would go his. That was their agreement.

Besides, he'd watched her drive away in her Beemer a half hour ago. The coast was clear.

Eric opened the door of the apartment and found Mrs. Manderley standing outside on the landing. She was wearing some sort of smock over her civilian clothes, and she was armed with a vacuum sweeper, a mop and pail, and a cleaning caddy filled with everything from disinfectant to furniture polish to window cleaner, from a toilet brush to a scrub brush to a feather duster.

The housekeeper was ready to do battle.

"Good morning, Mr. Law," she said in greeting. "Off to town, are we?"

"Yes," he said, and stepped back to allow her entrance. "May I help you with that?"

"No need." She pushed the Hoover past him into the apartment and went back for the cleaning caddy and other supplies. "I'm used to doing things my own way."

"I'll be out of your hair in a minute," Eric guaranteed, patting the pockets of his denim shirt and mentally running down a list of what he needed to take with him: wallet, sunglasses, keys to the pickup, dirty shirts for the laundry, grocery list, reminder to stop by the garage and see how they were coming with the repairs on Red. Damn, he knew he was forgetting something.

How about your cell phone, Law.

Which, naturally, brought up—maybe that was a bad choice of words—which reminded him of the pun Sydney had told him that first evening; her delighted laughter filling the night air: *Is that your cell phone or are you just glad to see me?*

"Take your time, Mr. Law," the housekeeper said, bringing out a can of lemon-scented Pledge and spraying the surface of the coffee table in front of the chenille slipcovered sofa. He was halfway out the door when she finally looked up from her polishing and said, "People around these parts say you've changed a lot since you were in high school."

Eric paused with his hand on the doorknob, the scent of lemon permeating the air. He had no idea where she was going with this. "Everybody changes as they get older" seemed like a nice, safe, innocuous response on his part.

"Some more than others." *Spray. Wipe. Polish.* "Sometimes for the better." *Spray. Wipe. Polish.* "And sometimes not," Mrs. Manderley said, hitting her stride and next turning her attention to the end tables. *Spray. Wipe. Polish.*

He couldn't argue with that.

The woman took her own sweet time. "I hear tell you're a highfalutin lawyer now like your brother."

Personally Eric preferred the term *world-class attorney,* or *brilliant legal mind,* or, hell, even *legal eagle,* but this probably wasn't the time to argue semantics with Mrs. Manderley. "I'm a licensed attorney in both Massachusetts and Indiana." *And* New York *and* Washington, D.C., *and* several other places he was pretty sure would be of little or no interest to the housekeeper.

She looked at him askance. "Then do you mind if I ask you a legal question?"

Experience had taught him there was really no good answer to that. So he stood there half in, half out of the doorway, his head cocked slightly to one side, as if to appear interested and ready to listen, and said, "Unofficially? Off the record?"

Mrs. Manderley nodded as she sprayed the kitchen counter with disinfectant. He remembered that distinctive smell from his childhood and realized his mother must have used the same brand. It was another minute and several more swipes of her cleaning cloth before she volunteered, "I have a friend with a problem."

Nobody ever had problems themselves. Everybody had friends with problems.

Eric waited.

The housekeeper seemed fixated on obliterating a spot of who-knew-what on the tile countertop; she was scrubbing as if her life depended on it. She cleared her throat and said, "This friend knows something nobody else knows."

"I see. . . ."

"It goes back a long way."

Eric discovered he was curious in spite of himself. "How long?" he asked.

The woman's mouth tightened and she appeared to scrub even harder. "Forty-five years."

He let out a low whistle under his breath. "That's a long time to keep a secret."

"Yessiree, it is." She raised one arm and wiped her sleeve across a forehead shiny with perspiration. "Anyway, this friend is having second thoughts."

"About what?"

Mrs. Manderley didn't answer straight off. Instead, she changed her focus and ruthlessly tackled the dust on the woodwork with a short-handled mop. "She's thinking maybe she should have told someone about what happened back then, after all." She cleared her throat and amended her statement. "Or what didn't happen."

It sounded to him like a Chinese puzzle box: a puzzle within a puzzle within a puzzle. "Why is your friend having second thoughts now?"

The housekeeper's lips thinned and her face was suddenly drawn; she even looked older. "My friend feels like the burden has grown heavier over the last few years, and she doesn't want to die with this on her conscience."

Eric could understand that. He said in all sincerity,

"Most of us would like to make peace with the past before it's too late." Ella Manderley wasn't the first person he'd run into who had decided to come clean long after the fact.

She went perfectly still, but didn't look up at him. "So, what should my friend do?"

Eric blew out his breath. This was always the tricky part. "If it's a question of legalities, then your friend needs to consult an attorney." He added, "Officially."

The edges of her mouth turned up, but it wasn't a smile. "For the record?"

Something like that.

He made the only recommendation he could. "There are any number of capable lawyers your friend could call and talk to right here in Sweetheart."

"Maybe she'll decide to do that," the woman said, but there was a lack of conviction in her voice.

Eric could tell Mrs. Manderley was wavering in her resolve. Before he put the other foot out the door, he said, "If for no other reason, urge your friend to make the phone call for her own sake."

"Any calls or appointments?" Eric asked facetiously as he opened the door to Sam's law office and spied his brother's very efficient secretary, Gal Friday, and right-hand woman, behind her desk, in the process of hanging up the telephone.

Carolyn Hart peered at him over the rim of her reading glasses. "As a matter of fact, the phone has been ringing off the hook for the past few days."

Eric stepped inside the second-floor suite of offices and

closed the hallway door behind him. "I thought everybody knew Sam was on his honeymoon."

"They do. The calls have all been for you." Carolyn Hart was smart and experienced, professional and no-nonsense, so it was highly unlikely she was teasing him.

Eric frowned and raked his fingers through his hair, although he did manage to stop himself from scratching his head. "For me?"

She nodded crisply in the direction of the adjoining office. "There is a stack of messages waiting on Sam's—on *your* desk. I've arranged them in chronological order starting with the date and the time they came into the office." The secretary did a one-eighty in her desk chair, dropped a folder into the large mahogany file cabinet behind her, maneuvered around and quickly typed something into the computer on the L-shaped arm of her work station and said, "I would have notified you last week, but Sam made it clear you were taking some time off."

Eric thrust his left hand into the pocket of his jeans and jiggled his loose change. "I am."

Without glancing up from her work, she added, "He also said you were badly in need of a vacation."

"Did he?"

She nodded her head. "I was instructed not to bother you with business until you were good and ready."

Eric was curious. "And how were you supposed to determine when I was good and ready?" he inquired, folding his arms across his chest and leaning back against the door frame.

Carolyn Hart turned and gave him one of those looks that spoke volumes. "Sam said you'd show up here at the office."

Well, *duh*.

"When did the phone calls start?"

Her recall of the facts was instantaneous and impressive. "Last week. Wednesday. Five-thirty p.m."

Ah-huh. That just happened to coincide with the afternoon he'd encountered Mrs. Ledbetter out in front of the Sweetheart Bed & Breakfast. The poor old dear had been standing at the bottom of the steps, leaning on her cane, hesitant to climb them on her own. And rightly so. The flight of stairs were original to the old mansion, a bit steep, and made of granite. Granite was pretty unforgiving if you were an octogenarian, or older, and happened to fall.

Of course, as a result of that chance meeting with Mrs. Ledbetter, he'd ended up spending the rest of the afternoon tasting various herbal teas, which he discovered were definitely *not* his cup of tea, and making small talk.

"That was right after I"—Eric crossed one foot over the other and was about to say "got roped into," but settled for—"attended Minerva Bagley's tea party."

"Your kindness to Elsa Ledbetter and your presence at the weekly tea were specifically mentioned in about fifty percent of the phone calls," Carolyn Hart confirmed.

That was an unexpected development. "Just out of curiosity, who's calling me?"

"Prospective clients. Mostly women. In fact, running about five to one, women to men." Sam's secretary bit the corners of her mouth against a smile. Maybe he'd have to rethink his assessment about her sense of humor.

"Well, I'll be damned," he muttered under his breath.

"I'd say the word is out."

Something told Eric it wasn't his reputation as a brilliant attorney she was referring to. He dreaded asking, but in the end he did. "Exactly what word would that be?"

"That Eric Law is back in town *and*"—Carolyn Hart looked straight at him—"back on the market."

He felt his face go hot. He didn't have to ask *what* market?

The woman behind the desk seemed sympathetic if vaguely amused by his situation. "Under the circumstances, I took the liberty of organizing your messages into three categories."

That got his interest.

She went on to explain her system. "The messages flagged with a green Post-it appear to be legitimate. The ones marked with yellow might require caution on your part."

He hazarded a wild guess. "And, at all costs, avoid the ones tagged with a red Post-it."

She moderated his statement with, "Well, proceed at your own risk, anyway."

He pushed off from the doorframe. "Thank you, Mrs. Hart. I appreciate your help with this."

"Call me Carol. Sam does."

He smiled. "Thanks, Carol."

"You're welcome, Eric," then she turned her attention to the telephone ringing on her desk.

More than an hour later, having worked his way through the stack of phone messages tagged with green stickers and having duly noted the appointments he'd made for the following week on Sam's computer, Eric steepled his fingers behind his head, sat back in his brother's office chair, and put his feet up on the windowsill.

He noticed there were scuff marks, including some pretty old ones, on the wood's dark patina. Apparently he wasn't the first to use the edge of the floor-to-ceiling window as a footrest.

In fact, he could picture Sam sitting here at the end of the day, mulling over his most recent and challenging case. Dusk would be descending on Sweetheart; the evening sky awash with vivid pinks, deep purples, and stratified blues from robin's egg to royal to navy.

His brother might lean back, as he was now, and gaze out at the town square and across the street to the Sweetheart County courthouse: a majestic limestone edifice dating back to 1903, the same year the Bagley Building, itself, was constructed.

If it were evening, one by one the spotlights would flicker on, illuminating the front of the courthouse and the marble statue of Lady Justice mounted above its portico. The figure was carved in the classic pose: blindfolded, a two-edged sword held in one hand and the scales of justice balanced in the other.

Justice was blind.

It was supposed to be, anyway, Eric thought as he leaned back even farther in Sam's chair.

Mice were blind. At least the three in the nursery rhyme were. Of course, he remembered how surprised he'd been to learn the bloody history behind that seemingly innocent childhood poem, since the three blind mice were actually three English noblemen burned at the stake by Bloody Mary, Queen Mary I, daughter of Henry VIII. That had been "justice" sixteenth-century style.

Men were often blind. Blind to the truth. Blind to their

own faults. Blind to what was right and to what was wrong.

Love was blind. Or so they claimed.

Had he ever really been in love? The kind of love that lasted a lifetime? The till-death-do-us-part kind? The kind of love his parents had shared for more than thirty-five years? And his grandparents for more than sixty?

Hell, he wasn't sure he even believed in that kind of love anymore, at least not for him. He had wondered more than once if he'd ever been in love with his ex-wife. Marla had seemed like someone he *should* love. Not the same thing as someone he simply loved . . . if love could ever be described as simple.

One thing was for damned sure: The strongest emotion he'd felt after his divorce was relief.

Water under the bridge, buddy.

Eric blew out his breath expressively, turned his head, and studied the stack of publications piled on top of the barrister's bookcase to his right. They were weighty tomes with titles like *Indiana Criminal Law*, *Indiana Law and Property*, *Jurisprudence for You*, *Torts and Taxes*, and *Divorce: It's Not for Amateurs Anymore.*

No doubt that last one had been a best-seller, he thought with a sardonic smile, swiveling around in the high-backed office chair.

Then he noticed a smaller three-shelver tucked into the corner of the room and got up to investigate. He needed a bookcase just about this size for his apartment. But since he was pretty sure that Sam wouldn't appreciate him "borrowing" this one, he'd just have to buy himself something similar.

Driven by curiosity, Eric reached down and took out the first slim volume, turned it over to the front cover, and read the title to himself: *Sex, Lies, and Lawsuits.*

Intriguing.

He went on to several more on the top shelf: *Jurisprudence for Dummies* and *Torts R Us.* He chuckled and picked up the next book on the stack. *It's a Moo Point: A humorous look at the law through the eyes of a cow.*

He was still chuckling when he came to the last book. *More Balls Than Hands: Juggling your way to success by learning to love your mistakes.*

Eric put his head back and began to laugh. He laughed until he thought he would split a gut. He laughed until the tears ran unabashedly down his face. In fact, he couldn't remember the last time he'd laughed so hard.

Sure, you do, Law. It was two weeks ago when you were with Sydney St. John.

Forty-five minutes later Eric drove down the tree-shaded street and turned onto Pearson Boulevard, named for the two very distinct branches of the Pearson family. Everybody in Sweetheart knew that one branch of the Pearsons lived on the south side of the street, and the other on the north side.

A town with its own Mason-Dixon line, he thought with an ironic smile.

The historic houses along both sides of Pearson Boulevard were all two or two-and-a-half stories tall. They were painted in neutral shades: white or off-white, gray or beige, with shutters in forest green, dark brown, or black. The same was true for the front doors.

The house numbers were always brass, always polished, and always mounted next to the mailbox. The lawns were immaculate. The shrubbery was neatly trimmed. The flowers were colorful, but discreet; nothing too flashy or gaudy or overblown.

There were no lawn ornaments to mar the perfection: no politically incorrect figurines holding lanterns aloft; no semiobscene fountains with water spouting from dubious body parts, no concrete ducks dressed up in cutesy seasonal garb.

This afternoon cars were parked as far as the eye could see. They were lined up and down the boulevard in both directions, along every side street, and in every available driveway.

Eric finally found an open parking space, got down from the cab of the pickup, and started walking. Should he begin his search for a bookcase on the south side of the street or the north?

He passed a woman carrying an ornate Victorian lamp, complete with tasseled lampshade. A man strolled past him, whistling, a fishing pole over his shoulder. Two excited and chattering young women went by, carrying cardboard boxes with who-knew-what inside.

As Eric got closer to the two large and nearly identical houses in the middle of the block, he noticed sale items overflowing from open garages onto the lawns, the driveways, even the sidewalks. There was everything from Coca-Cola collectibles to golf clubs to bicycles to leftover Christmas decorations.

And signs.

Everywhere there were signs.

Carolyn Hart had warned him that the two Pearson cousins—rivals for as long as anyone could remember—were attempting to raise money for their political campaigns. Walter P. and Walter E. were fierce opponents in the race for dog catcher.

Well, technically, they were running for animal control officer, which, Carol had explained, included domestic animals, wildlife, *and* fisheries. (She would know since she and her husband, Truman Hart, were the leading members and main supporters of the local chapter of the SPCA.)

On one side of the boulevard was a simple sign in stark black lettering against a white background: MORE THAN JUST A DOG CATCHER!

Directly across the street were two even larger signs mounted on posts in the front lawn. The first read: BAD FOR FISH! WRONG FOR SWEETHEART!

The second: YOUR POND COULD BE NEXT. BEWARE THE FRANKENFISH.

Yep, Eric thought, this had to be the place.

"My cousin is making a big stink about a bunch of dead fish," Walter E. shouted into the megaphone he was holding up to his mouth. The megaphone was several feet long, fashioned of brushed aluminum, and was painted a shade of deep golden yellow. There was a large black *P* embossed on one side and CLASS OF '59 on the other.

The *P*, however, didn't stand for *Pearson*. It stood for *Purdue*. Walter E. had been the head cheerleader during his university days at the West Lafayette campus.

"You tell 'em, Walt!" somebody shouted from the far side of the gathering.

Walter E. disliked being called Walt, and everyone in Sweetheart knew it. But he was a trooper. He carried on in the face of adversity. "Mark my words, friends and neighbors, there is far more at stake in this campaign than fish," he warned.

"You have signs posted all over town accusing Walter P. of being a slippery, flat-bellied bottom-feeder," pointed out one of his future constituents. "Sounds pretty fishy to me."

That brought twitters of laughter from the crowd milling around Walter E.'s front yard.

"My opponent would have you believe he is a friend to the fish. But don't be taken in by such unscrupulous and unprincipled tactics. Believe me, he's not above using fear to convince you to vote for him," said the man with the megaphone. Then he added, "Sadly, folks, politics is a dirty business."

"What is a Frankenfish?" asked a boy staring at the large billboard across the street.

Walter E. cleared his throat. "Would anyone care to answer young Tommy's question?"

There was dead silence.

"Maybe it's a figment of Walter P.'s imagination," volunteered someone in the front.

His cousin sniffed and said disdainfully, "We all know that Walter P. has no imagination. I'm sure you recall his petition last year to keep the water tower a nondescript gray color."

"I liked your idea of painting a big yellow smiley face on it," endorsed one woman.

"So did I," agreed another.

Walter E. beamed with pleasure and said, "Thank you for the vote of confidence, ladies."

"But what is a Frankenfish?" Tommy asked again, persistent as only a curious ten-year-old could be.

Sydney finally spoke up from the other side of the

crowd. "Actually, 'Frankenfish' is the description scientists have given to the northern snakehead fish."

"I've been an avid fisherman all my life," touted a middle-aged man. "I've never heard of a snakehead fish."

"Neither have I," came from somewhere else in the throng of bargain hunters.

Well, she had. "Unfortunately, there was one recently discovered in Chicago's Burnham Harbor," Sydney said. "And I can tell you that the news sent a shock wave through the entire scientific community. They even called in the Army Corps of Engineers, along with their electronic detection equipment, to help in the search for more of the dreaded fish."

"What's all the fuss about?" asked the self-proclaimed expert angler as he tugged on the brim of his baseball cap. The inscription on the front read: WOMEN LOVE ME. FISH FEAR ME. "And what the hell's it got to do with us, anyway?"

The woman standing beside him tugged on his arm and said, "Fred, there's no need for that kind of language."

Sydney continued with her explanation. "The northern snakehead was imported into this country primarily for aquariums. Regrettably some pet owners dump their fish into the nearest stream or lake or body of water when they can't *or* don't want to care for them anymore. Once a northern snakehead—the so-called Frankenfish—is released or escapes into the wild, it becomes not just a nuisance, but a real danger."

"In what way?" someone challenged.

"By surviving under extremely adverse conditions. For example, in oxygen-depleted water."

"Your point being . . ."

"It has the ability to move from pond to pond, gobbling up native fish and wreaking havoc on freshwater ecosystems," she said. "The northern snakehead has already been spotted in Virginia, Maryland, Pennsylvania, and Wisconsin. It could show up in Indiana one day."

"You mean it might become a threat right here in Sweetheart County?" speculated the fisherman.

"There's no evidence at this time, but it's always a possibility," she said.

Walter E. cleared his throat and neatly cut her off. "Thank you, Sydney. Your input as a scientist was most interesting and edifying. But we don't want to go running around with our hair on fire and frightening folks, now do we? I leave those kind of hysterics to my cousin." He turned his attention to his audience. "I'm sure Dr. St. John will agree that the chances of this so-called Frankenfish coming anywhere near our beloved community are pretty remote."

Sydney opened her mouth to correct him—first, she wasn't a doctor, and second, she certainly was no scientist—but their host was already on to his next point. "The reason I've invited you all here today is to raise campaign funds so that I can be elected animal control officer for the coming two years. Rather than go around town with my hand held out like a beggar, I decided to hold a yard sale and give you something in exchange for your hard-earned money."

"Besides, Walter P. is holding a sale right across the street and you wouldn't want to be outdone by your cousin, would you?" hollered a male heckler.

Walter E.'s gaze swept the motley group assembled on his property and came to rest on a man dressed in dirty coveralls and leaning against the side of his garage. "Is that you, Billy Bob?"

"Yes, sir," Billy Bob spoke up, touching the brim of his baseball cap with a two-fingered salute; his hat was inscribed with the succinct message: LIFE'S A BEACH.

The man with the megaphone frowned. "You never could hold your tongue."

"But I sure can hold my liquor," was Billy Bob's response amidst another smattering of laughter from the people looking over furniture, dishes, bric-a-brac, racks of clothing, assorted sporting and fishing equipment, a variety of tools—both hand and power—lawnmowers, and sundry other items.

Walter E. wisely decided to come down off his soapbox and mingle with the public interested in what he had to sell.

"How much do you want for this piece of furniture marked 'chester drawers'?" inquired one woman.

Walter Pearson studied the price tag dangling from a drawer pull. "It's an antique, circa 1875. Original hardware. Excellent condition. Never been refinished, of course." He took a deep breath and went on. "It belonged to my maternal grandmother: Her last name was Chester before she married my grandfather, and I understand this is where she kept her drawers." Walter E. stopped and snorted at his own joke. Once he'd regained control of himself he said, "Naturally, I hate to part with it, but it's yours for six hundred dollars, Shirley."

"I'll give you three hundred and fifty, and not a penny more," she countered. Shirley was a shrewd shopper.

"Sold!" was Walter's response.

"This bureau says it's a 'Chip and Dale,' " pointed out another interested buyer. "Do you mean Chippendale?"

Walter E. turned beet red and got a peculiar expression on his face. He hemmed and hawed for a minute and then said, "It was meant as a joke, Janet."

"Oh, of course it was," she said, giving a polite laugh. Janet was known for her tactfulness.

Apparently Minerva decided this was the perfect time to intervene. "Do tell us another one of your jokes, Walter E.," she urged from where she and Sydney were standing on the driveway.

"I'd be happy to oblige. Thank you for asking, Minerva." The man scratched his head for a moment, then snapped his fingers and said, "Why does a bee hum?"

"I don't know," came a voice from somewhere over by knicknacks, "why does he?"

Walter E. chortled, slapped his thigh with the flat of his hand, and just barely managed to deliver the punch line. "Because he doesn't know the words."

Sydney leaned toward her aunt and whispered, "I see his jokes haven't improved."

"Walter E. has been telling the same bad jokes since we were in grade school together, and that's been more than five decades ago," Minerva said to her in an aside. She turned her attention to a three-tiered stand being used to display pieces of china and other odds and ends. "I suggest we buy several small items here, and then go across the street and do the same at Walter P.'s yard sale."

Sydney kept her voice low. "Tit for tat?"

Minerva bit the edges of her mouth against a smile. "Something like that. The reason for the feud between the two branches of the Pearson family may have been forgotten long ago, but one still walks a fine line with Walter P. and Walter E. We wouldn't want to be accused of showing favoritism."

Sydney looked at her aunt out of the corner of her eye. "I seem to recall that at some point in the past both Walter E. and Walter P. danced attendance on you."

Minerva gave a ladylike snort. "Unfortunately Walter E. behaves as if everything *and* everyone are part of some great cosmic joke. On the flip side, Walter P. takes life too seriously. He fails to see the humor in anything." She selected a sugar bowl and creamer set with a delicate floral pattern, turned them over, studied the markings on the bottom, said, "This is quite nice for the price," and picked up the thread of their conversation without missing a beat. "If you want my opinion, I think there's just enough intelligence, wit, and common sense between the two of them to make *one* good man."

"A good man is hard to find," Sydney agreed as she examined a pair of fake Staffordshire dogs.

Then, for some inexplicable reason, an image of Eric Law popped into her head, along with an irreverent thought: *And a hard man was good to find.*

"My cousin thinks this is all just a joke," Walter P. confided to Eric as he wiped his greasy hands on an old towel apparently meant for that very purpose; it was already stained with paint and motor oil. "He doesn't seem to understand that politics is serious business."

It also makes for strange bedfellows, Eric thought as he perused the area for a bookcase.

The man beside him went on talking as he finished cleaning up an ancient bicycle marked: FOR SALE AS IS. NAME YOUR OWN PRICE. "It wasn't until after my victory last year regarding the water tower that I decided to throw my hat into the political ring."

Speaking of hats, Eric couldn't help but notice the traditional baseball cap Walter P. was wearing. (Did every man in town own one of the damn things?) A pithy saying was emblazoned across the front: I'M CONFUSED. WAIT ... MAYBE I'M NOT.

Walter P. had mentioned the water tower. Did he really want to know what the man meant by his "victory"? *Naw.* The water tower was plain, old gray. For as long as Eric could remember it had been plain, old gray. He glanced up at the familiar structure standing guard over the town. It still was plain, old gray. All was right with the world.

"Once I made the decision to run for animal control officer, someone else, who shall remain nameless"—here Walter P. paused, shot daggers across the street at his cousin's house, and gave an indignant sniff—"decided that *he* would run for the same office."

Gee, I wonder who, Eric thought with a wry smile. After all these years, the rivalry between the Pearson cousins was obviously alive and well. So much for letting bygones be bygones.

Walter P. seemed especially pleased to find someone he assumed was sympathetic to his cause. "There aren't too many people around these parts who would understand, Eric." He lowered his voice a notch. "But I'm intrigued by the psychology of fish."

Oh, boy.

Walter P. finished oiling the bicycle. He wiped off a greasy patch here and there, and then leaned it up against the corner of the garage since the kickstand was missing.

"I've been trying to get inside their heads." Then he said with a heartfelt sigh, "I wish I could talk to them."

Eric frowned. "To the fish?"

"Yes." Walter P. had the good sense to blush. "I suppose that sounds a little crazy."

Nothing sounded crazy to him these days, Eric realized. That's what a couple of weeks back in his hometown had done to him. "You mean like Doctor Doolittle?"

"Doctor Doolittle?"

"The character in the classic novel who can communicate with animals," Eric explained as he looked over an upholstered footstool marked down from forty dollars to a bargain price of two-fifty. Unfortunately the geometric pattern in shades of bright orange and even brighter chartreuse was not only ugly as sin, but clashed with every piece of furniture in his apartment.

Walter Pearson smiled; it was a rare occurrence. "Then I wish I were like this Doolittle person." He patted Eric on the back and declared, "I must say it's gratifying to run into a bright young fellow who understands my vision for the future of Sweetheart County."

Eric cleared his throat. "You don't happen to have any bookcases for sale, do you?"

"I certainly do," was Walter P.'s response. "There's a

handsome floor-to-ceiling unit in my garage. Solid walnut. I'll give it to you for ten percent off."

Eric hated to break the news to the man but "I was thinking of something smaller."

"Smaller," Walter P. repeated, pondering his request. "Yes, I do believe there's one above half that size on the other side of the driveway. You'll find it tucked between the life-size statue of Venus de Milo and the painting of Elvis on black velvet."

Sydney was paying for the solid maple bookcase—she had the perfect spot for it beneath the window in her bedroom; the bedroom she was in the process of redecorating—when a familiar voice behind her said, "I'll take it."

"We're supposed to dicker on the price," Walter P. informed his customer. "You're not supposed to just give me what's marked on the bookcase."

In a half-amused, half-befuddled tone, Eric said, "I figured you'd want to make as much as possible for your fund-raiser."

"True enough, boy."

Sydney could just imagine the expression on Eric Law's face at being called "boy."

Walter P.'s sales assistance and next-door neighbor swept past the two men with a SOLD sticker in her hand and slapped it on the bookcase. "It's a moot point now. This piece is already spoken for."

"I'll give you double your asking price," Eric offered, opening his wallet.

Walter P. shrugged his shoulders and said, "I'm afraid

it's out of my hands now, Eric, my boy. You'll have to ask the new owner."

"Who would that be?"

"The young lady is standing right behind you."

Chapter
fifteen

 "It was certainly thoughtful of Eric to lug that heavy bookcase all the way to your car for you," Minerva was saying to Sydney later that same afternoon.

The two women were sitting side by side in a pair of traditional Adirondack chairs, relaxing under a sprawling shade tree in Minerva's backyard, sipping a glass of cool mint water, and enjoying a few quiet moments together.

"Yes, it was," Sydney said, and meant it. She was no shrinking violet, but she could never have managed the bookcase on her own. The darn thing weighed a ton.

It was another minute or two before her aunt remarked, "Eric is quite the gentleman."

She took a sip of mint water. "Yes, he is."

"He reminds me more of his older brother every time I'm with him," Minerva said.

"I can't say I ever knew Samuel Law all that well." Sydney watched as a small sweat bee landed on her arm. She knew better than to swat at it. She waited patiently for the tiny creature to take flight again before she finished her thought. "Sam was three years ahead of me when we were back in high school."

"Well, I'll tell you, my dear, with Uncle Bert gone, there's no man in Sweetheart I trust more than Samuel Law."

High praise, indeed, since her aunt wasn't someone prone to hyperbole or exaggeration.

Minerva kicked off her gardening clogs (on first returning home from the yard sales, she had gone into the mint patch for a few fresh sprigs to add as a garnish to their glasses of mint water) and stretched her legs out in front of her. "During the last several years of his life, this was your great-uncle's favorite place to sit and while away an hour or two on a fine summer day."

Sydney was pretty sure she understood how Great-Uncle Bert must have felt. This was the first time in a long time— Weeks? Months? *Years?*—that she'd been utterly at peace.

She eased back in her chair, slipped off her sandals, and wiggled her toes in the grass. "It's a lovely spot."

Minerva nodded. "Even when he reached his nineties and had been instructed by his doctor to take it easy, Uncle Bert still insisted on going into his office every morning. Then he'd meet old friends or professional colleagues for lunch and have a good gab.

"But on warm summer afternoons like this one, he'd sit here in the shade, a straw hat on his head, and gaze out at the garden. Sometimes I'd notice his chin drop forward onto his chest and realize that he'd dozed off," Minerva said nostalgically. "I never mentioned it to him, of course. Uncle Bert didn't like to admit he was getting any older."

"He always seemed ageless to me," Sydney said, reaching across the small space that divided them and interlacing her fingers with her aunt's. "I miss him."

It was a moment before Minerva said, "So do I."

They sat hand-in-hand and watched birds on the wing against a blue July sky, and butterflies gracefully flitting about in the garden, and a soft breeze stirring the lavender, sending a whiff of its lovely and familiar fragrance in their direction.

It was late afternoon—almost early evening, as a matter of fact—when Minerva broached another subject that had clearly been on her mind. "Speaking of Uncle Bert and his law offices," she said in preamble, "I've been thinking of selling the Bagley Building."

Sydney removed her sunglasses and turned halfway in her chair. "Have you?"

Her aunt nodded her head. "Water from the Moon keeps me very busy, as you know. For the past five years, business has been growing at a phenomenal rate. Frankly, I don't have the time to deal with the Bagley Building anymore. I don't need the money, or the tax write-off, or the aggravation." She heaved a sigh. "I've never cared much for being a landlord, anyway."

The answer seemed simple enough to Sydney. "Then you should sell it," she said, and then as an afterthought, "I would in your shoes."

Brown eyes, shrewdly observant eyes, seemed to be watching for a reaction from her. "Are you sure you don't mind?"

Sydney laughed light-heartedly. "Good heavens, of course, I don't mind. Why would I? Besides, the Bagley Building is yours to do with as you see fit."

Minerva admitted a little sheepishly, "I was going to leave it to you someday as part of your inheritance. Although I'm not certain if bequeathing a century-old historic landmark to you would be regarded as a blessing or a curse."

Sydney regarded the woman beside her with genuine affection. "Like the family curse—the famous Bagley Curse—you told me about when I was a girl."

Minerva's hand flew to her mouth. "You remember."

"I remember. In fact, to this day," Sydney said, sitting forward, "I can close my eyes and still see the apron you were wearing: big red poppies against a bright yellow background, with splotches of white flour dotting the front."

"I must have been baking cookies."

"Chocolate chip." Sydney could almost smell them, too. "That family curse idea was very quick thinking on your part. It wasn't until years later that it struck me you probably concocted the whole story on the spot just to make me feel better."

Minerva smiled in that unique and special way·she had of smiling: It was both sweet and enigmatic. "But I was right, wasn't I? You *are* tall. You *do* have the perfect size feet for the woman you grew into as an adult. You've learned to appreciate *and* make the most of your auburn hair and your other natural assets." Her aunt patted her hand several times in quick succession. "And you're beautiful, just as I promised you would be, but yours isn't any old ordinary kind of beauty, my girl. You're different in the best sense of the word, and you have learned how to embrace that difference, haven't you?"

Sydney tried to swallow the lump that had suddenly appeared in her throat. "Yes, I have."

"And you still have plenty of time to discover what your destiny is, and where it will lead you." Minerva leaned closer and looked her straight in the eyes, just as she had all those years ago. "You are the luckiest woman I know, Sydney Marie St. John."

"The very luckiest," she echoed.

"I am so proud of you. More proud than you will ever know." Then Minerva cleared her throat, took a sip of mint water, and said, "Now back to this business of selling the Bagley Building."

Sydney switched gears and put on her professional thinking cap. "Do you have anyone particular in mind?"

"Yes. Samuel Law."

"Is he interested in buying?"

"I'm sure he would be for the right price."

"It seems like the perfect solution to me," Sydney said, voicing her approval. "The Bagley Building has housed a law firm since it was first conceived and constructed. Samuel Law is a highly respected lawyer in Sweetheart." She even went so far as to say, "I think Uncle Bert would give his blessing."

"I think he would, too," Minerva agreed.

Sydney sensed there was something else her aunt wasn't telling her. "What?" she asked.

"I have a favor to ask of you."

She didn't even need to know what it was. "Anything. Anything at all."

"Someone has to finish going through Uncle Bert's books and papers that are still in storage at the Bagley Building. I tried to clear out some of his things after he died, but there was just so much and then my business took off . . ." Minerva's voice trailed off.

Pack rats, Sydney thought, the whole lot of them. That was the true curse of the Bagleys.

Her aunt took a deep breath and then let it out slowly. "Anyway, I never took the time to go back and finish the job. Finally, last year I did arrange for most of the boxes to be moved downstairs into that empty rear office. The one Uncle Bert used to refer to as the archives."

"I know the one," Sydney said, thinking of the dark, dank, broom-closet-size room with a lovely scenic view of the alleyway. "Of course I'll do it."

Minerva was visibly relieved. "Thank you, my dear. You have no idea what a weight that is off my mind."

"It's settled, then. I'll start first thing next week." In the distance Sydney heard the church bells chiming the hour. She counted along. It was five o'clock and she'd missed lunch. "How about an early dinner at McGinty's? My treat."

Minerva glanced down at her watch. "I would love to, but I have a conference call in ten minutes with my Web designer." She suddenly became animated, energized, eyes sparkling, hands gesturing. "We're going for a whole new look for the Web site for Water from the Moon. Something bright and cheerful and inviting, rather than the shadowy and evocative moon theme we've been using this past year. I'm recommending yellow."

"Yellow?"

"As the dominant color scheme," said Minerva. "After all, don't you think of the moon as being a shade of yellow?"

"Well, I think of the sun as yellow. The moon has always struck me more as silver."

"Silver, yes," her aunt said contemplatively, tapping a finger against her cheek. "Perhaps Cissy and I should do something in shades of silver and blue with yellow lettering."

"Perhaps." Sydney had failed art class; she wasn't the one to be asking.

"Maybe it's time to think outside the box," Minerva speculated. "Or is it outside the bun?" She paused and seemed to be lost deep in thought. "Maybe go with a whole new color scheme that evokes the emotions I'd like to have associated with Water from the Moon." She paused again. Then she became excited. She moved her head and hairpins went flying. "Purple, perhaps. Or magenta. Or a lovely shade of vivid pink that bleeds into a brilliant orange."

Sydney simply nodded.

Her aunt sprang to her feet and said abruptly, "I'm so sorry, my girl, but I must run. I hope you don't mind showing yourself out."

"Of course, not."

Minerva went up on her tiptoes and dropped a quick kiss on her cheek. "I'll see you in a day or two. I'll bake some of your favorite chocolate chip cookies. And we'll work in the greenhouses together and chatter away the whole afternoon. It'll be just like the old days." She hurried off toward her office. "Lovely. Just like the old days. Lovely."

"I'd love to, Aunt Minerva," Sydney said, shaking her head and laughing under her breath as she headed for her car.

"My word, is that really you, Sydney St. John?" Hilda McGinty greeted her the minute she walked through the front door of McGinty's Pub.

"Hello, Hilda."

"Why, I haven't seen you in years. When did you get back in town? I'll bet you came home for the wedding. Come to think of it, I did see you across the park that day. You were wearing a bright red dress. Very chic. Very expensive. And I hear you were dancing with the best man. He turned out to be quite the success story, didn't he? Who'd have thought? And you've turned into a real stunner, my girl. I always knew you were smart and I always thought you would make something of yourself. I told Mike as much. Didn't I, Mike?"

Mike McGinty shrugged his burly shoulders and kept right on wiping the bar with the damp cloth in his hand. When he spotted Sydney, he stopped in mid-swipe and said, "You haven't given the girl a chance to draw breath, let alone answer any of your questions, my love."

"So I haven't." But that didn't stop Hilda McGinty. "I remember the summer you waited tables here."

Sydney found humor in that memory. "*Tried* to wait tables. Let's face it, I was a disaster as a waitress."

"That's okay, deary. We all know you had plenty of other talents. Why, I even heard you're some kind of financial genius."

"Then you must have been talking to Aunt Minerva."

"She sure is proud of you. Couldn't be prouder if you were her own daughter." Hilda stopped and wiped her hands on her apron. "I suppose in a way you are. She never having any of her own."

"I suppose I am," Sydney conceded.

"The girl is probably hungry," piped up Mike. "Why don't we feed her?"

Hilda gave her the once-over. "You're too skinny. What are they feeding you in Chicago?" The woman held up both her hands. "No, don't tell me. Probably some of those fancy micro-mini meals and tiny vegetables that you need a magnifying glass to see." She made a disapproving sound. "Don't you fret. We'll feed you right. Put some meat on those beautiful bones of yours."

Mike finally took a step forward. "What can we bring you, Sydney?"

She was almost afraid to order. "A small salad, dressing on the side, and a glass of iced tea."

Hilda planted her hands on her ample hips. "That will do for starters. What about dinner?"

"Let's surprise her," Mike suggested.

Sydney couldn't argue with their sweet generosity toward her. The McGintys had always been kind to her. They'd even given her a job when no one else in town was willing to take a chance on an awkward sixteen-year-old. If they brought her enough to feed a dozen people, she'd just take it home for Sneaker.

Mike appeared with her salad and iced tea several minutes later. Ten minutes after that, a large sandwich and a
huge plate of French fries appeared on the table. And after
that a slice of Hilda's homemade cherry pie: her favorite.
They'd remembered. That's the kind of people the McGintys were.

A shadow appeared over her booth. Surely it wasn't
Mike or Hilda with more food. She was already stuffed to
the gills.

Sydney glanced up.

It was Eric Law.

He looked down at the table and she could tell he was
trying not to smile. "Are you expecting someone?"

She swallowed hard. "No."

"Then do you mind if I join you?"

Chapter
sixteen

 You didn't have to be a mind reader to know what Sydney was thinking. She wanted to tell him: *As a matter of fact, I do mind. I don't want you to join me. Go away. Sit somewhere else. Anywhere else. Just don't sit here.*

"This is the only available seat in the house," Eric said to her, knowing she was looking around the popular pub for another option. But he'd already done that: Every booth and table in McGinty's was full. Even the individual bar stools facing the mirrored wall behind the counter were taken.

The joint was jumping tonight.

"In that case, please be my guest and sit down," Sydney said politely. Maybe a little too politely.

Eric slid into the seat across from her, leaned forward, planted his elbows on the table, interlocked his fingers—

here's the church and here's the steeple, open the door and see all the people—and said for her ears only, "I realize this is a breach of contract."

She frowned. "Breach of contract?"

He was going to have to explain it without the legalese. "Our verbal agreement made that first night. To ignore each other. You go your way. I go mine," he reminded her.

The light dawned. "Ah, yes, our agreement."

It had worked out so well, too, Eric thought wryly. He'd only bumped into her every single time he'd left the Woodlands.

He deliberately kept his voice at a confidential level. "I know it's not your first choice to have dinner with me. But now that the Fates have intervened and thrown us together"—*again*—"it sure beats making a scene and creating gossip."

Sydney lowered her voice to a near whisper. "I think the gossip about us has already started."

"I think you're right," he said, trying his level best not to stare at the front of her T-shirt. It was hot pink with red sequins that spelled out: *If the shoe fits, buy it in every color.*

Shoes weren't the first thing that came to mind.

Eric forced himself to focus on her face. "In fact, I have it on the best authority," he said.

Sydney made some kind of movement with her mouth: It wasn't a smile, but it wasn't a frown, either. Maybe it was simply resignation. "I assume Mrs. Goldman got to you before you left the yard sales this afternoon."

Now who was the mind reader? "Goldie and at least three other people." Eric suddenly realized he was starved. Without thinking he picked up one of the French fries off her plate, dipped it in ketchup, used it as a temporary pointer, and finally popped it into his mouth. "Do you realize that half the town thinks we hate each other and the other half thinks we're having a clandestine affair?"

Hazel eyes narrowed. "I did warn you."

"Yes, you did," he said, helping himself to more French fries. He hated to see food go to waste, and she wasn't eating them. "I also recall telling you at the time it was inevitable."

Her mouth flirted with a smile. At least he thought it was a smile. "It turned out we both were right."

He bent forward and continued in a whisper, "So we're damned if we do . . ."

". . . and we're damned if we don't," Sydney said, finishing the thought for him.

Eric reached for a couple of paper napkins from one of those old-fashioned metal paper napkin holders that were placed on the far end of each table at McGinty's. He wiped off his greasy fingers and scrunched the used napkin into a ball. "Then what do you say we agree to ignore the whole bloody lot of them?"

"That's a great idea," Sydney said, her face clearing.

"Deal?" Eric held out his hand.

"Deal," she agreed, reaching across the table and giving it a firm shake. She raised her voice to a normal conversational level and said, "So how did your hunt go for a bookcase?"

"I wasn't as lucky as you."

"You didn't find one."

"I not only didn't find a bookcase, but I had to listen to some of the worst jokes I've ever heard."

Sydney took a sip of iced tea and, with her lips still

pursed around the plastic straw, murmured discreetly, "Walter E.?"

"Yes." Then he said, "Do you know why a bee hums?"

She nodded her head.

He tried again. "How about this one: What's yellow and lays in a tree?"

She choked on her drink.

Eric sat back in the vinyl-covered booth. "I guess you've heard that one, too." Third time was a charm. "He even insisted on giving me the weather forecast: 'Chili today; hot tamale.'"

Sydney chuckled and said, "Luckily, I missed that one."

Eric reached for a menu: it was encased in a protective plastic sleeve and was propped up between the napkin holder and the salt and pepper shakers. He opened it to Dinner Selections, studied his choices for a minute, then looked up and said, "Where does the man get them? Bad Jokes to Go?"

Sydney laughed out loud.

Eric replaced the menu. "Then the guy started talking to me about trying something called Kickapoo Joy Juice, and that's when I hightailed it out of there."

A waitress stopped at their booth and hovered for a moment or two. She stood with an order pad in one hand and a snub of a pencil in the other, poised to write. She snapped her gum and said to Eric, "So, do you want to order something?"

They didn't stand on formalities at McGinty's.

He glanced down at the half-consumed meal in front of Sydney. "I'll have the same thing she's having."

The woman barked out loud. "That'll be a steak sandwich rare with avocado."

He quickly corrected her. "Make that well-done, skip the avocado, but throw on a slice of tomato."

"Iced tea?"

"Make mine a Guinness draft."

"French fries?"

"Home fries."

"Cherry pie?"

"Apple pie. With a scoop of ice cream."

The waitress didn't miss a beat. "Vanilla?"

He shook his head. "Chocolate."

It was Sydney who grimaced and said with gastronomical horror, "Chocolate ice cream on apple pie?"

Eric looked across the table at her in challenge. "Have you ever tried it?"

She wrinkled up her nose. "No." And it was a real no, an emphatic no, not some wishy-washy no.

He smiled at her and instilled a little something extra in his voice. "Then don't knock what you haven't tried, honey."

That brought a raised eyebrow from the woman waiting to finish taking his order.

Interesting. Fascinating. He noticed that freckles started appearing on Sydney's face. Just a smattering of small ones across her nose and along the line of her cheekbones. Eric wondered if it was her own unique way of blushing when she got embarrassed.

"I'm sure it's an acquired taste," Sydney said quickly, attempting to do some damage control.

Eric realized he was having fun. "Some of the best things in life are an acquired taste," he said meaningfully.

Then he looked up at the waitress, who frankly appeared a little bored by now; no doubt she'd heard just about everything in her time and was shockproof. She repeated his order, asked if that was all, he said it was, so she stuck her pencil behind her ear, and took off in the direction of the kitchen.

"You are incorrigible," Sydney said under her breath.

"Yes, I am," he said, unrepentant.

She went back to her normal tone of voice and changed the subject—apparently as fully aware as he was that the people in the booths on either side of them seemed abnormally quiet. "I'm sorry to hear you didn't find the bookcase you were looking for, Eric. You could always try the antique mall or one of the furniture stores in town."

"Thanks for the suggestion, Sydney. I think I will."

"Thank you again for hauling that heavy bookcase I bought back to my car."

"You're welcome, Dr. St. John."

She turned beet red and more freckles magically appeared. "So you heard about that?"

Eric nodded his head and waited for the waitress to set his Guinness down on the Formica table in front of him before he said, "I understand you gave quite an enlightening lecture on the subject of the northern snakehead." He picked up the glass of dark stout and took a drink. "Sounds like a fish tale to me."

Maybe he shouldn't have teased her. Sydney sounded defensive when she responded, "Every single word I said at Walter E.'s yard sale was true. They have spotted the dreaded creature in Chicago's Burnham Harbor."

He backpedaled. "I don't doubt that for an instant."

Nevertheless, she got that stern schoolteacher expression on her face. A crease formed between her eyes. Her mouth thinned. Her chin came up a notch in the air. This was one dead-serious woman. "It's an ecological disaster just waiting to happen," she informed him, fretting with her napkin until it was in shreds.

Eric threw up both of his hands in surrender. "Hey, I believe you. A lot of people believed you. They were still talking about the Frankenfish long after you'd made your getaway."

"I did not make a getaway." Sydney seemed to pick and choose her words with care. "When we were finished shopping, I went home with Aunt Minerva." Just for a split second Eric thought he glimpsed her chin tremble. "I knew this town loved to gossip," she said. "I'd just forgotten it was a spectator sport."

All of a sudden he felt six inches tall and guilty as hell. *You're such an insensitive ass, Law.* He reached out and touched her arm reassuringly. "I'd forgotten, too. I'm sorry, Syd."

"Why should you be sorry?" She drew a breath and then slowly exhaled. "You didn't do anything."

Sure he had. "I've maneuvered my way through these treacherous waters since I was a kid," he said to her. "I'm not sure you're prepared to handle the dangerous currents and the undertow."

Sydney clasped her hands together very tightly on the edge of the table. "Don't you worry about me. I'm a big girl now. And an excellent swimmer. I can take care of myself."

Eric frowned and tried to tug another napkin from the holder. Half a dozen came out all at once, so he used the whole lot of them to mop up the single ring of moisture left on the tabletop by his glass of Guinness. "Think you can?"

She drew another deep breath and straightened her shoulders. "You forget that I've been on my own for a long time. During a good part of my childhood, my parents were off deworming orphans in Somalia, or working in the backwaters of some godforsaken place halfway around the world from Sweetheart, or searching for rare plant species in the jungles of the Amazon."

Eric turned his head very slightly in acknowledgment as the waitress set his dinner down in front of him. "Thank you," he said to the woman, and then looked back at Sydney and commented, "Yep, it's a jungle out there all right."

"Hell, it's a jungle in here," she said, deadpan.

Eric put his head back and started to laugh. Some of their fellow diners turned and momentarily watched the pair of them. "Yes, I suppose it is." He salted his home fries, poured a generous amount of steak sauce onto his plate, speared a thick wedge of potato with his fork, dipped it into the sauce, took a bite, savored that wonderful combination of crunchy and salty and a little bit sweet, and finally said to her, "You always could make me laugh."

Sydney seemed to relax. She sat back, took her spoon, scooped up one of the leftover cherries on her pie plate, and popped it into her mouth. "Is that good or bad?"

"It's good. In fact, it's very good. Too bad more people don't have the ability to laugh at themselves or know how to make others laugh along with them. It's a gift." He studied her with an unwavering gaze. "Believe me, it's a rare gift."

Something akin to skepticism flashed across her face. "I'm not sure everyone would agree with you."

He tried to keep the tone of their conversation light. "What happened? Some boyfriend didn't find you funny? Or appreciate your sense of humor? Or your brains?"

She gave him a speaking glance. "Is this multiple choice?"

Eric dug into his steak sandwich. It was maybe half a minute before he finished chewing the bite in his mouth, swallowed, took a drink of his Guinness and said, "Sure."

"Then all of the above."

He shook his head from side to side in mock dismay. "I thought in this modern day and age a man wasn't supposed to be intimidated by a beautiful woman with brains."

She pushed another cherry around in circles on her dessert plate. "I think men are always intimidated by a woman with brains." Eric noticed she'd left out the word *beautiful*.

"Some men."

She sighed. "Most men."

Eric polished off his steak sandwich and home fries. "Okay, I'm willing to concede that there are still some men out there who are intimidated by a woman who's smarter than they are." He made a disparaging sound. "Whoever he was, he was an immature jerk."

"And an ex-fiancé."

He nearly choked on his beer. "Oops." He grabbed a napkin and swiped at his mouth. "Sorry about that."

Sydney seemed unconcerned. "Don't be. I'm not."

Eric glanced up just in time to see his dirty dishes disappear from the table in front of him, and a moment later a huge slice of apple pie arrive with a giant scoop of chocolate ice cream on the side. He looked at Sydney. "Would you like anything else while I eat my dessert?"

Sydney gave her full attention to the waitress. "A cup of black coffee, please."

"I'll have the same," he said to their server. Then he turned to Sydney. "Black coffee, huh? No cream? No sugar? None of that fake sweetener stuff?" She shook her head each time he rattled off one of the items on the list. Then he gave her an approving nod. "You're a girl after my own heart."

Sydney seemed to snuggle back into one corner of the booth. She slipped a leg up under her and rested an elbow on the large leather handbag beside her on the seat. She looked comfortable. Somehow that made him feel comfortable, too.

"By the way, any news about your car?" she asked.

"They've had Red for two weeks," he said, losing his smile. "Fourteen days. Count them." He started to hold up his fingers and realized he'd run out before he'd made his point and he wasn't about to resort to using his toes, too. "They still don't have a clue what's wrong with him."

Sydney seemed to be biting the inside of her mouth against a smile. "Him?"

"It, then."

"I doubt if any of the guys down at the local garage have worked on a Porsche before," Sydney said, sounding reasonable about the whole unreasonable mess.

"Which is why I'm thinking about bringing in an outside specialist." Chocolate ice cream slipped off his spoon and onto his chin. Eric managed to catch it in time before it plopped onto the front of his denim shirt. It was time to change the subject. "So, how's Sneaker doing?"

"Well, I'm convinced that credit applications in this country are going to the dogs."

He looked at her for a long moment and said, "You'll have to explain that one to me."

Sydney seemed more than happy to oblige. "Sneaker got his first pre-approved credit card offer in the mail today," she said and took a sip of her coffee.

"No joke?"

"No joke. He's even been given a five-thousand-dollar limit based on a thorough background check of his employment and his sensible and mature handling of credit in the past."

Eric leaned forward and said in a confidential tone, "Maybe Sneaker takes after you. I was informed by several reliable sources today that you're something of a financial genius."

"Well," she said, looking a little like the cat who had swallowed the canary, "I heard that you're a hotshot attorney *and* a millionaire."

He could top that one. "And I have it on the best authority that you negotiated such a shrewd contract with your last employer that you never have to work another day in your life."

She appeared vastly amused. "Sneaker and I won't starve, anyway. Although I do believe he's going to the dogs. His natural instincts seemed to have surfaced living on a farm."

"Such as?"

"He's a Shetland sheepdog. That's a herding breed.

When I left him this afternoon, he was attempting to round up the butterflies in the fenced-in garden. I'm sure he'll be trying to herd the barn cats next, and eventually he may try his hand at the Canada geese or even the mallard ducks down at the pond."

"So he's taking to country life like a duck to water."

Sydney half laughed and half groaned, and was forced to put her coffee cup back down on the table.

"I know. I know," Eric confessed, finishing the last bite of his apple pie. "Pun is the lowest form of humor."

"I always say: What's a day without a little pun in it?" she said, and then they both laughed.

Eric realized that while he'd managed to finish every bite of his own dinner and even some of Sydney's, there was still half a steak sandwich and nearly a full order of French fries going cold on her plate. "Are you going to take your leftovers home to Sneaker?"

"Maybe the steak."

"What about the fries?"

She shook her head and said firmly, "Sneaker isn't allowed to eat French fries."

"Why, because he's from the British Isles?"

She chuckled and said, "No, it's vet's orders. French fries aren't good for dogs." Then she just had to go and rain on his parade by informing him, "In fact, the latest scientific evidence indicates that French fries aren't good for human beings, either. They're pretty much a health hazard period."

Eric thought of the oversize serving of home fries that he had just enjoyed, savored right down to the last crispy bite. "I take it back," he said, reaching for his wallet.

Sydney frowned. "Take *what* back?"

"What I said about your sense of humor," he was saying to her as they waved to Hilda and Mike and exited the busy pub. "Sometimes you're not funny at all."

Chapter

seventeen

Five minutes later, outside McGinty's Pub, Eric and Sydney were talking as they strolled along the sidewalk in the direction of the parking lot.

"Let me get this straight," Sydney said, handbag slung over her right shoulder, doggie bag clasped in her left hand. She knew her skepticism was showing. "You're telling me that Guinness is a health food?"

Eric walked beside her: tall, dark, and relaxed. "As a matter of fact," he said with a conclusive nod of his head, "a glass of Guinness may be the perfect food."

It took her an instant to laugh. "Based on what evidence, *Dr.* Law?"

"To begin with, it's lower in alcohol content, has fewer calories and less carbohydrates than most other beers, not to mention low-fat milk and orange juice." He didn't even pause to take a breath. "Guinness is loaded with flavonoids, the same antioxidants that give the dark color to many fruits and vegetables. It also helps to lower bad cholesterol and keeps the arteries from becoming clogged. Not to mention that, like milk, it helps your bones stay strong."

Sydney opened and then closed her mouth in amazement. The man was a walking encyclopedia on the subject.

"Scientists also think that Guinness protects against heart attacks, blindness, and maybe even impotence." There was a flash of straight, white teeth.

"Well, I can certainly understand why men would be interested in that last benefit," she said, no longer able to keep the amusement out of her voice.

Apparently Eric wasn't finished. "And it all happened by accident," he said.

She came up with an example of her own. "Like Dom Pérignon and champagne."

"Exactly."

She liked champagne. Especially champagne cocktails. Or maybe it was the cube of sugar dissolving on the bottom of the glass and all the tiny bubbles sparkling, rising to the surface. "A seventeenth-century monk makes a mistake down in the wine cellar of a monastery and—voilà—we all have him to thank for champagne."

"Or so the legend goes," Eric said, and she knew there was more to the tale and that he intended to tell her what it was. "Actually, there were other French monks who'd managed to create the same effect with wine a century before. But Dom Pérignon, a Benedictine who just happened to also be the cellar master at his monastery, was the one who came up with a method of storing champagne by using glass bottles and Spanish corks. And *that*, as they say, made all the difference."

"Vive la différence," she said, knowing full well that the French meant something entirely different when they used that phrase.

Eric smiled and continued with his story about Guinness, the perfect food. "Well, something similar happened with stout. Apparently some poor blighter in London accidentally burned his barley and the brew came out very dark, almost black in color, so he sold it to working men at a cheaper price. But, lo and behold, it caught on and the next thing you know Arthur Guinness had heard about it and he decided to burn the barley on purpose. And the rest is history."

Sydney had a confession to make. "I've never tasted Irish stout or Guinness or whatever name it goes by."

Eric gave her an appraising look. "You'll have to try it the next time we eat at McGinty's."

We?

They walked past a small hole-in-the-wall bar. There was no name on the place, just a single dingy window in front with OPEN spelled out in neon lights. It was dark inside even though it was still early evening outside. The door was propped open, and smoke and laughter and music poured out onto the sidewalk. Somebody was having a good time. They must have put a couple of quarters in the jukebox. The song playing was "How's the World Treating You."

Sydney slowed down and listened to the words about lost love and shattered dreams. "That's such a sad song," she said.

"Yes, it is," Eric agreed.

"Alison Krauss and James Taylor."

He frowned. "Who?"

"Alison Krauss and James Taylor: that's who's singing the song. I've always like James Taylor's music," she said, thinking of that night—that long ago night in the rain when she had been with this man when he was a boy and she was a young and foolish girl.

That was then, Sydney. This is now.

"So how is the world treating you?' she asked, looking up at Eric and realizing again just how blue his eyes were.

"Not bad. I'm sleeping a lot." They seemed to be walking slower and slower. "How about you?"

"I'm sleeping a lot, too."

He didn't seem embarrassed to tell her, "I didn't even get out of bed the day after the wedding."

"Neither did I."

"I didn't shave. I didn't even bother taking a shower."

"I only got up to get something to eat and use the bathroom," she confessed.

"It was great."

"Yes, it was."

"But I guess it had to come to an end." he said, his mouth curving up at the corners.

Like all good things? Sydney thought.

Eric laughed and said, "Even *I* couldn't stand being around me after twenty-four hours in the same pair of Jockey shorts."

Since they were being so candid with each other . . .

"It was three days before I ventured outside the house," she told him. "And then I didn't go any farther than the front porch. I curled up on the glider and decided to read a book. I think I fell asleep somewhere in the middle of chapter one."

It was a minute before Eric said, "I know. I saw you from my window."

Sydney quickly tried to recall what she'd been wearing that day. All she could think of was a pair of short shorts that were way too snug across her butt and a halter top that was at least one size too small. She'd found them in the bottom drawer of her bureau. Maybe dating from college. Oh, Lordy, maybe even from high school. No makeup. Hair pulled up into a ponytail and secured with a plain old rubber band that had pulled on her scalp and made her wince.

She cleared her throat. "I believe I was dressed in vintage that particular afternoon."

Eric grinned at her and said in a meaning-filled way, "So . . . that's what you call it."

"What do you call it?" she said, challenging him to a duel.

He had that look on his face. "Hot," he said.

She frowned. "I don't recall that it was particularly hot that afternoon."

Eric put his head back and crowed. "The weather wasn't hot, Syd. You were." He laughed again and slapped the back pocket of his jeans with his hand. "Hell, woman, I would have come right over if it hadn't been for our agreement. But a promise is a promise, and I knew we were both worn out and needed some time alone."

"Yes, our famous agreement."

"Works like a charm, too," he said with self-deprecating humor. "I've left my apartment to go into town a grand total of two times in the past two weeks. The first time I end up at a tea party where you're pouring, and the second time was this afternoon at the Pearsons' yard sales."

"Where I literally steal a bookcase out from under your nose."

"First come, first serve. Finders, keepers, et cetera," he said, with a nonchalant shrug.

"So, logic dictates that we only run into each other when we leave the Woodlands," she proposed, not altogether seriously.

There was something akin to a smirk on his face. "I think it's called irony."

"Or coincidence."

"Maybe fate," he suggested

Sydney snapped her fingers. "Serendipity. I've always liked the sound of that word."

"Or bad timing. Or good timing. Or maybe the gods are laughing at us mere mortals."

"I suppose it has its humorous side if we look hard enough," she said as they reached the parking lot.

"Where's your car?" he asked.

"Third row back. Silver BMW sedan."

"I know what you drive, Syd," Eric said, and she thought, *Well, of course, he does.*

As she approached her car, Sydney noticed a slip of paper stuck underneath the windshield wiper on the passenger side. "Well, it can't be a parking ticket," she said with confidence as she circled around the front of her Beemer. "After all, this is a free parking lot."

"Maybe it's an advertising circular." Eric glanced around at other nearby vehicles. "Although there must be thirty or forty cars parked in here and yours is the only one with something on it."

Sydney reached across and retrieved whatever it was. "It looks like notebook paper. You know the kind with wide-ruled lines like we used back in elementary school." The piece of paper was folded in half and then in half again, so she opened it up. The message was written in block letters using a crayon. Without saying a word, she handed it to Eric.

He read it out loud.

> *Roses are red*
> *Violets are blue*
> *Your feet stink*
> *And so do you*

"I don't get it," he said, scratching his head.

"A joke," she suggested.

"Maybe it is some kid playing a joke on you. Maybe not even you specifically. Maybe it was shoved under your windshield at random," he said, sharing his first impressions.

"That's certainly one theory."

"Except . . ." Eric stopped and just stood there.

"Except what?"

"It almost looks and feels somehow like it's an adult pretending to write as a child," he said, scrutinizing the piece of paper again.

"I had the same impression," Sydney told him.

"I can't imagine what the reason would be for an adult to write it though," he said, puzzled.

"I think it's a voice out of my past."

His head snapped up. "Why?"

"Because this isn't the first note I've received. I found this one in my mailbox yesterday." Sydney opened her handbag and took out an identical piece of wide-lined school paper. She handed it to him.

He read it to himself in silence, but she knew it by heart, of course.

> *You're a poet*
> *And you don't know it*
> *But your feet show it*
> *They're longfellows*

"Someone's idea of a bad joke," he muttered. "Or just very bad poetry."

Chapter
eighteen

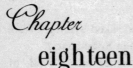 Eric didn't like it. Not one bit. Okay, so maybe he was overreacting, but in his line of work he'd seen seemingly innocent "jokes" turn into serious cases of harassment. There were people who became obsessed with someone who had done them a wrong, real or imagined. Then there were always the stalkers. Some of those situations had been life-altering, or had even ended in tragedy.

He stood there in the parking lot, both notes in his hand. He read them again and asked Sydney, "What did you mean when you said: 'I think it's a voice out of my past'?"

"I don't know," she said with a shrug.

She did know; she just wasn't telling him.

It was as natural as breathing for him to question every word, every action, every intention. To cross-examine the witness—okay, some used the word *grilled* in his particular case—and to keep digging until he was certain he'd gotten right down to the heart of the matter. Maybe it was those instincts that had helped to make him what he was, Eric thought. A damned fine lawyer.

Which doesn't necessarily equate to being a damned fine husband . . . or even a damned fine human being, does, it, Law?

He shoved that thought aside and asked Sydney, "Were you teased as a kid growing up here in Sweetheart?"

She got an incredulous look on her face. "Well, of course I was. Everybody was. Weren't you?"

He nodded. "My middle name is Anscomb."

"Eric Anscomb Law," she said, as if she were trying it out and rolling it around on her tongue. "I like it. It's unusual. Distinguished-sounding. Different."

He grimaced. "It's different all right."

"I thought you said different was good."

"I did and it is, but I also said different wasn't easy. Especially not when you're seven or eight years old. I got called everything from 'ants come' to 'ass comb.'" Sydney looked stricken for a moment, as if she knew—*felt*—what it had cost him as a boy. "Those were just a few variations on a theme after our teacher let the cat out of the bag."

"How did she do that?"

"She called out our full names the first day of class. I didn't live it down for years."

"I remember now," Sydney said with a reflective expression on her face. "Not your middle name, I didn't remember that. But I do recall Mrs. Bogan saying 'Sydney Marie St. John' and then making a comment about how it was a good thing my middle name was Marie because it saved me from being mistaken for a boy.

"Well, I spoke right up and informed Mrs. Bogan that *Sydney* with a *y* was from the Old French and a derivation of Saint Denis as in 'from Saint Denis, France,' and that it was the feminine form of the name *Sidney*, which is how boys usually spelled it: with an *i*. Although there were exceptions to that rule as there were to almost every rule." Sydney finally paused and took a breath. "Now that I think about it, I'm sure Mrs. Bogan didn't appreciated me correcting her."

Eric couldn't help himself. He shook his head and laughed and said, "How old were you at the time?"

"I was young for our class—the youngest, as a matter of fact—so I guess six."

"Six years old," Eric repeated, shaking his head again.

Sydney looked at him, puzzled. "What?"

"Nothing," he said, and then he added, "You were . . . *are* amazing, that's all."

"Well, amazing or not, I got teased about everything from the size of my feet to my freckles to being the teacher's pet. Smart kids always seem to get teased."

"Not so smart ones get teased, too," he said. He'd learned that firsthand.

There was silence, and then Sydney inquired, "What does *Anscomb* mean?"

He knew it by heart. His mother must have told him a hundred times—a thousand times—when he was growing up. "It's from the Old English and a rough translation would be 'an unusual man who dwells in a special place.' "

After a moment, "Now I like Anscomb even more," she said. "And it suits you."

"Well, I didn't like it for a long time," he admitted.

They must have been thinking along the same lines because the next words out of Sydney's mouth were exactly the same words on the tip of his tongue. "Kids can be so cruel."

He moved his head and frowned. "Sometimes they don't outgrow their cruelty, either. They become cruel adults."

They both glanced down at the papers in his hand.

"There's no threat in those notes," she said, sounding all grown-up and reasonable. "There's not even an implied threat. They're just someone being rather silly and childish."

Eric folded up both notes and slipped them into the pocket of his jeans. "I'm going to keep these if you don't mind." He really wasn't giving her a choice.

"I can't imagine why you'd want them," she threw off nonchalantly. "I was going to toss them in the trash."

Right . . . which was the reason she still had the first note in her handbag, he thought.

"Heading home?" he said with the same nonchalance.

"Not straight away."

Eric didn't have the right to ask her where she was going, so he waited to see if Sydney would volunteer the information.

She did. "I'm going to stop at the library and pick up something to read."

"Hey"—he snapped his fingers—"what a coincidence. I was headed to the library myself."

She gave him a look that spoke volumes. "You were planning to stop at the public library this evening."

Eric spread his hands wide, palms up, and shrugged. "How can you doubt it with our recent history of running into each other no matter where we go?"

Maybe she was convinced, maybe not, but her brow unfurrowed. "I suppose it makes sense in a strange kind of way."

He winged it the best he could. "What are you looking for? Bookwise, that is?"

She took his question seriously and answered him with the same single-minded intensity. "I've been thinking about rereading the entire Jane Austen collection."

"That's only what . . . five books?"

"Six."

"I didn't take you for a romantic."

"What are you looking for?" she asked him without responding to his comment.

He'd been about to say he was going to check out a couple of John Grisham novels, but that seemed like such a cliché for a lawyer. "I think I'm in the mood for Louis L'Amour."

"I didn't take you for a cowboy," she said, opening her car door, tossing her handbag and the doggie bag for Sneaker onto the passenger seat, and then sliding in behind the wheel.

Eric chuckled. "Touché."

The corners of Sydney's mouth turned up. "Thanks."

He leaned against the open door. "You don't happen to be stopping at DQ after the library. . . ."

"As a matter of fact, I am," she managed to answer with a perfectly straight face, and then added a little dig, "I've been in the mood for ice cream all day."

"So have I," he said.

"Really?" she said, letting her eyes go wide. "Even after that huge scoop of chocolate you had with your apple pie no more than"—she glanced down at her watch—"a half hour ago?"

Think, Eric. Fast. "Well, you know what they say, Syd."

She hesitated; not wanting to ask, but obviously knowing she would. "What?"

Eric grinned down at her and, determined to have the last word for once, started to close her car door as he said, "There's always room for ice cream."

He'd lied to her.

Not about the books. He'd check out two of L'Amour's Sackett novels: *Ride the Dark Trail* and *The Daybreakers*. Then at the last minute he'd added a John Grisham and a Scott Turow to his stack just to make sure he had something to read that he'd enjoy.

Nope, he'd lied about the ice cream.

He'd had every intention of ordering the smallest item on the menu—even if it was a "kiddie" cone—but then Sydney had practically bolted out of her car and said it was her treat since he'd picked up the tab for dinner. What she'd carried out to his truck five minutes later had been a banana split the size of Montana, and he told her so.

They sat on the back with the tailgate down and he said, "You're kidding, right?"

Laughing, Sydney handed him a plastic spoon and a couple of paper napkins with the DQ symbol blazoned in red print across the front. "One banana split. Two spoons. And we can let most of it melt for all I care," she said, and then she added as a confession, "It was worth it just to see the expression on your face."

Exactly two spoonfuls later, she jumped down from the rear of the pickup, brushed off the back of her jeans—they were white and fit her like a glove—and announced to him, "I'm going home now, so quit worrying about me. Like I told you before: I'm a big girl. I can take care of myself."

Had his concern for her been that obvious? He'd been so positive that he'd had his poker face on. The one he was famous for. The one he used in the courtroom—and sometimes in the boardroom—to such advantage.

Bad news, buddy. When did you start to feel protective toward the woman?

"Well, shit," Eric muttered under his breath as he put the tailgate up, got behind the wheel, tried to keep Sydney's sleek silver Beemer in sight, and drove toward home.

Chapter
nineteen

Sydney could *feel* Eric behind her all the way home.

She'd spotted the headlights of his pickup truck in her rearview mirror not long after she had pulled out of the parking lot at DQ and taken off down Main Street. Sometimes she caught a glimpse of him when a vehicle passed her coming from the opposite direction, or when she drove underneath a streetlight.

Once they were through town and out into the countryside—when had day turned to evening and then to night?—she even imagined she saw his face (it was all shadows and shapes and sharp angles) when the moon drifted out from behind the clouds, and the words of a song, or maybe it was a line from a poem, flitted through her mind: "Long evenings wet with the moon."

There was the familiar sign for the Woodlands. She turned onto the tree-canopied lane that would bring them to her family's house. He was practically riding her back bumper now.

She hit the brakes. She left the keys dangling in the ignition and more or less sprang from her car. The white pickup screeched to a halt alongside her, wheels spinning, gravel flying. Eric got out in one easy movement—he didn't even bother shutting the cab door behind him—and came toward her in long measured strides.

He didn't say "*I'm going to kiss you*," he just walked straight up to her and did it.

She'd known what was coming and she met him halfway, lips parted and then mouth open as she wrapped her arms around his neck and he pulled her up and into him.

Hot. Feverish. Burning. Scalding flesh without the pain and yet there was pain.

Hard. Beautifully hard and strong and unforgiving, but there was no need or reason for forgiveness. Yielding, when there was nothing to yield because it was offered, given freely, without asking and without a word spoken.

Out of control. Insistent. Soft hands and rough hands. Her fingers wrapping around a black curl, first one and then another. His fingers slipping through her hair.

Closer. Wilder. Frenzied. Sinking down into passion, only to be lifted up by it again, higher, ever higher.

He kissed her hard and she kissed him back harder. He licked her throat and she traced an erotic line from ear to ear with her tongue. His hands were on the back of her jeans; hers on the front of his. She was wet with desire and he was poised on the brink.

This was the way it could be, should be: mindless, with no past and no future, only the moment, a single moment, Sydney thought.

Time didn't stand still. Time simply had no meaning. Just as place ceased to exist. Reality began and ended with the two of them as she matched him demanding kiss for demanding kiss, ragged breath for ragged breath, stroke for stroke.

They didn't speak. No words passed between them. No lies. No insincerities. There was only the truth: They both wanted this—whatever this was.

It wasn't calculated. It wasn't one desiring more or less than the other. There were no questions and there weren't any answers. It had a beginning, but there didn't seem to be any end.

Suddenly, close by, there was the shriek of a bird of prey in the air, carried along by the wind. It split the night in two. Maybe it was an owl on the hunt; its victim—a rabbit or a mouse or maybe even a harmless snake—clasped in its beak or gripped between its sharp talons.

They broke off. Staggered backward. Stared at each other. Breathing hard and fast.

"This fucking town drives me crazy," Eric swore crudely, unapologetically. "*You* drive me crazy."

"I feel crazy."

He turned his head and stared off into the dark, dark woods, his chest rapidly rising and falling, his lungs gasping for air. Then he looked back at her and said, "This is not the smartest thing I've ever done." He laughed without a trace of humor and admitted to her, "But it's far from the dumbest thing I've ever done."

She didn't feel smart or dumb.

"And why are you wearing that"—Eric made an accusatory gesture with his hand—"shirt?"

Sydney frowned and glanced down at herself. "What's wrong with my shirt?"

"It's too . . ." He never bothered finishing the thought. Or maybe there had been no thought to finish.

"You don't make any sense," she said, champagne bubbles in her head.

"*This* doesn't make sense," he growled, standing no more than a foot or two from her, not backing off, but not coming any closer.

"Does everything in your world make sense?" She really wanted to know because her world had made sense right up until a few moments ago. Or at least she'd thought it had.

Eric stared at her as if she'd grown another head or two or three. "Are you kidding?"

"No."

His voice deepened with frustration, dropped half an octave or more. "Here's a news bulletin for you, Syd. Right now absolutely nothing makes sense to me."

"Good."

Eric's eyes blazed. "Good?"

She nodded her head. "I don't want to be the only one who's a little confused."

"Trust me, you aren't," he said, and her heart stopped at the look in his eyes. "Why did we do this?" he demanded to know as if she would suddenly, magically, have an answer for him.

Sydney shrugged. "Curiosity?"

He took a half-step closer and she forced herself to stand her ground. "Curiosity about what? Sex? I think we're both a little bit too old and a little bit too experienced to plead that kind of ignorance."

Speak for yourself, she wanted to tell him.

"Curiosity about the past?" he suggested.

"Possibly." But she didn't think that was it. "Maybe it's just been too long."

"Too long?" And a hint of a smile appeared on his lips. "I thought conventional wisdom was size *does* matter."

"I'm not talking about size," she said, impatient with him. "I'm talking about length."

That didn't seem to clear up anything. In fact, Eric appeared to grab a fistful of his own hair and seemed tempted to pull it out by the roots. "You don't make any sense."

"You already said that."

"No. *You* said it. I said *this* didn't make sense."

Well, we don't know what this is, *do we?* was right there on the tip of her tongue.

Instead she asked, "Do you believe that passion and humor can exist side by side?"

Eric's eyes narrowed. "That sounds suspiciously like one of those trick questions."

She shook her head. "No tricks."

"Well, I doubt if much research has been done in that particular area of human relationships."

"Maybe it should be."

"In the interest of science?"

"Yes," she said.

Eric let his head drop forward onto his chest and Sydney heard him heave a sigh that seemed to come from somewhere deep inside. He finally raised his eyes to hers and said, "Why are we having this conversation, Syd?"

Because we've stopped kissing?

"I was just wondering how you could be both sexy as hell and funny as hell at the same time," she said to him.

Christ, did he want to strangle the woman, or kiss her until she couldn't see straight, stand on her own two feet, know up from down, in from out? Neither option seemed like the ideal solution to his problem.

And what exactly is your problem, Law?

The problem was he did not want to be attracted to anyone right now, not even a swan. Especially not a swan. Especially not a gorgeous, long-legged, redheaded, intelligent, and sexy swan.

"I haven't kissed a woman like that in a very long time," he finally said.

"Neither have I." Sydney laughed self-consciously. "I meant I haven't kissed a man like that in a long time."

"I know what you meant."

A crease formed between her eyes. "It's difficult to have a personal life when you're married to your career."

"Were you?"

"What?"

"Married to your career?"

She nodded her head, but it seemed to be a little floppy on her neck. "Yes. Until recently, of course."

"I tried to be married to both my career and to a woman. Doesn't work. You've got to choose."

"You did choose," she pointed out.

"So I did."

"I did, too." She went on to say, "Careers are easier to deal with than people."

"Now you're making sense to me," he admitted.

She got a certain look on her face. "Then the moment of insanity has passed, hasn't it?"

"Yes."

"Just as well, I suppose."

"Yes."

She cocked her head to one side and studied him for five or ten seconds. "Do you always say yes?"

Eric shook his head. "It's almost always no."

"Well, at least that's something."

"I'd say in our case that's quite a lot." For some reason he noticed the door of her car was ajar and the overhead light was on. He turned his head and looked back at his pickup for an instant. He'd bolted out of his truck like a bat out of hell and hadn't even realized the door was standing wide open and the engine was still running. She was right. It'd been a moment of insanity. And the moment had passed. "Would you like me to carry your bookcase inside?"

"Thanks, but not tonight. It can wait until tomorrow."

"Tomorrow's another day," he said, and then frowned because he was pretty sure he'd said the same thing to her before.

Maybe it had been that first night when he'd stopped a foot or two from her BMW and planted his feet, thinking at the time it was a little like putting stakes in the ground. *This* was his territory. *That* was hers. No-man's-land was the narrow strip of gravel driveway between them.

Well, they'd crossed that no-man's-land, that line drawn

in the sand, that boundary tonight. But only for a few crazy minutes. They'd stepped back in time and played it safe. No harm done.

Eric was still thinking about that when he crawled into bed an hour later. He rolled over onto his back and crammed a pillow behind his neck.

Murphy's Laws said that sex took up the least amount of time and caused the most amount of trouble.

Damn, if Murphy wasn't right again.

Chapter
twenty

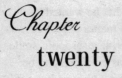 *Mrs. Murphy's Law: If a man is talking but a woman isn't there to hear him is he still wrong?*

Eric was pondering that question and others—like the meaning of life in general and his life in particular—as he hiked up into the pine forest above the Woodlands. Despite the unusually warm July day, he needed to get his head on straight, and there was nothing like a long walk to clear away the cobwebs.

He was talking to himself. He noticed he'd been doing it a lot lately. "You're always claiming it's water under the bridge, buddy. That the past is the past. That it's over and done with. Kaput. So, why don't you put it behind you once and for all? It's time to not only live in the present, but plan for the future."

Okay, where did he see himself in a year? In five years? Hell, in ten years? What would he be doing?

Did he envision himself back in Boston? Back within the hallowed mahogany halls of Barrett, Barrett & Hartmann? Back being "Eric the Red," the hotshot of BB&H, whose killer instincts and utter ruthlessness had been rewarded with promotions, a partnership in the firm, bonuses, perks, prestige, and a reputation that left grown men quaking in their shoes? Is that what he wanted?

He was good at his profession. As a matter of fact, he was brilliant. Modest, too, Eric thought with a sardonic smile. But sometimes success wasn't all it was cracked up to be.

There were always choices. Options. Other paths to follow. Other ways to utilize his education and his talents.

Other ways to be happy.

Look at Sam. He'd not only used his head. He'd not only followed his gut instincts. But he'd listened to his heart. His older brother had refused to compromise his integrity. He'd made difficult decisions and he'd made sacrifices. He had resisted the lure of money, glory, fame, and fortune. And now he had it all. Sam was successful—by his own definition of success, not somebody else's—and he was happy in his professional life *and* in his personal life.

Hell, I don't even have a personal life, Eric thought, feeling a little sorry for himself.

For the first time in a very long time, he realized that he was envious of his older brother.

Then he stopped in the middle of the hiking path roughly hewn out of the forest and listened.

Music.

Singing, anyway. It was a man's voice somewhere up ahead, somewhere deep in the evergreen forest, and he was crooning "White Christmas."

Eric followed the sound. Another several hundred yards into the woods he glimpsed a middle-aged man (on second thought maybe a well-preserved sixty-something) of average height, sturdy in build, muscular, and pretty roughly hewn himself, like someone who had spent a great deal of time out-of-doors. "Hello," he called out to him.

The man stopped singing and paused in what he was doing, pruning shears grasped in his gloved hands, and turned his head. Between the bill of the baseball cap pulled down low and the aviator sunglasses, it was next to impossible to make out his features. "Hello, yourself," came the gruff response.

Not exactly a warm welcome.

"Warm day," Eric said, removing his dark glasses and wiping the back of his hand across his forehead.

"Yep."

"I guess it's to be expected in July."

"Guess so."

Eric realized he was standing in a forest of evergreens. In the distance were the mature trees; they were tall and majestic and old. In the immediate area the evergreens and firs were five or six or seven feet in height, and were being pruned for the upcoming holiday season, although it was still months away, of course. Just on the other side of the path were rows of smaller trees, and beyond those a field of seedlings. This must be where the St. Johns grew their famous Christmas trees.

"Beautiful forest," he said.

The man grumbled, "Just don't start talking to me about that age-old philosophical question." Then he turned and topped off the tree directly in front of him before moving on down the row to the next one. "I've heard it a thousand times."

Eric realized he was squinting into bright sunlight. He put his sunglasses back on and said, "Exactly which age-old philosophical question would that be?"

"You're either a smart man for not asking or you're as sly as a fox," said the tree farmer.

Eric almost said: *Thank you*, but in the end, he didn't. Sometimes the best response was no response.

He looked around and wondered how many people wandered up this far into the woods except at the holidays. That's when the ground was strewn with straw and ropes of colored lights marked the pathway, strung from one end of the forest to the other. That's when members of the public were welcome to come out to the Woodlands and select the tree they wanted cut down and sold to them for Christmas.

Eric was curious. "So, what is the question you get asked all the time?"

The man moved on to the next evergreen and clipped off five or six inches of the leader. "If a tree falls in the forest and no one is there to hear it, does it make a sound?"

"Ah, *that* age-old philosophical question."

"There have been a hundred or a thousand variations on it, of course," the man said. "Some thoughtful. Some humorous. Some interesting. Some just plain idiotic. I've heard them all."

"Can't say that I have," Eric admitted.

There was a pause and then, "If a tree falls in the forest and no one is there to hear it, do the other trees laugh?"

That must be one of the idiotic versions.

Another variation followed. "Or if a tree falls in the forest and it hits a mime, does he make a noise?"

Eric laughed that time.

The man with the weathered complexion shook his head from side to side and said, "I'll spare you the rest. They pretty much go downhill after that, anyway." He put his shears on the ground and picked up a long blade; it looked like a machete. He used it to expertly shape the tree he'd just topped. "You're Eric Law."

"Yes, I am."

"I heard you were back in town."

"You heard right. And you're Bimford Willow."

"The one and only." The man stopped his shearing a few minutes later and said, "I like you. You can call me Bim."

"You don't know me. How can you like me?"

"I heard through the grapevine that you were real nice to Minerva Bagley. That's recommendation enough for me."

"Minerva Bagley was very kind to me a number of years ago, and, believe me, at the time I didn't deserve it." Eric smiled, remembering. "She sat me down in her kitchen and fed me homemade cookies."

"Sounds like Minerva."

"Are you and Minerva old friends?"

"Something of the kind. We've known one another since we were kids," Bim said. "We don't see a lot of each other these days. I don't go into town much."

"And she probably doesn't get out here often."

"Only at Christmas to get her tree. She comes every year on December Seventh like clockwork." It was a minute before he said, "Has for forty years or more."

"December Seventh. That's Pearl Harbor Day."

"Didn't think of that at the time," Bimford Willow mumbled under his breath.

Eric took a step closer and said, "What?"

Bim raised his voice. "I said, that was before our time. I was a toddler. Minerva would have been a baby, not even walking yet, when Pearl Harbor was bombed." The man went back to his work. He said, "Hand me that pair of pruning shears, will you?"

It was several trees later before Eric said, "Minerva has come out here on the same date for more than forty years? I wonder if it has some special significance for her."

"Not my place to say. She's entitled to her privacy."

"Yes, she is."

"People would be better off if they kept more things to themselves," Bim said, his lips disappearing into a thin, disapproving line. "Too little privacy and too dang much gossip in this town as it is."

Eric nodded his head and topped off the next tree. "I couldn't agree more."

Bim paused and looked at him like he'd taken leave of his senses. "In your case, what the blue blazes do you expect? You're living twenty yards from her door."

Apparently word got around. "Actually, it's more like thirty yards." From behind the dark-tinted glasses, Eric knew the other man was giving him a steely-eyed glare. "Okay, it wasn't my best idea," he said, his jaw squaring. "But it wasn't planned ahead of time, either. It was purely a coincidence."

Bim muttered under his breath, and even though he couldn't make out the words, Eric knew exactly what the other man was saying.

"You're taller than I am and you don't have arthritis in your shoulders," Bim said clearly enough this time. "Do you mind reaching the ones I can't anymore?"

Eric trimmed the tops off trees that afternoon until his own shoulders ached. But it was a good kind of ache. The kind that came from doing hard physical labor and working up a sweat and toiling side by side with someone for an hour or two with little or no conversation.

"I don't imagine you get many visitors up here in the summer," Eric said as they finished up for the day.

"Nope. But I don't mind," Bim said, and then he added, "Trees are a good sight more reliable than most people."

"So are dogs."

Bim took a handkerchief from his back pocket and wiped the sweat from his face and neck. "You got a dog?"

"No, but Sydney does."

"Then she's luckier than you are. She's got someone constant. Someone who's always happy to see her when she comes home at the end of the day. Someone who will curl up beside her in bed and give her unconditional love."

Eric had to admit he was surprised. He hadn't thought of Bimford Willow as someone who even used the word *love*. Bim had always been something of a loner and a hermit. He hadn't expected the outdoorsman to be so astute when it came to human emotions.

"Tell you one thing, Eric." Bim took off his work gloves and tossed them into the wheelbarrow at the end of the last row of trees, along with his toolbox. "If you think you love a woman, if you think there might be something worthwhile between the two of you, don't walk away from it."

His voice changed. "Better to make a mistake, better to fall flat on your goddamned face, better to fail miserably, better to have your heart broken even, than to live with regret for the rest of your life."

"Regret?"

"Because you were too damned scared to try."

Oh, he'd tried all right, and he'd made plenty of mistakes, Eric wanted to inform the man. Yet a thought niggled at him: *Did you really try? Or did you marry the wrong person at the wrong time and definitely for the wrong reasons, and then just give up on love and marriage because the first time had been a mistake from the beginning?*

Eric had to hand it to Bim. "You know a lot about people for someone who spends most of his time up here with the trees."

"Trees can teach you a lot if you're willing to listen." Bim shook his head. "I'm sixty-three. I only wish I'd listened a hell of a lot better a long time ago."

Eric was thirty-four years old, but he knew exactly how the other man felt.

"A little of this goes a long way, doesn't it, Sneaker?" Sydney was saying to her faithful companion as she opened another box and saw that it was filled with old newspaper clippings. She groaned and said, "Uncle Bert, why did you save all of this"—she wanted to say *junk,* but settled for—"stuff?"

Sydney made a vow right there and then. Once she'd finished doing this favor for Aunt Minerva, she was going to clean out every drawer, every closet, every box she had stored at her parents' home. Clutter was the true curse of the Bagleys, and she was, after all, half Bagley.

For now, she was stuck in the "archives" at the back of the Bagley Building, as she had been for the past two weeks. She had consulted both the historical society and the public library to find out what, if anything, they'd be interested in having from her great-uncle's collection. But in truth, Uncle Bert had donated all the important or interesting papers in the year before his death. What was left was either personal items or plain old junk or simply a mystery.

At least she had a system in place.

She'd put three containers on the other side of the small room. One was marked PERSONAL. One had the word TRASH written on it in indelible black ink. And the third had a large question mark on the side. She was nothing if not organized.

Sydney peered down into the box of newspaper clippings: The one on top was a column dated 1954 and it mentioned the date of a Rotary Club meeting. She made an executive decision. "I think these can wait until another time, don't you, sweetie pie?"

The Sheltie seemed to agree with her from the safety of his Port-a-Pooch. He gave one short yelp and rested his head on the edge of his carrier, his eyes following her every move.

Sydney got up from the ancient office chair, stretched out her legs, and made a slow circle around the perimeter of the small office.

She'd learned several important things in the past fourteen days: Cleaning out Uncle Bert's papers was a dirty job and the room—it wasn't much larger than a decent-size walk-in closet—was stifling during the day, even with a small fan blowing the air around and disturbing the dust that had to be a decade or two in the making. So, she wore the oldest and the coolest clothes she owned, and she mostly worked during the evenings.

She'd also learned to keep the office door open to the hallway, and had managed to pry open the back door (someone had nailed it shut at some point, probably for security reasons) in order to create a cross-draft. Her car was parked right outside in the alley.

"I'm going to do one more drawer tonight and then we're heading to DQ," she promised Sneaker.

Sneaker seemed to approve of her plan. He was particularly fond of ice cream. Especially soft ice cream. Especially vanilla-flavored soft ice cream. It had become a nightly treat before the drive back to the Woodlands.

Sydney opened a file drawer at random, and inside, toward the back and behind several dozen faded green folders, was a manila envelope, yellowed from age, and with the words *Unfinished business* written across the top. The penmanship was old-fashioned and one she didn't recognize. It wasn't Great-uncle Bert's handwriting. Or Minerva's. Maybe it had been his secretary's at the time.

She took the manila envelope over to the small desk she'd been working at, opened the back—the small metal tabs were so brittle they broke off when she tried to straighten them—and dumped the contents out on the desktop in front of her.

There were a few old photographs, several handwritten notes of no consequence, a canceled check or two dated decades before, a birth certificate—she recognized the name on it as Uncle Bert's deceased son—and then another official-looking, business-size envelope.

Sydney opened this second envelope and took out the single piece of paper inside. It was a document. A certificate of marriage. She glanced at the name of the town where the license had been issued: It was somewhere in Kentucky she wasn't familiar with. She noted the date and realized it had been registered nearly forty-five years ago. Then she read the names on the certificate and she was dumbstruck. Under "bride" was written: Minerva Bagley.

"Aunt Minerva married?" she said in a whisper.

Sneaker growled softly.

Sydney sat there in disbelief. Then she said it again, out loud this time, as if that would somehow help her make sense of it. "Aunt Minerva was married."

Sneaker shot up in his Port-a-Pooch, his eyes alert, his ears perked up, his nose twitching and his body quivering as if he'd caught the scent of some wild thing. Then he gave a sharp, ear-piercing bark.

Sydney glanced up at the door she'd propped open, the one that led into the hallway. She thought she heard something . . . or someone. Then footsteps.

She stood and walked across the room and stuck her head around the corner. The hallway was empty. "Is someone there?" she demanded to know.

Again, footsteps.

Receding. Growing fainter.

Running away.

Nevertheless, that's when Sneaker began to bark in earnest.

Chapter
twenty-one

Eric finished dictating a letter to his newest client, typed a couple of memos to himself and several more to Carol, turned off the system, and put the computer into sleep mode.

Theoretically he was still on vacation, or at least only working part-time in his brother's absence, so enough was enough. Carolyn Hart would find plenty to keep her busy when she came into the office tomorrow morning.

It was time to call it a day.

Eric swiveled in Sam's high-backed chair. He didn't think it was an expensive piece of furniture, nor that the genuine Corinthian leather was either genuine or leather. The office chair wasn't stylish, or fancy, or ergonomic, or even particularly attractive. But, damn, it did seem to fit him to a T.

Anyway, he turned around and gazed out the row of

windows that faced the town square. That's when he realized the spotlights were on across the street. The front of the courthouse was fully illuminated, including Lady Justice, the flowerbeds meticulously tended by the Ladies Auxiliary, and the ever-present flags—both Old Glory and the state flag of Indiana—that unfurled on the night breeze.

He glanced up at the clock on the wall. Past nine. It was time to call it a night.

Maybe he'd stop by McGinty's and grab a bite of dinner and a Guinness on his way home. Then, again, maybe not. He had pretty much avoided the pub since the evening he'd invited himself to share a booth and dinner with Sydney.

He'd pretty much avoided Sydney since that night, too. And she'd done an exceptionally fine job of avoiding him. In fact, they hadn't spoken two words to each other since the "incident" in the driveway.

You mean the wild and crazy, erotic, mind-blowing sexual episode that has kept you awake every night since, Law?

Yep, that was the one.

Eric went around turning off the lights and locking up the office. For the past several weeks it had been all work and no play. Hell, he might as well be back in Boston.

That wasn't quite true. The work he was doing here in Sweetheart seemed more . . . *personal*. That was the word he was looking for. He seemed to be personally helping the clients that came to him. Frankly, it made him feel good.

And that surprised him.

He'd assumed he was here to do Sam a favor. It might well turn out that Sam was the one doing the favor by giving him a chance to see the law and the honorable profession of being a lawyer from an entirely different perspective.

Besides, he had to stay busy or he'd go nuts, bonkers, off his crumpet, as the English said. He had to do something to keep from thinking about Sydney all the time.

Eric swore softly under his breath, locked the outer office door, and stepped into the second-floor hallway. That's when he heard the "noise" loud and clear. It sounded like a dog barking. And not just any dog, but a very particular dog: Sneaker.

He'd know that bark anywhere.

What would Sneaker be doing in the Bagley Building at this time of night?

More important—since it was highly unlikely that the Sheltie was here on his own—what was Sydney doing in an empty office building at nearly ten o'clock?

Of course, Minerva did own the whole kit and caboodle now that Bert, the last of the Bagley law dynasty, had moved on to that great courtroom in the sky.

"It's none of your damned business what she's doing here, buddy," he muttered under his breath as he started down the central hallway and toward the flight of stairs that would take him in the direction of the front door.

Sneaker was still barking up a storm.

What if something was wrong?

What if something had happened to Sydney?

There was no way he could just turn his back on her and walk out that door. It seemed he was going to make it his business, after all.

Eric followed the sound of barking down to the first floor and then along a narrow hallway toward the back of the Bagley Building. At the far end of the last corridor he could see light spilling out onto the marble floor.

This must be the place.

He gave her fair warning by calling out her name: "Sydney, is that you?"

Her head appeared around the corner of the doorway. "Eric." She seemed relieved to see him. "Were you just outside this room a few minutes ago?" she asked.

"No, I've been upstairs working. I was locking up for the night when I heard Sneaker barking and came to investigate."

Her questions were pointed. "Is there anyone else in the building?"

"I don't think so. I suppose the woman who comes in to clean could still be around here somewhere, but I haven't seen her tonight." He walked past Sydney into the room. It was small and dingy and dusty. There were several ancient file cabinets against one wall, a rickety old desk and chair pushed to one side—she had obviously been using them as a place to sit and sort papers—and boxes upon boxes, stacked head-high in some places. "What in the hell are you doing?" he said.

Sydney straightened and put her shoulders back in that way he'd seen before. This was one proud woman. "If you must know, I'm doing Aunt Minerva a favor."

He lost his patience on her behalf. "Well, I'm doing my brother a favor, too, but his office is at least clean and more or less air-conditioned. This place is filthy and it's hot."

Sydney tried to smile and failed. "It's not too bad if I keep both doors open and the fan running."

His eyes narrowed. "And work at night?"

She moistened her lips. "It's like an oven in here during the day, especially in the afternoon, so I have to wait until it cools off a little."

Eric wanted to say, *Oh, Sydney, what are you doing to yourself?*

"I know I must look an awful fright," she said, trying to tuck a few damp tendrils of hair back up into a ponytail that was coming half undone as it was.

She looked hot and tired and dirty and adorable.

"I don't think it's a good idea for you to work here by yourself at night. There are always a few unsavory types running around even in a place like Sweetheart," Eric said, trying to sound reasonable about the whole thing.

He wanted to add: *Jesus H. Christ, Sydney, don't go looking for trouble.* But he knew the biggest trouble she'd run into since returning to their hometown was him.

"I'm not alone," she pointed out.

As if on cue, Sneaker gave a small yelp to remind them of his presence.

"No offense. But I don't think a fifteen-pound dog qualifies as a guard dog."

"Well, I think he frightened away whoever was lurking around outside in the hallway earlier."

Then she went pale, and Eric's mouth went thin, and he asked her, "Are you all right?"

"I've had something of a surprise," she said, walking toward the dilapidated desk some five or six feet away. "More of a shock really." She gazed up at him with those trusting eyes of hers. "I know I can count on your discretion."

"Absolutely."

"Like lawyer-client privilege."

"Yes, like lawyer-client privilege." Or maybe just as a friend she could confide in with confidence.

"I've found something. It concerns Aunt Minerva. It may be none of my business or yours." Eric waited for Sydney to tell him in her own words. "I was getting tired and the last box I opened up looked like a bunch of old newspaper clippings that Uncle Bert had saved, and since the Bagleys are famous for being pack rats, I decided I couldn't face cleaning out one more box tonight. So I opened that file cabinet over there and inside was a manila envelope marked 'unfinished business.'" She stopped to take a breath and brush a cobweb away with her hand. "Inside were a number of things like old photographs and letters. And there was another envelope. A regular business-size envelope." She picked it up off the desk and handed it to him. "As you can see there's nothing written on the outside, but this is what I found on the inside." She passed him a single sheet of paper. It was a certificate of some kind.

Eric took it from her and stepped a little closer to the light. He read it twice just to make sure it was exactly what he thought—what he knew—it was. "It's a marriage certificate."

"Yes, it is."

He read on. "Between Minerva Bagley and Bimford Willow."

"The date on the certificate is nearly forty-five years ago," she pointed out unnecessarily.

"December seventh," Eric said, and then paused. "That date means something."

"It's the anniversary of the bombing of Pearl Harbor," Sydney volunteered.

"Yes, but I've recently heard that date in relationship to something else." He held up one hand. "Give me a minute. It'll come back to me." Then he snapped his fingers. "Of course. It was the day I was up at the tree farm helping Bim top off the trees for this year. He said that Minerva always came on exactly the same date every year to pick out her Christmas tree."

"December seventh," they said in unison.

"I wondered at the time if there was some significance to it." Eric rubbed his hand back and forth along his chin. "It was the day they were married!"

Sydney heaved a heartfelt sigh. "If Aunt Minerva wanted me or anyone else to know that she and Bim had been married at one time, she would have come right out and said so. She must have her reasons for not talking about it. She's certainly entitled to her privacy. We all have something in our past that's nobody else's business."

"I agree."

"Here's what bothers me, though," Sydney said. "I assume there was an annulment or a divorce."

"That's a logical assumption."

"So why was the marriage certificate in a file marked 'unfinished business'?"

Eric shrugged. "It might mean something; It might mean nothing. I wouldn't go jumping to any conclusions." He gave the so-called archives a second look. "Especially considering the condition of this room."

"It's a mess."

"That is an understatement."

"Well, I found one more piece to the puzzle while I was sorting through a different file yesterday." Sydney handed over a newspaper obituary and a copy of a death certificate.

"This took place only one week after Minerva and Bim were married," Eric concluded.

"Poor Great-uncle Bert," Sydney said with feeling and shaking her head. "I'd almost forgotten that he lost both his wife and his son in a car accident."

"It was long before you were born," Eric reminded her as he studied the details.

"Uncle Bert was a stickler for details," she said. "Most good lawyers are, I suppose. But it crossed my mind that if he was the one handling Minerva's annulment or divorce and if that annulment or divorce happened to take place not long after she and Bim were married. Well . . ."

"What if it slipped through the cracks?"

"I know I may be reading more into this than there is, but she was only seventeen and Bim was eighteen, and it appears that they went to Kentucky to get married."

"Where the age of consent was younger."

"That's my conclusion. So, maybe they eloped because their families didn't approve. Or thought they were too young. It's all conjecture, but it's not outside the realm of possibility."

"I'll tell you what I can do," Eric said, knowing exactly what had to be done. "I can go over to the courthouse and check the records without arousing any suspicions. If I find the record of their annulment or divorce, then this whole discussion becomes a moot point."

"And none of our business. Papers destroyed. Lips sealed. Secrets kept."

"Exactly," he agreed. "Meanwhile, I'm going to keep these papers with me if that's okay with you."

"Thank you, Eric," she said, and he could tell she was grateful for his help.

"Where's your car parked?" he asked.

She thumbed toward the open back door. "Right outside."

"Well, it's time you and Sneaker called it a night and headed home. Lock up and I'll walk you to your car."

She opened her mouth to object and closed it again. "We'll be ready in five minutes."

She and the Sheltie were ready to go in two. They stepped out into the back alley, which wasn't particularly well lit. There was a streetlight on the corner that cast a faint glow onto her car.

Sydney was busy buckling Sneaker's Port-a-Pooch into the passenger seat when Eric spotted something she hadn't seen. "Sydney?"

She raised her head. "Yes."

"You might want to take a look at this," he advised from where he was standing in front of her car.

She walked around beside him. "Oh, no," she said, her hand flying to cover her mouth.

There, spray-painted in bold letters across the hood of her silver BMW, was a single word:

FREAK

"What is that all about?" Eric said, pointing to the graffiti defacing her expensive sedan.

Sydney stood there like a statue, without moving a muscle, her hand flattened across her mouth.

Eric took a wild guess. Why not? It wasn't his first for the evening, and so far he was batting a thousand. "You know what it means, don't you?"

Sydney finally moved, nodding her head, as she took a step closer to her car. She reached out as if she were going to touch the loathsome word and then drew her hand back without doing so. "It was a nickname that someone labeled me with way back in grade school. I never understood what I'd done wrong, or why the dislike ran so deep. It was as if they hated me." She exhaled on a sigh. "I remember I always hated being called the Freak."

"I can't imagine that anyone, especially any child, would *like* being called the Freak," he said, as kindly as he could.

"I have a pretty good idea who did this," she said to him in an unguarded moment.

Eric bristled with anger on her behalf. "Who? Tell me who? I'll have the son of a bitch arrested."

Sydney laughed without humor in her voice. "I'm not going to tell you who it is because I want . . . because I need more information before I take any action."

He was incredulous. "You're refusing to tell me?"

"It's not what you think."

It seemed pretty darned obvious to him. "I think it's vandalism," he said.

"We both know it's vandalism," she said, as if she were trying to explain the matter to a small child. "But I want to understand what's behind it. Why this? Why now? We're adults, not children anymore. This is someone I literally haven't seen in years . . . if I'm right about the person's identity."

"Sydney . . ."

"Give me a few days, a week, then I promise I'll tell you everything. I'll turn the whole sordid mess over to you and you can handle it through legal channels, if necessary."

"Promise?"

"Cross my heart and hope to die," she said.

He wasn't taking any chances.

Okay, maybe he was overreacting again, but "Better safe than sorry" was his new motto. "I'm driving you and

Sneaker back to the Woodlands. We'll take your car and I'll come back in the morning and retrieve the pickup." He was in no mood to argue about it, and he made that very clear to her.

Sydney fought him for a minute or two, but in the end she and Sneaker rode in the passenger seat while he took the wheel. He waited while she unlocked the door to her parents' house and then he did a quick sweep of each room before letting her enter. Maybe he was frightening her, but being scared wasn't necessarily all bad.

"I wish this house had a security system," he muttered under his breath.

Sydney reached out and touched his arm. "Eric, I honestly don't believe this person means me any harm. The notes weren't threatening, they were childish. The vandalism was done out of frustration more than anger."

"Now you're a psychologist?"

"No. But I'm a woman who was often teased and who often had her feelings hurt when she was a girl. Teasing is the number one issue for girls between the ages of eight and seventeen in this country."

"Which makes it a problem of emotional violence. Because teasing and gossip and name-calling is a form of psychological abuse, and we both know it," he said, speaking from personal and professional experience. "Violence of one type often begets violence of another type."

She didn't argue with him.

He changed the subject and said to her, "Do you want anything to eat?"

She shook her head. "All I want is a shower and clean clothes. I feel like I'm covered in several decades of dirt and dust. And I think I may burn this shirt and pair of slacks. They stink to high heaven." Then she thought to inquire, "Did you have any dinner tonight?"

Eric shook his head.

"Help yourself to whatever you can find in the fridge while I go get cleaned up." She barely got the words out before she started to yawn. "I'm sorry. I'm so tired all of a sudden."

"Go shower," he said firmly. "I can look after myself." In fact, he had the door of the refrigerator open and was studying its contents before she even left the kitchen and padded up the stairs.

"I'll be back in ten minutes," she called back down from the second-floor landing.

It was a half hour later that he decided he'd better check on her. "Come on, pal," he said, tossing the last bite of steak to the Sheltie. *Food was Sneaker's friend.* "Let's go see what your mistress is up to."

He made his way upstairs, following the trail left by the fluff ball—the dog definitely had his uses—and they found Sydney sound asleep on top of her bed.

"Stay," she murmured as she rolled over and saw him standing in the doorway of her bedroom.

"Are you sure?"

"Very sure." She snuggled down into the bedcovers. "I've always wanted you to make love to me in the rain."

"It's not raining, Syd," he said quietly.

Her eyes didn't open. "I know."

"And when I make love to you it will be in the clear light of day." That way they would both know exactly what they were getting into, Eric reasoned.

Sydney was clearly exhausted, physically and emotionally. "Promise you'll stay, anyway."

"I will. I promise," he said, but she was asleep already.

Eric kicked off his shoes and tried to make himself comfortable. Then he made sure Sydney was tucked in under the covers before he crawled on top of them. Sneaker jumped up on the bed, did a couple of turns, and then lay down beside him. He put his head on Eric's arm, dark, shiny eyes facing Sydney. He made a soft sympathetic whimper.

Eric reached down and stroked the Sheltie. "We'll both watch over her, pal."

Chapter
twenty-three

The summer sun was streaming in her bedroom window when Sydney awakened sometime in the early morning hours and discovered that Eric and Sneaker were both gone. Maybe he was taking Sneaker out for his daily walk around the yard that had specifically been set aside for a dog and his duty.

Or maybe he was gone. Maybe Eric hadn't wanted to be here when she woke up this morning.

Sydney turned over and buried her head in the bed pillows. Last night she had practically begged Eric to stay and make love to her. She had thrown herself at him just as she had back when she was seventeen. She'd made a fool of herself—again.

Then she heard someone on the stairs and soft footsteps coming down the hallway toward her room. The door was gently pushed opened and a man, a very sexy man, tiptoed into her bedroom.

Eric was barefoot. He was wearing a pair of clean jeans and a shirt that he hadn't bothered to button. His hair was still damp from the shower, and along the back of his neck it was curling into tiny dark ringlets. There was a small nick on his chin; he'd cut himself while shaving.

He turned. His eyes were as blue as a clear blue sky. He took her breath away.

"You're back," she said simply.

"I never really left." He was watching her closely. "How are you feeling this morning?"

"Better. Rested." She stretched. "Wonderful." She saw something in his eyes. "Why?"

Eric was holding one hand behind him.

She had to ask. "What's that you've got there?"

"Rain."

"Rain?"

He smiled and the sun came out again. "You said you'd always wanted me to make love to you in the rain. I told you last night that the first time I made love to you, it had to be in the clear light of day." He grinned. "But I think you'd fallen asleep by then and you didn't hear me."

Perhaps not. But she heard him now.

"It's morning," she pointed out. "The sun is pouring in through the windows. This is definitely the clear light of day."

"And, luckily, I have the rain." Eric brought out a paper sack from behind his back. He opened the top, reached inside and took out a handful of golden rain and began to sprinkle it all over her bed.

"Flowers from the Golden Raintree," Sydney said in awe, tears brimming. "I'd almost forgotten it was that time of year."

"I could only find one tree that was in full bloom, but since your family has a whole grove of them, I didn't think they'd mind."

She sat up and held out her hands. "Golden rain."

"Golden rain," Eric said. He tossed his shirt aside, slipped out of his jeans, and crawled back into bed beside her.

"You don't have to do this, you know."

"Oh, yes, I do," he said adamantly, and there was an edge to his voice that she'd never heard before.

"I don't want you to do this out of pity."

"You're the one who has to take pity on me, who has to put me out of my misery," he informed her. "I've been trying *not* to think about making love to you for the past few weeks. Sometimes it seems like I've been waiting to do this forever."

"I know how you feel," she admitted as his mouth came down on hers and his arms slipped around her and he kissed her as sweetly, as restrained, as beautifully as she had ever been kissed.

But Sydney wanted something more, something different. And she knew Eric did, too.

She sat up in bed, eased her nightgown over her head and let it drop to the floor. Then she took the bedcovers and tossed them aside.

Now they were both naked as jaybirds.

The first words that popped out of her mouth, when she saw him in the flesh and fully aroused, were "Talk about a banana split the size of Montana."

* * *

She laughed and then he laughed. They were both still laughing when she took him into her mouth and then Eric could feel her laughter on his erection like erotic ripples along that most sensitive of masculine skin, and he stopped laughing and moaned with the sheer, unbelievable pleasure of it.

"I think that's the answer to your question," he murmured sometime later—who knew how much later; time had ceased to exist or even to matter. He was satiated, happy, relaxed, as relaxed as he could never recall being, lying in the warm sun that came streaming in the window and seemed to bathe them and the golden flowers strewn all over the bed in a brilliant light.

"What question? What answer?" Sydney murmured into his shoulder as if talking took more energy and concentration than she possessed at the moment. She seemed content to simply lie there, unself-conscious in her nudity. Just as he was fully comfortable letting everything hang out.

Eric laughed, and his chest rose and fell along with the swath of fiery hair covering it. "I made another pun."

"Did you?" Sydney said, pushing up on one elbow. "Maybe a pun a day keeps the doctor away."

"I thought it was an apple a day," he said, his forehead creasing in thought, although he didn't feel much like thinking.

"Personally," she said, reaching down and stroking the length of him, "I think that particular rule of thumb should be revised to 'a banana a day keeps the doctor away.' "

Eric gave her a horror-stricken look. "Only one?"

"Well, how many do you think we can manage to eat in any given twenty-four hours?" she asked.

"I suppose that depends on how hungry you are?"

"*You* meaning *you and me*," Sydney said, as if needing some clarification from him.

"Naturally." He gave the matter serious consideration. "There is, as I'm sure you're aware, more than one way to peel a banana. Metaphorically speaking, of course."

She brought up another subject. "And, metaphorically speaking, there are all those other edibles available."

Eric turned onto his side. "Yes, I see what you mean. In fact, I do believe I've spotted a ripe red berry." He dipped his head and took a taste of her nipple. "And there's a second one," he said, nibbling on the other. "And what do we have here? Fresh, plump melons?"

"Not very large fresh, plump melons, I'm afraid," she said, sounding a little wistful.

"Well, you know what they say?" Eric covered one breast with the palm of his hand and squeezed just hard enough to create a sensation that was part pain and part pleasure, sheer unadulterated pleasure that made Sydney wiggle her body on the bed.

"Anymore than a handful is wasted?" she finally managed to choke out.

There was a twinkle in his eye when Eric said, "Anymore than a mouthful is wasted," and then he showed her how perfectly she fit into his mouth. How delicious she tasted on his tongue. How wild the feeling could be when he used his teeth on her. It was an erotic feast like none she'd ever known before.

"Let me see," she said some time later as she pushed him back on the bed. "What other goodies do you have to offer? Nuts," she said, then laughed and corrected herself, "Not those nuts. These little brown berry-size nuts on your chest."

She leaned over and licked him, discovering the taste and texture for herself. "Slightly almond in flavor, I would say. A hard little nut to crack. Might take a bite of my teeth to do it," and then she used her teeth on him until he cried for mercy.

"Did I hear you cry something like 'uncle'?" she said, raising her mouth from his chest.

Eric moved his head, and it was both yes and no.

"Well, I think it's time to move on to another"—she slid down his body and touched him on either side of his penis; now hard as a rock and having risen again to point skyward—"pair of . . . hmm . . . large walnuts?" Sydney shook her head and her hair brushed across his lower body like a silk whip. "No, they're too large for nuts. Lemons, then? No, not exotic enough. Giant kiwi? Yes, they're kiwi, aren't they?" She licked one with her tongue. "Definitely kiwi. A little hairy on the outside. A slight hint of both sweet and sour. Firm. Or at least until they ripen and become softer. Yes, definitely kiwi."

"Does that mean kiwi is on the menu for breakfast this morning?" Eric said, laughing, and then it was quickly no laughing matter.

"This morning and every morning," Sydney said before she thought about what she'd just implied.

"I think you've had enough 'fruit' for one day," he said. "Now, let me see, I've tasted ripe red berries and a bit of delicious melon. I think I'll try a bit of meat for a change. Some thigh meat would be nice."

Eric pushed her back on the pillows and nipped his way from her breast, past her abdomen to her thigh. Then he eased her legs apart and confessed, "The most tender and moist meat is always on the inside of the thigh."

Sydney started to protest; it was a small inconsequential sound that came from somewhere in the back of her throat and amounted to no more than a whimper.

Eric would have none of it. "Remember our motto: 'One good turn deserves another.'"

She just managed to move her head from side to side on the pillow, but it quickly became more of a thrashing as he eased her thighs apart and went for that tender flesh, taking nips with his teeth.

Then he licked her, tasted her, tested her with the tip of his tongue. He paused for a moment—and she almost died when he did—to say: "Rose petals: soft, fragrant, moist with dew." And then he plunged his tongue inside her.

Her hips flew off the bed. Her back arched. Her fingers became talons as they clawed at the sheets. "Dear God, stop," she said with the last breath of air to escape her lungs.

Eric apparently didn't believe her.

"Don't stop," she said once she found another scarce breath with which to speak.

Then he plunged deeper and she came undone in his hands, under his mouth, with his tongue buried inside her.

"I can't . . ." she started to say and lost her train of thought.

"You can't what?" Eric asked as he kissed his way back up her body and covered her mouth with his and she tasted herself on his lips, and tasted remnants of him in her mouth as well and it was an intoxicating drink: the drink of the gods.

"The nectar of the gods," she murmured, and didn't even have the energy to laugh at her own ridiculous description.

"Greedy little goddess," he said, from beside her.

"Well, I haven't eaten or had a drink like that in longer than I can remember."

"Neither have I," he confessed.

Sydney turned her head and said, "Truth to tell, I haven't tasted anything like it before."

"I've never tasted anything quite like you," Eric said, blue eyes staring straight into hers with truth evident in them.

Then he rolled over on top of her and moved between the thighs he had just left wet and quivering with his teeth and lips and tongue—and with his eyes wide open and staring straight into hers—he pushed against her, sensed she was ready and willing and able, and they watched each other as he eased himself into her inch by inch.

She went crazy waiting for him, wanting all of him, but knowing that good things come to those who wait, and so she waited, anticipating that what was next would be all the sweeter, all the more thrilling, all the more satisfying for the wait.

Then he thrust into her hard. Again. And again.

Sydney wrapped her legs around him, opened herself up to him even wider, grabbed at his shoulders, they were dewy and her hands slid down to his waist and then she reached beneath them and found his testicles, swollen, round, hard, flapping against her body and she loved the thought of it, the reality of it.

This was primal.

This was pleasure and lust and desire. It was hunger and thirst that needed to be fed, drunk, filled, satiated.

Then his hips pumped into her, once, twice, three times and a great wave, an inevitable wave, crashed over her and over him and they somehow rode the wild ride together toward shore.

It was how she'd always imagined it would be: Eric making love to her in the rain. But not once had she envisioned the rain would be soft flower petals from the Golden Raintree. Never had she realized what it would be like now that he was a man and she was a woman.

She was suddenly thankful that it hadn't happened back when they were teenagers. It was so much better to make love as adults with all that they were and with all that they had become.

"I thought it would be at night and we would be mere shadows and shapes to each other," she confessed, reaching up to trace the features so clear in the light of day.

Eric studied her intently. "Nighttime may seem more romantic . . ."

"But it's kid stuff."

"And we're not kids. We're adults who want to see each other for what we really are."

"You make love beautifully."

He smiled at her. "I do to you." Then he added, "All that spirit, all that passion, all that intelligence, all those lovely little freckles have never been put to better use."

She would have blushed, but she was way past the blushing stage. She had no secrets from him and he had none from her.

Except, she thought, for the secrets in our hearts.

We can clearly see what's on the outside. We may glimpse what's in the mind and what the mind wants the body to do. But we can't see into each other's hearts.

Perhaps it was just as well.

She had told herself—promised herself—that she wouldn't take anything Eric said or thought or did seriously ever again. Maybe this was a one-night affair. Maybe this was an affair while he remained in Sweetheart. But she would not look back and she would not look ahead too far. She would enjoy, savor, treasure whatever they had together for as long as they had it.

That's what an adult did.

So much for his poker face.

So much for his protective feelings toward her. He hadn't stopped to think that the real danger might be protecting Sydney from himself, Eric thought.

Or was he the vulnerable one?

He'd just had the best damned sex of his life and he wanted more. But it was more than sex. He could feel her in his blood and in his bones. He wanted to make love to her again in a huge bed with white satin sheets, maybe even with the song "Nights in White Satin" playing somewhere in the background.

He wanted to make love to her on a sandy beach and on a cold winter's night in front of the fire. And maybe outside on the dewy grass at dawn.

Who was the vulnerable one? Eric asked himself again. Which of them would walk away first and leave the other in the lurch?

He'd always done the leaving before. He'd always protected himself by walking away while he still could, while he still wanted to. Did he want to this time? Or was it already too late for him?

Hell, you've spent one night with the woman, he thought. The direction of a man's life didn't change in one night!

Oh, yeah, and why not?

Chapter
twenty-four

"Good morning, Mr. Law," Ella Manderley called out to him as Eric was cutting across the lawn in the direction of his apartment above the garage. For the past few weeks he'd been spending his nights with Sydney at the main house, although he usually tried to get back to his own place before the rest of the world stirred. This morning he'd overslept . . . again.

"Good morning, Mrs. Manderley," Eric said in response. There was no reason for him to be embarrassed or feel like he was sneaking around behind anyone's back. He and Sydney were adults. What they did behind closed doors was nobody else's business.

Then why do you feel like you're somehow compromising Sydney?

Mrs. Manderley stopped in her tracks and said, "May I have a word, sir?"

Eric suddenly wished that he'd tucked in his shirt, that his hair wasn't rumpled, that it wasn't quite so obvious where he'd been and what he'd been doing. "Of course," he said, clearing his throat.

The woman cast her gaze down for a moment and when she looked up there were tears brimming in her eyes. "I've been doing a lot of thinking about the matter we discussed."

Eric frowned. It was a little early for guessing games. "The matter we discussed?"

"I mentioned to you one day that I knew something from a long time ago," she reminded him.

"Forty-five years ago," he quickly recollected.

The housekeeper squinted against a bright August sun. "You've got a good memory."

"It's a necessity in my business."

"Yes, it would be." Mrs. Manderley moistened her lips. "Anyway, I don't believe it's a legal matter, but I'd still like to explain something to you and ask your advice."

"Why don't we sit on the porch?" he said, gesturing toward the house he'd just left.

Ella Manderley agreed and they sat down in a pair of matching lawn chairs. It was another minute or two before she began. "I know it's not a good excuse, but I was only sixteen at the time." A ghost of a smile flitted across her middle-age features. "I suppose we all do stupid things when we're sixteen."

He certainly had.

She continued. "This is difficult for me to confess, but I was young and foolish"—she stopped and swallowed before adding—"and pregnant. The father of my baby disappeared right after I gave him the news. The only person I could rely on was Bim."

"Your brother must have been awfully young himself at the time," Eric speculated.

"Bim was eighteen, but he was always mature for his age. He'd worked for years while he was going to school and by that December he was out on his own and self-supporting. He rented a small place just outside of town in the trailer park." Ella Manderley shaded her eyes with one hand and stared off toward the fields and the trees beyond. "He agreed to let me move in with him, and he looked after me."

"Bim's a good man."

"He's one of the best men I've ever known." There was a pause and then the housekeeper said, "That's one reason I still feel so bad about what I did." She gave a thoughtful sigh. "Or what I didn't do."

Eric waited for her to explain. Instead she went to tell him, "Several years later I was married and then I had more children and the whole incident seemed like it had happened in another lifetime and to someone else." Ella Manderley finally turned and looked directly at him. "You know Bim was married for a short time to Minerva Bagley, don't you?"

"Yes, I do." He was pretty sure he knew how the housekeeper had come by that information, too.

"Well, there's something you don't know. Something even Bim and Minerva don't know."

"What's that?" he prompted.

The woman picked up her story where she'd left off. "They'd only been back from Kentucky for a day or two when Minerva and Bim broke the news of their marriage to her family. The Bagleys weren't pleased to say the least."

"They were both very young."

"Among other objections." The woman reached down and smoothed the front of her cleaning smock. "Anyway, there was a big row. Things were said and feelings were hurt. In the end Minerva went back to her family and Bim returned alone to his trailer."

Eric didn't know what to say.

"What I never told Bim was that Minerva came to see him a few weeks later. He wasn't at home, but I was. That's when Minerva asked me for a favor."

"What was it?"

"She'd written Bim a letter and she wanted me to give it to him. Made me promise."

"But you broke your promise. You didn't give the letter to your brother."

Ella Manderley moved her head. "I burned it."

"Why?"

"I was afraid if they got back together I'd have to move out of the trailer." She went on in a rush of words, "I had no other place to go, no other means of support than Bim. I was frightened and I was desperate for myself and for the child I was going to have."

Eric reached across and patted the woman's hand. "You weren't much more than a child yourself."

"Still, I shouldn't have done it."

Then something occurred to Eric. "Did you read the letter before you burned it?"

Ella Manderley confirmed that she had. "Minerva had

written that she loved him and wanted them to be together whatever her parents' objections. She asked Bim to meet her so they could talk about their future."

"Bim never knew," Eric said softly.

Ella added, "And Minerva must have assumed that he'd changed his mind. I don't think they spoke or even saw each other for almost a year. By then Bert Bagley would have taken care of the legalities to dissolve the marriage."

Eric sat there in silence.

"Do you think I should tell Bim?" the woman finally said.

It was a minute before Eric answered her. "I think you should tell both Bim and Minerva."

"It's the only way, isn't it?"

He rubbed a hand back and forth across the morning stubble on his chin. "The past can't be changed, but they deserve to know. And it means you can finally forgive yourself."

"You're right. I'll do it," the woman said emphatically as she got to her feet. "It's time to put the past behind me once and for all."

Easier said than done.

"Now I have a favor to ask you," Eric said, standing. "Don't say anything to Bim and Minerva until I give you the go-ahead. Can you do that?"

"Yes, I can," she said, apparently determined to get it right this time around.

"Thank you for confiding in me, Mrs. Manderley."

"I should be the one thanking you." Her face was flush with emotion. "Just give me the word and I'll go see Minerva and my brother."

*   *   *

Oh, what a tangled web we humans weave, Eric was thinking to himself as he drove into Sweetheart later that week.
Finally he had assembled all the pieces of the puzzle—
well, nearly all the pieces—and it was time to put them together and take action. Not that it was going to be easy. In
fact, it was going to be damned difficult.

At least he'd taken care of that little matter involving
the culprit who had spray painted FREAK on Sydney's car.
She was being a lot more forgiving and generous than he
would have been under the circumstances. But he'd discovered something about Sydney St. John in the past couple of
months: She had a kind heart.

Much like Minerva.

They were going to have to tell Minerva, of course. He
and Sydney. That very afternoon once the special election
results were in. Ella Manderley only knew half the story.
After a meticulous and methodical legal search, in which
he'd left no stone unturned, the truth had to be faced: Minerva and Bim were still married.

Chapter
twenty-five

"Well, folks, as you know, we have the votes counted for the special election recently held in Sweetheart for the position of animal control officer. The two candidates, listed in alphabetical order, are Walter E. Pearson and Walter P. Pearson," the official was saying from the podium at the front of the meeting room.

"I wonder who's won," Sydney said in an aside to Minerva, who was seated to her left. Eric was sitting on the other side of her with a bemused expression on his face.

The gray-haired man accepted the envelope handed to him, opened it up, and read for a moment. He walked over and conferred briefly with the auditor who had certified the count before returning to the microphone and the podium.

He cleared his throat. "We have a most unusual situation, folks. I can't say we've run into this before in Sweetheart."

"Just spit it out, judge," someone urged from the back of the room.

"Here. Here," came another voice.

"The votes have been counted and recounted for accuracy, and these are the results: Walter E. Pearson has received a total of one thousand four hundred and two votes." There was a polite round of applause. "Walter P. Pearson has received a total of one thousand four hundred and two votes." The gentleman looked up and said almost apologetically, "In other words, it's a tie, folks."

The room buzzed with excitement.

The gavel came down on the podium. "Now, in the event of a tie, there is no legal recourse according to our local laws. The two candidates involved can decide which one wants to serve."

That created another buzz in the room.

The man tapped the microphone and said a little louder, "Or they can choose to serve their community in the truest spirit of altruism and accept the position as a team and work together."

The applause started small and grew from there to a virtual roar, and before the crowd emptied the room, history had been made in Sweetheart, Indiana. The longtime Pearson feud had been put to rest, and there were now two dog catchers serving as one.

"Your first job will be finding Sneaker," Eric informed them after the crowd had broken up. "Sydney left him right here outside city hall with the Bigelow boy holding his leash. Apparently the kid got distracted and now Sneaker is missing."

"Dognapping," Walter P. suggested, looking across at his co-elected dogcatcher.

"Maybe he's just off chasing after some girl dog," Walter E. said, with his usual flair for what sometimes passed as humor.

Sydney wrung her hands. "Sneaker has been neutered."

Eric said, "Ouch."

"We'll get right to it, Sydney. Don't you worry. We'll rally the troops," one of the cousins assured her.

"I'll take this side of the street," Eric volunteered. "Syd, why don't you go check out the city park? That seems like the kind of place Sneaker might hightail it to given half the chance."

Sydney agreed and headed across the street to the park. "Sneaker," she called out and tried not to sound desperate. "Sneaker, where are you?" She kept calling his name and looking behind every tree and bush, but there was no sign of the Sheltie. She was on the verge of giving up—she'd just have to look somewhere else—when suddenly a woman appeared in front of her.

"I . . . ah . . . I brought your dog back," the woman said, and held out the leash with Sneaker on the other end. "I found him running around a few streets over. I read his dog tags. His name is Sneaker, isn't it?"

Sydney went down on her haunches and hugged her sweetie pie. Then she looked up and said, "Yes, his name is Sneaker. And I can't thank you enough for returning him. I was frantic."

"I had a dog once a long time ago. He got hit by a car. I cried when that happened."

Sydney stood and looked at the woman. "You're Molly Manderley, aren't you?"

"I was until I married Billy Bob Maddox. Kept the same initials, anyway."

"We went to school together."

The woman brushed the ground with her sneaker. "Yes, we did." Then she raised her head and said in a different voice, "You're the one who did it, aren't you?"

"Did what?"

"You're the one who got me the scholarship so I could attend beauty school, all expenses paid, including enough to live on until I get back on my feet."

Sydney shook her head and said, "I'm afraid I don't know what you're talking about."

Molly almost smiled. "You never were a good liar, Sydney St. John. At first I couldn't figure out who would do something like that. Or even have the money to give away. Then I remembered you tried to help me once before."

Sydney crinkled up her forehead. "I did?"

"In grade school. With long division. I wasn't very nice about it, I'm afraid." Molly cast her eyes down for a moment, and when she raised her head there were tears on her face. "I've been doing a lot of thinking since I got the notice about the scholarship. I feel so ashamed. So guilty. I don't deserve what you're doing for me."

Sydney wasn't going to be coy. It was time for some plain speaking. "It's what you do for yourself that's important, Molly. No shame. No guilt. Think of it as a new beginning. A new start. A way of putting the past behind both of us once and for all."

Molly's face brightened. "You mean like pick yourself up, brush yourself off, and start all over again."

"That's exactly what I mean." Sydney wrapped Sneaker's leash around her wrist. "We're not kids anymore."

"No, we're not," the other woman agreed.

"We may not be able to change the past, but we can change the way we think about it." Sydney took a deep breath. "I hope whatever hurt feelings we may have caused each other as children can now be forgiven."

Molly's voice choked. "Hope," she said out loud. "I'd forgotten all about hope."

"We all need hope and forgiveness. We all need to let bygones be bygones."

"I'll try," Molly said. "I really will."

"I will, too," Sydney vowed.

"Maybe it's time to live life out loud." The other woman blushed. "I heard that in a song one night down at the bar."

"Live life out loud," Sydney repeated. "I like that."

The former Molly Manderley looked her straight in the eye and said, "If I'm going to make a fresh start, then there are some things you should know."

Sydney gave her the opportunity to say them. Sometimes that was as important or even more important than the words themselves. "I'm the one who picked the lilies of the valley and put them in your kitchen that first day to welcome you home. I don't want you to blame my mother. She'd specifically told me *not* to use that flower because you'd once been poisoned by it."

Sydney sighed. "I didn't blamed your mother. I just assumed she'd forgotten about the incident. It was a long time ago."

"My mother doesn't forget anything," Molly said, and Sydney was pretty sure Molly didn't forget anything either, especially slights, real or imagined. "I'm the one who left those silly and hurtful and mean notes in your mailbox and on your windshield. I was in the Bagley Building that night, listening outside your door. And I'm the one who spray-painted your car." The woman stopped to catch her breath. "When I found Sneaker, I knew I had to bring him right back to you. I knew you'd be frantic with worry."

"I was."

"I wasn't mean to your dog. I wouldn't ever hurt one of God's defenseless creatures," Molly declared.

"I know you wouldn't."

"I'm sorry, Sydney."

"So am I." Sydney held out her hand and the other woman finally understood and shook it. "What do you say we just call it even-steven and begin again. Deal?"

Molly pumped her hand. "Deal."

Chapter

twenty-six

"I was younger than you are when I let my chance pass me by," Minerva said to Sydney after she and Eric had broken the news to her. "By the way, it was kind of Eric to come himself and explain the legal ramifications."

"He wanted to, Minerva," Sydney said as she sat beside her aunt and held her hand. "He knew it would come as a shock."

"Married all these years and we never knew, we never realized." Minerva shook her head. "Uncle Bert took care of those things. But then, you know the tragedy that happened within our family about the same time and we let it slip between the cracks."

"It does happen," Sydney said, but she knew her words were inadequate.

"I've only loved one man in my life: Bim. We were young and we thought love was enough. It should have been enough," said Minerva. "But we ran into our first obstacle, my family's objections, and we let it defeat us. We allowed our future to slip away just like that."

"Oh, Minerva," she said, putting her arms around her aunt.

"No use blaming other folks. The truth is Bim and I *were* too young. If we'd been a little older and a little wiser maybe we would have fought for ourselves and for each other." Minerva shook her head. "I should have talked to him. I should have made him talk to me. But we were afraid of being hurt."

"I think most of us share that same fear," Sydney said sympathetically.

Minerva stood up and straightened her back. "Well, I've got news for them: Some people may think I'm too old for love. You're never too old for love. I may be past sixty, but if Bim tells me I haven't changed a bit over the years, I'll believe him. Maybe he can still see me as the seventeen-year-old he fell in love with. Maybe I can still see the eighteen-year-old man in him. Oh, we may look a bit different on the outside, but something inside may never have changed."

"You're going out to the farm to tell him yourself?"

"Yes. And if he swears to me that he's been in love with me all these years, I'll know it's true. Bim was never a man to tell an untruth. I suppose that's one reason he's always been better with trees than with people. People don't always take to the truth real well."

Facing the truth took courage, Sydney thought. Sometimes she'd been a coward about the truth.

"Anyway, that's how we met, you know. A mutual love of growing things, of tending our gardens. His, of course, turned out to be a forest and a lot bigger than mine." Minerva's expression softened. "I've never told anyone this before, but my feelings for Bim are the reason I've never married. And it's also the inspiration behind Water from the Moon."

"Water from the Moon," Sydney repeated thoughtfully. "It means something one can never have."

"Or someone," Minerva added. "I thought Bim had lost his nerve. I'm sure he thought I'd changed my mind. It really isn't Ella's fault for not telling us otherwise. She was just a kid at the time."

"I still wish Mrs. Manderley had told you later on."

"So does she. But it's all water under the bridge now, my dear girl," her aunt said.

"Yes, I suppose it is."

"Fear is the mind killer. I read that somewhere. I think in an old Frank Herbert novel." Minerva went on. "And it was Bertrand Russell who wrote that 'to fear love is to fear life, and those who fear life are already three quarters dead.'" She reached up and held Sydney's face between her hands. "Don't be afraid. Don't let your chance pass you by.

"I know all about the psychologists and marriage counselors and whatnot who claim there are any number of people we can be happy with. Hogwash. Not true for some of us. Some of us fall in love and are in love with one person all of our lives. A one-man woman. That's what I am."

Her brown eyes brimmed with tears and intelligence and understanding. "I think that's what you are."

Sydney smiled. Minerva had seen right through her. "What will you do now?" she asked.

"I'm going out to the tree farm, and I'm going to have a long talk with Bim. And then we'll see if there's a future for the two of us together. I'd rather know than always wonder what might have been." She looked Sydney straight in the eyes. "What will you do?"

"I'm not sure."

"Maybe it's time you thought about your destiny, my girl."

"My destiny," Sydney said softly. "You talked to me once a long time ago about my destiny."

"Yes, I did."

"Have I ever told you how precious those conversations were to me? How they helped me as a young girl and how your loving acceptance of me has been an anchor for my life?"

There was a tear on Minerva's cheek. It rolled down her face and dropped off her chin onto her blouse. "You have always been like a . . ."

". . . daughter?"

"Yes. You've always been like a daughter to me. The daughter I never had. But I never wanted or tried to take your mother's place. I never wanted to step on her toes."

"And you never did," Sydney assured her. "Mother chose her own path and it was often on the other side of the world when I needed her. But you were always there, in your apron, baking cookies and making tea and listening when I needed someone to listen. And offering gentle advice when I needed guidance. I want you to know how much I've always loved you for that."

After Sydney had gone Minerva sat in the library—it was her favorite room in the house—and did some hard thinking. Then she decided what she needed was a long walk in her garden. Bim had sought his sanctuary among the trees. She always sought hers in the garden. Perhaps they were kindred spirits after all. Maybe they always had been.

Walking between the rows of sunflowers—the stalks had grown tall as it neared summer's end; the seedpods were heavy and bowing their heads—and the patch of rambling roses, their blooms fading as the days grew shorter, made Minerva think of the moonflower, *Ipomoea alba*, or "evening glory."

The exact opposite of its country cousin, the morning glory, the moonflower was secretive in daylight and shimmery by night, with its large white blooms that emerged butterfly-like from green tubes attached to the twining vines. They had deep green, heart-shaped leaves. Sweet scented like cloves or lemons, the moonflower opened at dusk and lasted only one night.

"You were a little like a moonflower, weren't you, Minerva?"

But that was a long, long time ago.

"It's time to find out if you're a morning glory, after all,". she said to herself as she headed back toward the house.

* * *

"Who are you really, Sydney Marie St. John?" Sydney whispered to her reflection in the window glass. "What do you want?"

She had stood at this same window and had asked herself those same questions her first night in Sweetheart. Back then she'd been clear about what she *didn't* want. Now she knew what she wanted.

She wanted success, but on her own terms and according to her own definition of what success was.

She wanted to live mindfully, taking the time to be aware of the days and the seasons and the years.

She wanted to be happy.

She wanted a home and a husband and children. She wanted to teach her own daughter the recipe for Minerva's lemonade and the wisdom of her herbs and garden, to pass along the precious knowledge from one generation to the next.

And she wanted to love and to be loved in return.

Now that she knew what she wanted, it was time to listen to her heart as well as reason with her head. She couldn't be afraid of making mistakes. It was better to make a mistake and risk looking like a fool than to live with regret for the rest of her life.

As she closed the drapes against a moonless night, the words of a Longfellow poem flitted through Sydney's mind: *"Deep as love, deep as first love, and wild with all regret."*

Chapter
twenty-seven

 The second wedding ceremony between Minerva and Bim took place on December seventh, of course. It was simple and tasteful as befit a mature couple who were renewing their vows after forty-five years of being married to each other . . . and yet always waiting to be together.

Sydney had been a little surprised when Eric had slipped out early from the party—it was an intimate gathering of family and close friends—after whispering the words in her ear, "I'll see you back home later."

She pulled up in the driveway. There was Eric's red Porsche parked where she was used to seeing a white pickup truck. It had taken the mechanics down at the garage, along with an imported specialist, months to find out that the problem was wedding rice in some crucial part of the engine or the carburetor or the manifold.

Life had its little ironies.

The sky was cloudy and gray and a light drizzle was falling. Sydney got out of her car and started toward the porch. That's when she noticed Sneaker sitting there, waiting for her. He let out with what sounded like a happy hello.

His leash was tied to the Christmas decorations she'd helped to put up herself: a garland of natural pine boughs wrapped around the porch railing and accented every few feet with a large red bow. Now there was another bright red bow attached to Sneaker's collar, along with a hand-printed sign that said: LOVE ME; LOVE MY DOG.

"Sneaker, what's going on here?" she asked. Then she looked around, and in the distance she could see Christmas lights, strung in a pathway that led from the farm up into the trees.

Of course, the tree farm was closed for business today, but someone must have turned on the lights all the same.

"I wonder who," Sydney said. But she knew who. Eric Law, that's who.

She quickly changed from her dress shoes into a pair of boots from the mud room, then reached down and unsnapped Sneaker's leash. Before she could say, "Lead the way," the Sheltie was off at a fast clip running toward the forest.

Sydney pulled the hood of her raincoat up over her head and followed the pathway through the trees. Then she heard music—not Christmas music—but Trisha Yearwood singing something about how do I live without you.

She came around the last bend in the path, and there, in the middle of the pine forest, was a beautiful tree covered with small white lights. Eric was standing beside the tree dressed in a pair of blue jeans, the white dress shirt he'd had on earlier for Minerva and Bim's second wedding, and a black leather jacket. Sneaker ran to him and sat down at his feet. The two "men" in her life were waiting for her.

"We think we know what you want for Christmas this year," Eric said in a voice that came out a little nervous and a little loud.

Sydney couldn't speak. She could scarcely breathe. Her heart was pounding in her ears. "You do, do you?" she said at last.

The drizzle dripped from Eric's hair onto his shoulders. "Sneaker and I have talked it over."

A smile tugged at the corners of her mouth. "You have, have you?"

He nodded. "We want to give you everything: our unconditional love, our promise to be beside you every morning when you wake up—breakfast fruit optional."

She laughed.

But Eric wasn't finished. He went on. "We want to give you a house—a home—of your own and children someday and whatever is your heart's true desire."

Sydney's throat was filled with tears.

"Oh, and did we mention a wedding?" Eric glanced down at his furry companion and said, "We definitely want to give you a wedding."

"Who am I marrying at this wedding you're giving me?" she finally asked.

"Me." The man in front of her glanced down at her dog. "Us." Then Eric grew very serious. "You are my destiny. I believe I'm your destiny. That's more important to me than where I live, or what I do for a living, or how successful I am. Although Sam has offered me a partnership in his law firm and I've accepted."

"A partnership?"

"It turns out that between the two of us we have enough clients and court cases to keep half a dozen lawyers busy. Business is booming for the Law brothers."

"What about Boston?"

Eric shrugged. "Boston will have to manage without me." Then he added, "I can certainly manage without Boston."

"Why are you doing this?" She had to know.

"Because I've always been a sucker for long legs," he said not altogether serious.

"Did you have any particular pair of long legs in mind?" she asked in the same vein.

"Yep. *Your* long legs." Eric heaved an exaggerated sigh. "I was a goner from the first moment you stepped out of your Beemer and rescued me from a fate worse than death." Then he grew thoughtful again. "Much to my surprise, I've come back to my hometown and discovered it is home for me."

Her great-uncle Bert's words of wisdom echoed once again in her ears: *Sometimes we have to go home and deal with who we really are.*

Is that what she and Eric had both found in the past few months: who they really were?

"Minerva made me president and senior partner in Water from the Moon for Christmas," she mentioned to him.

"Tough act to follow," Eric acknowledged.

"My aunt has decided there's more to life than running

a business. In fact, she's going to live with Bim in the log cabin he built for her, for them forty-five years ago."

All of a sudden the drizzle turned to snow. The first snow of the season. Sydney threw back the hood of her coat and raised her face toward the sky. She opened her mouth and caught a snowflake on the tip of her tongue.

Eric put his head back and laughed as his hair was changed from black to white.

Sydney couldn't look away from him. "What do you want for Christmas?" she asked the beautiful man standing in front of her.

He went down on one knee and opened his hand, and there were two gold rings resting in his palm. "All I want for Christmas this year and for all the Christmases to come . . . is you, Sydney St. John."

He was her destiny. Just as she was his.

"I've loved you since I was sixteen years old," she confessed and took a step closer to him. "I think it was John Cheever who said: 'That sense of sanctuary that is the essence of love.'"

Eric stayed where he was. "Then you are my love, my sanctuary, the place I want to go at the end of the day when the outside world has been cruel and harsh. You are what I want to see first thing every morning and the last thing at night."

"I've never taken a chance on love before," she said.

"Then this is the time and the place and I'm the man," Eric told her.

He took a deep breath and said the words every woman waits to hear from the man she loves: "Will you marry me, Sydney Marie St. John?"

Sydney opened her mouth, but nothing came out. She took a deep breath and walked straight up to him and said, "Yes, I will marry you, Eric Anscomb Law."

Then Eric pulled her into his arms and he kissed her while the snow gently covered them and the tree lights sparkled against the winter to come and Sneaker ran in circles around them, barking in celebration.

She always had been the luckiest girl in the world.

Author's Note

I have big feet. Always have had. And I'm tall, and I once had eleven freckles on my nose. Yes, I counted them. My hair is curly and dark brown. I grew eight inches within a two-year span as a young girl. I felt gawky and awkward. I wasn't physically coordinated, and I had a propensity to say and do the wrong thing at the wrong time.

But I grew into my feet. I grew out of the awkwardness. The freckles disappeared. And I came into my own.

So this story is in part dedicated to all of those women who have shared this experience with me.

This book is also a loving tribute to my mother, Mary Noeding Simmons, who convinced me that being tall and having the feet to match that height was some-thing to celebrate! She encouraged me to be all that I could be. She gave me the praise, the unfailing support, and the confidence that she had often lacked herself as a girl.

Alis volat propriis.

"She flies with her own wings."

Additional Author's Note

For those interested in knowing exactly what pieces of classical music or other popular music I refer to in this story (they're all among my personal favorites), I have listed them below, classical composers before the music they wrote; popular performers, when specifically mentioned, after the song title:

CHAPTER 2:
Johann Sebastian Bach's "Suite for solo cello No. 1 in G Major, BWV 1007," performed by Yo-Yo Ma

"Fire and Rain," James Taylor
(How could I not love this particular song when he's singing about a woman named Suzanne?)

CHAPTER 6:
"You Don't Know Me," Ray Charles

CHAPTER 7:
"Goodnight, Sweetheart"

CHAPTER 10:
"My Way," Frank Sinatra

CHAPTER 17:
"How's the World Treating You," James Taylor and Alison Krauss

CHAPTER 20:
"White Christmas"

CHAPTER 23:
"Nights in White Satin (Notte Di Luce)," Mario Frangoulis, duet with Justin Hayward

CHAPTER 27:
"How Do I Live," Trisha Yearwood

Sweetheart, Indiana
by
Suzanne Simmons

Socialite Gillian Charles has just inherited
a town. There's only one catch: she has
to live there. What can a small town
possibly offer this big city girl?
For starters, Sam Law, the handsome
executer of the will, who has his
own mysterious plans for
Sweetheart—and for Gillian.

"HOT, SMART, AND LAUGH-OUT-LOUD
FUNNY...THIS IS THE ROMANCE
YOU'VE BEEN WAITING FOR!"
—ELIZABETH LOWELL

"IN A WORD: FABULOUS."
—JAYNE ANN KRENTZ

"GET READY TO BE CHARMED."
—STELLA CAMERON

0-425-19779-4

Available wherever books are sold or at
www.penguin.com

THEY'RE EXPERTS IN CRIME—AND PASSION.

Dangerous Curves
by
Jacey Ford

THEY CAN BREACH THE SECURITY AT ANY
BANK IN ATLANTA AND STILL BE DONE IN
TIME FOR COCKTAILS.

*Aimee, Daphne, and Raine are former FBI
agents who have started their own security
company: Partners in Crime. But when
Raine's old boyfriend, Agent Calder Preston,
has a job for the Partners,
sparks—and bullets—begin to fly.*

0-451-19685-2

**Available wherever books are sold or at
www.penguin.com**

B231